Vulture

A. M. Blanco

Vulture

A Novel

9th House

Books

Hialeah

9TH HOUSE BOOKS, LLC.
Hialeah, Florida 33013

Vulture / A. M. Blanco
Copyright © A. M. Blanco, 2024
Published by 9th House Books, LLC

Book & Cover Design by A. M. Blanco
For more information contact 9th House Books at:
www.9thhousebooks.com
To reach the author directly contact A. M. Blanco at:
amblancowriter@gmail.com
ISBN: 979-8-9920687-0-2
First 9th House Books LLC Edition December 2024

For my family

A. M. Blanco

Vulture

A Novel

Author's Note

This novel explores profound themes including mental illness, terminal illness, grief, and the darkness of suicidal thoughts. While these elements are part of the narrative, they are not meant to cause distress but to foster understanding and hope. Regardless of who you are, where you live or your specific circumstances, suicide is never the answer. No matter how alone or hopeless you may feel, please know that someone is always willing to be there and listen. Your wellbeing matters deeply. Please remember: you are not alone. Your life has value and meaning, regardless of your circumstances. Help is always available, day or night. If you or someone you know is experiencing thoughts of suicide, please do not hesitate to reach out:

Call 988 (US Suicide & Crisis Lifeline)
Message 741741 with the word "HOME" (Crisis Text Line)
Visit befrienders.org for international crisis resources

Every life holds infinite worth. Every story, including yours, deserves to continue. The services above are free, confidential, and staffed by compassionate people who want to listen—any time, day or night. Always remember that your presence in this world matters more than any story ever could.

"Whoever sows injustice reaps calamity,
and the rod they wield in fury will be broken."
-Proverbs 22:8

A. M. Blanco

Vulture

A Novel

1

Vultures devour carrion; tearing decaying flesh from bone. Crimson-stained beaks; doors of living sepulchers. *Autolysis*; an *enzymic* celebration of death. Flies; death's tiny dancing guests deposit their larvae in the carcass as gifts for the invitation.

The nature documentary showcasing the large scavenger birds feasting somewhere in the Florida Everglades plays softly and with captions on a robust overhead television set, its rabbit-ear antenna wrapped in foil.

I bite into my burger, its charred body a burnt offering to my soft palate. My taste buds flare barely registering the tasteless corpse, just another sensation lost in the effluvium of too many nights like this. I watch, transfixed, on the flickering screen above, vultures tearing into bloated, stiff remains with the cold and ruthless efficiency of a well-oiled machine, a gruesome display of nature's cyclical brutality; nature's own *noir*, playing out in vivid Technicolor.

Nature's janitors, that's what those honey-voiced nature documentary narrators call 'em. Cleaning up the mess predators leave behind. But who cleans up after us? After the likes of me? In this neon-drenched hellhole of a city, the vultures wear badges and suits, picking clean the bones of saints and sinners alike.

Welcome to Miami, city of homicides extraordinaire. Where the sun-kissed beaches hide needle-scattered alleys, and every scintillating high-rise casts a shadow long enough to drown a dozen lost souls. This is where hope comes to die, usually with a slit throat or a bullet between its eyes.

The city runs on a currency of decay and retribution, each viciously feeding the other in an endless cycle. For every body I pull from the bay, three more take its place. For every killer I cuff, five more are born in the humid, hopeless nights. And me? I'm just another vulture circling the bloated, putrefied remains, telling myself I'm cleaning up the mess when I'm really just another part of the sickness.

Some of the vultures on the screen are circling, their black wings slicing the humid air like a cheap hood's switchblade.

They're patient, these airborne undertakers, circling with the easy confidence of creatures who know death is always on the menu in this neon-drenched swampland. But as I watch, the television fades away, and suddenly I'm circling too. Round and round the wreckage of my own personal hell.

The headaches always start this way too. That nauseating inner spinning, always followed up by nosebleeds, fatigue and sometimes blackouts. My doctor says it's the Lymphoma causing all this shit; that it got worse after my wife and daughter's death because the grief probably lowered my immune system significantly. He says that's why I am getting so skinny too.

The carcass on the screen morphs, metal replacing meat, and

VULTURE

I'm back there again. That rain-slicked highway, the night my world ended. Sarah's lifeless body trapped in that wretched metal coffin. Emily's stuffed bear, torn and bloody on the asphalt; missing one eye. The vultures of my mind swoop down, pecking at the memories, tearing them open anew.

Twisted metal gleams under harsh streetlights, a mockery of the family sedan that once carried my hopes and dreams. Now it's just another roadside carnival of carnage, the kind of scene I've witnessed a hundred times before and since. But it's different when it's your family. It hits different. It tears you different. It devours you. This memory's got its claws in me, and it won't let go.

The drunk driver walked away without a scratch. My wife and daughter's life cut short because of some conscienceless asshole, too proud and *macho* to call a cab. I'm still there, circling that wreck, picking at the bones of what might have been.

The vultures and I, we're not so different. We both feed on the dead things. The only difference is, they get to fly away when they're done; while I remain a prisoner of that memory and this job; consuming death until one day it consumes me.

I blink, and I'm back in the diner, my hands gripping what's left of the greasy burger. The vultures on the TV are still at it, methodical in their destruction. I take another bite, my jaw working with all the emotion of an automaton. For a moment, I'm not sure which of us is really dead—me, or the corpse being picked clean on the screen.

This diner's the only twenty-four-hour joint in Little Havana; all the others close down at midnight. It's been here since the

3

mid-sixties, when its owner, a Cuban-Italian businessman from Havana, fled the communist regime in '59.

Its grimy linoleum floor catches the harsh fluorescent glare, casting a sickly pallor over everything. Under this unforgiving light, I catch a glimpse of myself in the smudged chrome of the napkin dispenser. Bloodshot eyes stare back at me, nestled in dark hollows that speak of too many nightmare-ridden nights.

My three-day stubble is racing towards a full beard, and my rumpled suit reeks of stale Camel cigarettes. I look like a haggard watchman at the gates of hell, one whiskey-soaked night from free-falling into the neon-lit abyss I've spent a career circling. My reflection's a grim reminder that in Miami, the line between watchdog and washout is thinner than the edge of my badge.

The air hangs heavy, thick with the stench of burnt coffee and cigarettes mingling with decades of accumulated grease. It's an olfactory cocktail unique to Miami's underbelly, one that reeks of countless broken dreams, half-baked schemes, and sins left to die on Formica tabletops.

Rain hits the window glass, harsh, cold, hypnotic like a Schoenberg symphony. To my left, the diner's neon sign's lights cast an ominous presence of pink and blue ripples on the parking lot's wet asphalt. My eyes follow those neon ripples through the torrent, until I can see the blurry shape of my black unmarked Dodge Diplomat, the only car in the lot.

I visit this place almost every night, on and off duty. The graveyard shift's my usual beat, but in homicide, you're always on call; overtime's as natural as breathing. On most nights, I commune with a coffee, maybe surrender to a burger or settle for a hot bagel with cream cheese, and let these nature documentaries wash over me, glancing occasionally over case files during commercials. The diner's clock's metronomic second hand ticking and shifting until my police radio signals the homicide code, followed by a personal summoning to another dance with death.

Sometimes, when on duty, my partner Mike Cordero joins me, but the guy's got timing like a broken watch; he'll barely plant his ass on the vinyl before dispatch calls and he's got to get his ass back up as if the booth's got thumbtacks.

I watch the vultures again, their mesmerizing death-consuming ritual holding my full attention, their razor-sharp beaks rending flesh from bone; their hooked bills ripping through layers of decaying skin, the sounds of their feeding echoing the rhythmic crunch of my own jaws working the remains of my burger.

"Easy there, detective. You're tearing into that burger like those buzzards on the tube. Might wanna come up for air before you start growing feathers." The words, raspy as a smoker's cough, slice through my reverie. A laugh follows, dry and hollow as bones rattling in a desert.

With the charred flesh still halfway down my throat, I wash down the last of the tasteless bit with a swig of even more tasteless coffee, its acrid scent reminding me to wonder, not for the first time, if there's any real difference between the predators and the cleanup crew. In this city, the line between the two is as blurry as my vision after a fifth of cheap whiskey.

Margaret Anderson materializes beside me, coffee pot in

hand, a specter in a faded powder blue uniform. Her age is hard to tell, but I'm forty-two, and I bet she was blowing out her sweet sixteen's candle when I was taking my first breath. Her hair is bleached and curls tightly around her head like slumbering albino snakes. Her face is a well-worn map of graveyard shifts and customer complaints, but her flat green eyes still hold a flicker of warmth; somehow she's still alive in there; a rare sight in this morgue of a diner.

"Just trying to keep the body and soul together, Marge, not sure which one's putting up more of a fight these days."

"Well, don't let either one fly the coop on my watch," she says, with a smile.

"Another shot of midnight oil, detective?" She asks, already halfway tipping the pot.

"Thanks, Marge," I nudge the nearly empty cup closer to her.

She pours the black oblivion to the brim of the cup. "You're the only one here tonight, again."

"Guess that makes me your most loyal customer." I watch the rising steam as it meets her eyes.

"Three nights in a row now, ain't it?"

"Yeah. Sounds about right."

I take a sip of the dark liquid. It tastes like it was filtered through a corpse.

"Must be all that news about those kidnappings and Satanic cults sacrificing people that's got all the folks curled up at home, even our sleepless regulars." She says, as her eyebrows raise so high they might wake the albino snakes.

I lean in, lowering my voice. "You hearing things, Marge?

6

About the kidnappings and the cults?"

Her eyes dart around the empty diner before she leans in and responds, her voice dropping to a conspiratorial whisper.

"I've heard all sorts of things. You heard anything about them missing kids? My sister swears she saw some hooded figures dragging a bag into a car last night. Bag was moving, if you catch my drift."

"Did she file a report?" I ask, already knowing the answer. Everyone in this city fears retribution.

"Hell no! She's not risking it, my sister's youngest kid goes to that daycare they're investigating now. Says they found some . . . things. Ritualistic stuff. And that ain't the half of it. People are whispering about human sacrifices down south by the Everglades."

"Listen, Marge, it's 1985. Nowadays, the media exaggerates things and people start . . . you know . . . seeing things that aren't really there. The mind's open to suggestion. At least that's what my department's shrink says."

I lean back, the vinyl seat creaking like old bones.

"Look, I've been on this beat long enough to know there's real monsters out there; plenty of psychos and sick bastards who don't need any devil to tell them to do evil. But Satanic cults? Human sacrifices? Pentagrams and black robes? That's just window dressing for the nightly news." My mouth snakes a chuckle. "Hell, that even sounds like a bad Hollywood movie plot to me."

Marge shakes her head, a mix of disappointment and fear in her eyes.

"I hope you're right, Tom. I really do. But if you're wrong . . ."

Her eyes trail off, glancing at the TV where the vultures are still feeding.

My eyes follow hers to the screen and I drain my cup, the bitter dregs matching my mood.

"If I'm wrong, Marge, then God help us all. Because we cops sure as hell won't be able to."

She refills my cup without asking, her hand trembling slightly. "Just . . . keep your eyes open, detective. Sometimes the truth is uglier than any story we could make up."

I nod, crossing my arms, feeling the weight of my Colt .38 against my ribs.

"You too, Marge, keep your eyes and ears open. And for Christ's sake, be careful."

"Don't think He's listening anymore, detective. Not in Miami."

Marge's face is grim. She pauses, her face growing serious. "But you be careful out there, you hear? This feels different. Like the city's holding its breath, waiting for something worse."

I nod, feeling the weight of her words settle on my shoulders like a lead jacket. "Always am, Marge. Always am."

Her face changes like Miami weather - sunny to storm in half a heartbeat. "Tom," she breathes, finger rising slowly, aiming right between my eyes. "you're bleeding."

I touch my nose, my fingers coming away slick with red. I stare at the blood, in awe. It's almost beautiful in the flickering fluorescent light.

"And your shirt, oh Lord." Marge whines. "That's gonna leave a stain."

"It's nothing," I mutter. "Just side effects of the meds."

She places the coffee jug down on the table and fumbles for napkins in the chrome dispenser.

"Meds? You sick or something?" She hands me a batch.

As I wipe my nose, a laugh jolts from my mouth that sounds more like a death rattle. "Something like that. Got myself a nice first-class ticket to the big sleep. Doctors say I've got about six months, maybe a year if I'm lucky."

The words linger in the air between us, heavy as an elephant. Marge's face sags, and I can see the pity taunting her watery eyes. It signals my exit cue.

"Christ, Tom. I'm so—"

"Don't, please." I cut her off with a smile. "Look, the way I see it, this is my chance to see Sarah and Emily again, without having to eat my gun."

"What's the diagnosis?" she asks timidly.

"Terminal Lymphoma," I say, my eyes meeting hers. "Stage four *Waldenstrom's.*"

Marge stares silently, she's gone mute. I can't blame her; there's really nothing else she can say, and I wouldn't have it any other way.

I stand abruptly, digging my left back pocket for my wallet. I finger the bills with my right and toss a couple large ones on the table, more than enough to cover the coffee, burger and a generous tip for Marge. It's not like I'm making it to retirement.

"Leaving already? It's still pouring like crazy out there," Marge asks.

I pick up my newspaper from the tabletop, fold it and stuff it under my left armpit. "Yeah, I am beat, Marge. Gotta try to get some shut eye before another stiff steals another forty-eight hours of it."

"See you soon, Tom." Marge smiles with her eyes.

"Counting on it. You take care now. Goodnight."

"Goodnight."

I stride to the door and pull the handle, its welcoming bell ushering me out. Standing under the awning my eyes meet the drenched neon-lit Miami night. Phosphorescent blues, pinks and greens linger and peek through the deluge in the distance before me like melting moths. I pull a pack of Camels from my suit, tap the box five times onto an open palm. A station wagon splashes through a large puddle, the spray hurdles over the lonely bus stop's bench. I pull a cigarette out, and its filter meets my lips. My thumb on the spark wheel—*flick!* goes the Bic pocket lighter, its flame kissing the bogey. I take a long drag and exhale watching the smoke make love with the rain.

I tread carefully to my left under the awning, as close to the diner's window glass as possible, until I reach the bend at the corner where the awning ends. The Diplomat looms ahead, a black beast waiting to swallow me whole. It's only about fifteen feet away and I plan to make a run for it. I take my final drag, toss the butt into the deluge, and watch it drown in the black abyss of the asphalt.

With my car keys in hand, I take my newspaper and open it wide over my head; a weak shelter of ink and lies. I step into the torrent, it hits me like a band of cold bullets. As I leap through the puddles, the parking lot looks like a black mirror of oily rainbows under the streetlights. Within seconds, my newspaper shelter falters and I'm soaked to the bone. My white bloodstained shirt is now as pink as a flamingo.

I unlock the car, open the door and slide into the driver's seat, the familiar smell of leather and stale cigarettes enveloping me, like a mother's embrace. For a moment, I just sit there and watch the neon signs blur into a psychedelic smear, and listen to the rain drumming on the roof; Miami's fever dream made manifest.

I start the ignition, the engine roars alive like a lion in heat. I turn on the wipers at max speed, their metronomic motion becomes a hypnotic pendulum and I am back to that rain-slicked highway of death. Sarah's face drenched in blood, her body halfway out the windshield; the other half wrapped in metal spirals that thread in and out of her entrails like whipstitch. Emily's lifeless body lying like a rag-doll in the backseat, a dark crimson pool buoys her hair.

I linger there momentarily until the coppery taste brushes my lips. Great, another nosebleed. I reach for the glove compartment, pulling out a wad of fast-food napkins, trapped under an extra revolver I keep in there. I press them to my nose, watching crimson blotches seeping through and morphing into a real-time Rorschach test, each one spreading a grim stain that reminds me of the clock ticking inside me.

I buckle my seatbelt and turn the radio on, hoping some jazz might ease the thoughts rattling in my skull. Instead of John Coltrane I hear:

". . . third victim this month, yet another disappearance rocks Miami

tonight. Police refuse to comment on rumors of occult involvement, but sources close to the investigation suggest disturbing ritualistic elements have been found at each of the scenes. Adding fuel to the growing panic, Miami police spokesperson Ruben Fernandez offered only a terse 'no comment' when pressed about rumors of cult activity. . . ."

I turn the radio off with a quick turn of my wrist to the left. No wonder Marge was rambling about Satanists, this shit's everywhere. This city's always danced with the devil, but lately? It feels like he's singing his own praises and everyone's riding the carousel of damnation he's handing out free tickets to.

With my foot on the brake, I turn my headlights on, grip the gear selector behind the steering wheel and set the gear to drive. I pull out of the lot, a black metal coffin sailing the heavenly waters. Time to head home, to an empty house that only haunts me. Another night, another dance with my sins and my ghosts. If I am lucky, maybe in six months, I'll be joining them. Until then, I am stuck here cleaning up the mess the predators leave behind, striving to balance the scales of justice; a reminder that in this city, death's the only thing that plays fair.

2

I glance at my watch, it's 1:33 a. m. The same time I got the call from Lieutenant Patrick Jacobs about the accident. When he called it was my second night off. I was in the kitchen, heating up a few slices of leftover pizza, and waiting for Sarah and Emily to arrive from North Carolina.

They'd gone up to visit Sarah's parents in Davidson two weeks prior; it was her mother's birthday two days after they arrived there and it was tradition for them to spend birthdays together and take yearly photographs to record three maternal generations, all while annotating their progressive aging. They'd compare their physical changes year to year, and celebrate life.

Sarah's mother—Jane Millar—is a charming and gentle woman, slim and unusually tall for a woman in her mid-seventies, a retired schoolteacher who'd taught second grade students for a bit over forty years. After her husband—Sarah's father—John—passed away, she moved in with her sister, Florence, in Charlotte.

John Millar was a retired family physician, a tall and robust man with extraordinary large but smooth hands and a heart just as big. The true altruistic man. His kind blue eyes would instantly make his patients feel better; he was the ideal doctor. His private practice remained Davidson's most popular medical office until his retirement just four years ago. He had a massive heart attack about a month after the accident.

Most of the time I stayed behind, my work gripping me as tight as a boa. The one time I should have gone with them I remained fighting off the boa's choke hold: a case of a twenty-three-year-old call girl found hanged in a motel's closet off Southwest 8th Street.

It was set up to look like a suicide. Turned out to be one of her regular clients that swept her off her feet—no pun intended. It was an open and shut case, but finding the guy took a few days. He'd been hiding out in Hollywood Beach with a cousin.

When we brought him in for questioning, he broke down and confessed right away. The poor schmuck ended up hanging himself his first night in prison.

When I picked up the receiver off the wall mount next to the pantry, Jacobs seemed as cool as he usually was. He greeted me, asked me how I was doing and after a short pause—as was natural of his conversational pace when he needed me to do something —said "Tom, I need you in my office ASAP."

I explained I would head over as soon as Sarah and Emily arrived, that they'd be here any time soon, being that they left Davidson around 3 p. m. today when I last spoke to Sarah before they headed out, and it was only about an eleven-hour drive to Miami from Davidson.

Jacobs insisted that his request was of the highest priority. I pecked around, almost interrogating him about the nature of his demand, hoping he'd spill some information that would allow me to negotiate a later arrival, but he never caved. I could tell he was being unusually patient with me, but I figured he was tired, and wanted me to take over a new case and show our two new detective rookies the ropes. Since Palermo, the second C-shift Sergeant had moved over to B-shift about a week prior, I was certain this had to be somewhat the nature of his enigmatic request.

Jacobs, is the type of brass bear you don't want to poke too much, if at all. I'd poke him occasionally because of our unique rapport; we'd been through the academy together, assigned to the same squad for three years, and when I transferred over to Homicide, he rose through the ranks. He later worked as a Sergeant in Internal Affairs for a few years, and eventually was assigned to Homicide Bureau after being promoted to Lieutenant.

I was promoted to Detective-Sergeant only after he strongly petitioned me to take the Sergeant test, about a year later. He said he needed a Sergeant he could truly trust and rely on. The department had recently suffered a major blow when numerous officers were convicted of several different felonies tied to widespread corruption. In light of this, I unenthusiastically accepted his proposal, mostly because I figured the pay raise would make Sarah happy.

Jacobs kept quiet for a few seconds after I quit prying, strengthening his authority through silence. I reluctantly agreed to leave immediately. Upon arriving to his office, he prepared me for the horror he was about to inform me about by insisting I take a seat. I knew something dreadful was about to spill from his mouth when he stood from his chair behind his desk and walked around the corner of the bend and sat on the edge of the desk right in front of me, our knees touching. He laid his left hand on my right shoulder and grasped firmly while he told me about the accident. His voice faded in and out while we walked out of his office, down the Bureau's hall, through the exit doors, to the elevators and down the back entrance of the station, all the way to his unmarked car.

He drove to the scene, speaking what I believe must have been words of condolences and encouragement which were muffled out with the tinnitus. I didn't speak a word that night, until Jacobs dropped me off at home and I turned to him and said "Thank you, brother." as I opened the door and entered my now desolate house.

The Diplomat cuts through the downpour like a sling blade, tires hissing on every turn I take. The wipers fight a losing battle against Miami's heavy tears. Each flash of neon slicing through the rain-streaked windshield like a strobe light.

I make a right off Coral Way and 22nd Avenue and then another right on Southwest 16th Terrace. I'll be home in less than a minute.

3

The Diplomat looms into my driveway, headlights washing out the already-stark white garage door. Under this drenching night rain, my three-bedroom home's light beige exterior hums a blue-grey.

I kill the engine, and sit in the darkness listening to the rain drumming a funeral march on the roof; it reminds me of the city. Miami's always been a playground for corruption; a gleaming façade, where people's lives are bartered like poker chips, where the pot's only getting bigger every night. Now, the city's on its toes; unexplained disappearances and whispers of cult activity waltzing under the moonlight. It's a new sick dance with depravity, a deeper disease flowing through the veins of Miami.

The stench of fear and panic hangs over this city like a shroud. I don't have much time left until the reaper comes knocking, but as long as my lungs have air, I'll drive these rain-slick streets chasing shadows and demons, because in this city the only thing standing between the monsters and the masses, is a thin blue line; and it gets thinner every night.

I grab my tattered newspaper and open it wide again as I prepare to exit my vehicle. Grabbing the handle in one swift motion, I open the door, push the lock knob down, step outside covering my head with the newspaper, and bolt to the front entrance of my house.

I stand under the roofed porch and toss the drenched newspaper on top of a pale green lawn chair; its cushion sucking the inky water like the residents of this city suck on the lies of its politicians.

The warm porch light illuminates the wall-mounted mailbox's five-letter etched rendition of my last name: VOGEL. I open the black metal box and take the three single envelopes inside; bills addressed to me. I shove my key into the lock, turn right and yank open my stiff door—the humidity always swells the wood; it does the same to the bodies found close to the river.

I stride inside and stand in the foyer. Shut the door and watch the water cascading down my suit onto the hardwood floor; it reminds me of the funeral, the rain drops hammering the caskets like an angry blacksmith. I remove my shoes, using foot to heel movements, abandoning them next to the brown door rug. I take off my drenched suit, heavy and limp and hang it on the portmanteau; a guilty criminal in a spaghetti Western. This place reeks of grief and despair with a touch of spilled whiskey.

I drift into my room, Loneliness creeps out and greets me. I acknowledge its presence and accept its burden. There's no warmth in here without Sarah. It's been almost six months now, and I still haven't changed these bedsheets; her smell still lingers on them and is my only true companion in here. Her pillow especially; it carries her scent quicker into my nostrils when I shove my sobbing face into it.

I miss her terribly; her blue sapphire eyes, her blonde luscious hair, her tender smile. Sarah was the light of my life. The mother of my one and only child. A classically trained musician, she selfishly abandoned her career as a professional violinist to take up the role of a full time mother. The perfect stay-at-home mother; she took care of our home and Emily. Breakfast, lunch, homework, school projects, and ballet rehearsals were always her priority.

Emily, a young carbon copy of Sarah, was only seven years old and carried her stuffed bear with her everywhere she went. When we dropped her off at school, the bear stayed in the backseat of the car waiting for her until we'd pick her up at 2 p. m.

Sometimes after school we'd take her to Shenandoah Park before I'd have to get ready for my shift; the bear would sit with us in the bench, waiting for Emily to finish at the playground. To be honest, he was the most patient of us four. His name was Teddy; now his name is Loneliness.

I cross my right hand over my left ribs, unholstering my .38 and lay it on the nightstand. My golden badge lands with a dull thud next to it. They both sit like gargoyles, guarding my favorite photograph of Sarah and Emily. I peel off my blood-stained shirt and toss it in a white plastic bin. My pants, socks and underwear follow it. They join the cluster of neglected dirty clothes waiting their turn for the dry cleaners. My naked body's reflection in the full-length mirror that stands beside my bathroom's door reveals the severity of my weight loss.

A strong nauseating feeling stirs my insides. My insides churn and rebel; the acidic fluid rising up my esophagus like a volcano about to erupt. I scuttle into my bathroom straight to the toilet. My knees hitting the cold tile and cracking as I lift the lid. My mouth opens and the torrent of bile, blood, and rotting flesh spews out. The acrid stench hits my nostrils and I retch again and again, with bulging watery eyes. My stomach heaves frantically as even more filth exits my burning throat. Bitter yellow bile closes the unholy nightly ritual and I slump against the wall, depleted and shaking. It's like my body is striving to get rid of me.

After a moment, I wipe my mouth with my left forearm and stand. I glance at the floor and notice my scale. I step on it and watch the numbers ascend to my weight; it confirms what the mirror revealed; I am three pounds lighter than my last weigh-in.

I turn the shower on and step inside. The lukewarm water hits my head and snakes down my body comforting me. I shake and regulate under the soothing waters. As I wash my hair, I feel a strange entanglement in my fingers, like the strands have weaved spider webs around them. I gently lift my hands up from my head and open my eyes to see a chunk of weak wet hair resting on my fingers and palms. I rinse them off and watch them spiral down the drain. I reach for my hair once more only to pull yet another batch. These meds are my executioners, slower than a bullet but just as deadly. Each dose hammers another nail into my coffin, a chivalrous effect of modern medicine.

It's 2:15 a. m. when I finish showering, towel drying, and putting on a pair of shorts. In the kitchen there's a quarter-finished puzzle that taunts me from the table. Dr. Stein—the department's shrink—says puzzles alleviate the grief by stimulating cognitive abilities. I've probably been working on this for at least two months now; however, I don't recall ever really starting it, so go figure. Somehow my hands are always compelled to move the pieces around anyway. I'm lucky if I can piece together ten of these tabs a night. Each failed attempt to connect them reminds me of how I've failed to put my life back together. Maybe there's a deeper psychological enigma Dr. Stein is trying to elicit. I however, just feel like the puzzle numbs out the feelings; although it could just be the whiskey that always accompanies me as I attempt to build it.

I jolt as the phone's piercing ring shatters my concentration. It's probably Cordero or Jacobs; they're the only ones who call at this time, usually with the news of another floating stiff. I grab the receiver and say "Vogel."

All I hear is static; in the background a voice too faint to make out lingers within indistinguishable whispers. "Hello?" I utter into the void. Still, no response.

I hang up and within seconds it rings again. I lift up the receiver and speak clearly into it "Hello, Vogel here."

The static now clears a bit and I hear the faint voice a bit stronger but still can't make out what it's saying. It sounds like an old Gregorian chant, breathy and haunting.

"Listen," I say, "I can't hear you well, just call back after I hang up again."

After the third shrill ring, I pick up and answer, this time the static ends within seconds and the voice becomes clearer; it's a dark and heavy voice:

"Hoooommmmooo . . . hoooomiiinnniii . . . vuuullllttttuuurrrissss," each word is a serpent's hiss; the sinister words slithering into my ear like venomous vipers. "Blood will lead the way. The reckoning has arrived. The hunger will be satisfied. It will consume those who consume others."

I want to hang up, but I must hear more, I must draw him in like a moth drawn to the flame. I stay quiet, allowing the voice to reveal more of itself. I do the same in interrogations. Nothing strengthens authority more than staunch silence. I learned that from Jacobs.

"You don't believe do you? Tom."

"Who is this?" I demand.

A haunting laugh permeates through the receiver; it sends a chill running down my spine, colder than an icebox. "How do you know my name?"

The laughter crackles over the line again, it sounds like old creaking bones. "I know many things, Thomas Herman Vogel."

I stay quiet, my hand tightening on the receiver, my knuckles turn white like sea foam.

"I know about the guilt that gnaws at your soul. It sings sweet songs to me," the sinister voice murmurs.

This must be some sick joke, maybe teenagers prank calling, trying to play on the whole Satanic cult thing; I'll scare them straight.

"Okay, listen up, if this is some sort of prank, you picked the wrong house to call buddy, I am a cop, you hear me? And if you call here again, I'll trace this call from the station, I'll know who you are, and I'll pay you a visit. I don't think you'll like me if I visit you, most especially when I get a harassment misdemeanor stamped on your back. You'll be opening a whole can of worms you don't want open. Are we clear?"

No response. I hang up annoyed. That'll show them. These damn city kids have nothing better to do.

As I stroll back to the puzzle, the phone rings again. I dash to the receiver, pick up and say "Now you really piss—"

"*Hoooommmmooo . . . hoooomiiinnniii . . . vuuullllltttuuurrrissss,*" the strong whispering voice cuts me off.

"You're so fucked!" I cut back in. "You hear me? You picked the fucking wrong guy to mess with!" I roar at the receiver, my free hand clenching a fist so tight I feel my nails digging crescents into my palm.

"You still don't believe, Tom?" The caller's calm in the face of my outburst awakens a fear that claws at my insides.

"Listen, Asshole—"

"I know all about Sarah and Emily," the voice continues, "I know all about the little stuffed bear you avoid making eye contact with every time you enter your room. The one you keep on Sarah's dresser.

"I know about the cancer eating you from the inside out. It all started with those little nosebleeds you avoided getting checked out. I am sorry about this, but there just wasn't any other way for you to understand, Tommy boy."

No one ever called me 'Tommy boy' except my father. He's been dead for six years now.

"Your father . . ."—the voice speaks as if reading my mind

—"was born in Munich. August 18, 1918. Raised in New York. Fought in the war in 1939 and was injured. He met your mother, Leonor, in the hospital. She was his nurse. You were born four years later in Indiana. They moved down to Florida with you the following year."

I should hang up. I should call this in, have Jacobs get a trace on the line.

"You should believe, Tom. You really should." The voice sounds strangely compassionate and creepy at the same time. "*Hoooommmmooo . . . hoooomiiinnniii . . . vuuullllltttuuurrrissss.* Goodnight, Tom," the ominous voice utters and hangs up.

The disconnect tone hums a menacing beat. My heart pounding, I rip the cord from the wall and hurl the phone to the ground. These Satanic cults seem to work in the darkness, slithering through Miami's insides like a poisonous serpent, releasing a venom of fear and panic that's turning this sun-soaked cesspool into a full-blown nightmare. The good news is that I'm already half-dead and the other half's the city's antidote.

In the meantime, I head to bed, although sleep brings me no peace. Sarah and Emily's faces haunt me every night; their smiles more painful than any nightmare. I shove my face deep into Sarah's pillow and sob myself to sleep breathing in the fading scent of the life I'll never have again.

4

I perch on a bench outside the hallway of Dr. Gabriel Stein's office, waiting for him to open the door, dismiss his current patient, and signal me to enter with his customary head nod.

Dr. Stein has been the department's clinical psychologist for eighteen years. He handles all mental health assessments, clinical interventions, and operational support trainings for the Miami Police Department. This includes assessments for all of the city's law enforcement officers, background checks during the pre-employment process, Fitness-for-Duty Evaluations, Critical Incident Stress Debriefing, and Stress Management Counseling.

From hiring to firing, if a badge's attached to a cracked skull in Miami, Dr. Stein—the gatekeeper of cops' marbles—is the one who tries to patch it up.

Prior to joining the department in 1965, I'd only met Dr. Stein's predecessor, Dr. Martin Harris, during my pre-employment process. Dr. Harris retired two years later in 1967, with Dr. Stein taking his place.

I've been seeing Stein for an hour, once every two weeks, since the accident. Lieutenant Jacobs suggested I see him—not as an official Fitness-for-Duty Evaluation, but as a grief counselor. I admit these sessions have kept me from eating my own gun, though I've never told him or Jacobs I'd considered it.

My eyes drift to the large round clock mounted four feet above my line of sight. 3 p. m. I've been waiting about ten minutes already, though I'm usually never early. Today, however, I'd stopped by the station at noon to organize files of cases I'd closed earlier this month. That took about two hours, and I figured I might as well stay in the area since Stein's office lurks in the building right across from headquarters, where Homicide operates.

At 3:03, Stein swings open the door. A uniform steps out, and Stein performs his farewell rituals before giving me the welcoming nod. He regularly extends sessions with his patients by at least ten minutes—he's done so with me more than once—which is why I've developed the habit of announcing "time's up" exactly an hour after we start. Today will be no different.

Stein holds the door as I step through. He lets it snap shut like a bad habit and turns toward his desk. I watch the door close, the reversed frosted engraving of his name gleaming under fluorescent lights, mocking me with its empty promise of healing.

The office wraps around me like an iron maiden disguised in soft muted tones and deceptively comfortable chairs. It strives to soothe but succeeds only in revealing Stein's obsession with wild birds and taxidermy. The walls press in as the beaks of preserved Quails, Parakeets, Cockatoos, Cardinals, Ravens, Crows, and Falcons that adorn the entire office stand ready to peck away at whatever remains of my sanity.

The birds pose in frozen imitation of life—wings spread wide, beaks parted in eternal silence, as if caught between flight and fury.

Behind his desk, mounted between two particularly aggressive-looking falcons, a wooden plaque catches my eye. Carved into its surface are strange characters—Sanskrit, Stein explained three sessions ago—their curves and angles writhing with unnatural life in the filtered light. It reads:

$$मृत्युः सर्वहरश्चाहम्$$

Though I can't decipher its meaning, something about it burrows into my consciousness like a splinter in my mind I can't quite reach. Every time I enter this room, my eyes gravitate toward those alien symbols, as if they're whispering secrets I'm not ready to hear.

The afternoon light slices through wooden venetian blinds, casting long striped shadows across the office. They stretch like prison bars. Maybe they are. Maybe this entire office is just one elaborate bird cage.

"Detective Vogel," he drawls, settling into his wingback chair. A clipboard with a yellow legal pad rests on his lap.

I follow his voice, my gaze darting between the entrancing birds and him. He gestures to the armchair across from him. "Please, have a seat."

I sink into the leather armchair and glance at the black Raven on his desk to my right. It faces me, wings spread with green and purple oblong streaks still seemingly alive with malevolent purpose. Its talons splay open and sharp, eternally attacking a rattlesnake coiled at the base of the mount, forever poised to strike. It mirrors Miami's finest locked in endless combat with the venomous criminal vermin that slither through the night.

Stein watches me with practiced patience, his silver hair, wire-rimmed glasses, and piercing blue eyes dissecting the silence with calm authority. Sixty-two years of knowledge and eighteen years of buried secrets sharpen his gaze. In my line of work, everyone's got secrets, and the good doctor knows how to pluck them out like feathers. He waits for the soft, chapped stones of my face to part so the tomb can speak. My skin crawls, but I don't yield.

His deep voice finally cleaves the air. "So, how have you been since our last session, Tom?"

I twist my lips into what passes for a smile. "Taking it day by day, Doc."

"How's sleep? Improving?"

"Slowly, but surely."

"What about the nightmares?"

My insides knot themselves into steel wool.

"What about them? They come and they go. It's my curse to carry."

"Sarah and Emily aren't your curse to carry, Tom. Their death is not your fault. We've been over this before. You've got to let go of the guilt. There's no solid base for it. You had nothing to do with their passing. And there's nothing you could have done to save them."

His words hammer into my gut.

"What's your point?"

Stein leans forward, his gaze boring through my defenses.

"My point, Tom, is that this unreasonable guilt is devouring you alive, like your cancer. In fact, spiritually speaking, this may be the root cause of the Lymphoma. Every physical disease has a metaphysical root. I've witnessed this in countless hypnosis sessions with private clients before ever working for the city."

I bark out a laugh, deflecting. "Listen, Doc, the cancer's been around since way before the accident. It was stage four already when it was discovered last year, so the accident has nothing to do with it. That was just six months ago."

"I know how it feels, Tom. The void you feel. Like there's nothing connected to it. But there is. Guilt is the heaviest weight someone can carry. Remember the story I told you two sessions ago? Eight years ago, I lost my son to a drunk driver. I felt guilty I had bought him the car he died in. Irrational, right? It didn't feel fair. My son was just twenty-two years old. His whole life snatched away in a blink. And the driver? Served some jail time. He just got out four months ago. You think guilt has nothing to do with it? Well, let me tell you that unprocessed guilt is the sneakiest of all sins. I had to heal. Just like you need to heal. The first step is awareness."

I remember the case with crystal clarity. Palermo's case. Eight years ago. The kid's car impaled on a concrete wall, death instant and absolute. The drunk *Marielito* walked away without a scratch. Stein's words slice too close to bone, and he isn't finished.

"Are you familiar with the Bible, Tom?"

Perfect. Now he'll sermonize about sin and redemption, as if guilt needs a spiritual filter to poison the soul.

"Sure. I've read some. What are you getting at?"

"There's a verse that says, 'The wages of sin is death.' Romans 6:23." His voice carries the weight of ancient wisdom. "But it's not just Christianity that speaks of cosmic debt, Tom. The same truth echoes through many traditions. The *Bhagavad Gita* speaks of karma—how our actions carry consequences we can't escape. For example, chapter 3:13 says, 'The righteous who eat the remnants of sacrifices are freed from all sins. But the sinful ones who cook only for their own sake eat only sin.' Like that Sanskrit verse on my wall—it's all connected."

My eyes drift back to those haunting characters between the falcons. For a moment, they seem to pulse with their own inner light.

"That's a bit heavy for a therapy session, isn't it, Doc?"

"Perhaps. But consider this—what if guilt isn't just an emotion? What if it's the psyche's way of collecting a debt? Every tradition, every culture has recognized this pattern. Actions demand balance. Nature itself operates on this principle."

I remain silent. The Doc's swimming into deep waters, and I'm not sure I want to follow. Something in his words scrapes against a truth I'm not ready to face.

"Listen, Tom," he continues, "What I'm saying is that sometimes, death might be the metaphysical or spiritual wage for an unresolved subconscious trauma. In your case, it's guilt, or the inability to forgive yourself for something you may have done in the past that you may not be proud of. Sometimes, there can even be a rare manifestation of it even when you aren't truly guilty in the first place. Similar to the phenomenon of false memories.

"In psychological terms, we call it 'Identification.' You see, Tom, we are empathetic creatures and we're prone to identify with anything; even more so when it's something that's built rapport with us, whether it be something real or not."

I lean forward, my voice dropping to a growl.

"Let me get this straight, Doc. Are you trying to tell me that this cancer is some sort of cosmic punishment for a sin I'm unaware of? Or that I'm imagining guilt that may belong to someone else?"

"Well," he tilts his head and furrows his brow. "Let me put it this way, Tom. You're ridden with guilt. But it doesn't make any sense. Sarah and Emily's passing isn't your fault, it was an accident—you weren't even there, so you can't blame yourself for that.

"You say the cancer started prior to the accident. So, psychologically speaking, you must be feeling subconscious guilt for a 'sin' you aren't fully aware of.

"This guilt you feel may or may not belong to you. Judging from our time together all these months, I'd wager it's probably a false memory of sorts. You're most likely holding on to a 'sin' that isn't even yours to begin with."

His words hover in the air between us, heavy as a loaded cargo plane.

"What if my sin is simply being alive when my loved ones aren't? What's the wage for that, Doc?"

"Cancer is killing your body, Tom," his voice muffles inside my head, "but guilt is killing your soul."

My heart accelerates and I launch myself up, pacing the room like a caged animal.

"You know, Tom," his voice trails me as I move, "avoidance isn't a solution. It's a temporary shelter at best, and a prison at worst."

I stare at the shadowy prison bars caging me in.

"And what would you have me do?"

"Tom, like I've told you before, you have a choice to make. You can let this guilt consume you, or you can find a way to consume it."

An ironic chuckle tears from my throat. "And how exactly am I supposed to do that, Doc? Huh? Do I just order it off the menu the next time I'm at the local diner?"

Stein leans back in his chair, extends his left hand toward his desk, and places the clipboard on it. "Well, that's what we're here to figure out, isn't it, Tom? Look, I suggest we try hypnosis; it's a great tool we can implement in future sessions to discover where this is all stemming from. If you're open to it, of course."

I offer a subtle nod, my eyes locked on his.

"Good. Well, I want you to think of it as a process, because that's exactly what hypnosis is, and in fact, what all this is. Every word, every interaction we have is hypnotic. I'm positive you remember when I explained all of this to you a few sessions ago."

Another affirmative nod. "That's right. I knew you'd remember. Think of all this as a puzzle we're working on together. Hypnosis only lets us solve the puzzle a bit quicker. Speaking of which, how's the puzzle I gave you coming along?"

The maiden and its iron spikes press closer. I might as well jump into the pit I've dug. That damn puzzle.

"It's . . . coming along," I mutter, evasively. I'm thinking it's just about 'time's up' for today.

"I'm okay with whatever you suggest Doc, I mean that's why I'm here right? Plus it's not like you're going to make me quack like a chicken, are you?" A death rattle chuckles out from my throat.

"That's great Tom. And no, of course I won't make you quack like a chicken, that's just unnecessary. But I do want you to remember these words . . ."

His compassionate voice is soft but makes my stomach churn.

"Sometimes," he continues, "The image we seek only becomes clear when we have all the pieces in the right place. Even the ones we'd rather not see. They're all part of the grand scheme of things."

What if he's right? The thought sends a chill down my spine, colder than a stiff on a morgue slab.

I check my watch: 3:56 p. m.

"Time's up, Doc. I've got a long night ahead of me. If I ever plan on finishing that puzzle—I should get an early start."

I stand to leave, raw from the session's intensity. Stein's words have gutted me like sharp talons, leaving nothing but a hollow shell.

Stein rises and opens the door. "That's a great idea, I hope you finish it soon, Tom. Keep me posted. See you in two weeks."

I stroll out the door, pause, and turn back to Stein.

"You ever think that maybe some puzzles aren't meant to be

solved?" I ask.

His response freezes my marrow. "Perhaps. But I think you'll find, Detective, that this one demands completion. Whether you want it to or not. You take care now, Tom."

Stein closes the door and I make my way down the long hallway, his words echoing with prophetic resonance. Eyes bore into my back, but I keep walking. My hands automatically reach for the pack of cigarettes in my suit's inner left pocket as I descend the stairs to the final exit. I'm already palming one as I emerge from the building. I cushion the coffin nail between my lips. The city's hellish breath could ignite it, but my Bic pocket lighter's flame leans in for a kiss anyway. I inhale deeply; the smoke floods my lungs with familiar fire. It ignites something inside me hot enough to keep searching for answers in a city that only offers questions. I take the last drag of the cigarette as I approach the Diplomat, drop it on the concrete, and crush it beneath my shoe.

I turn the key in the ignition; the engine snarls to life. The growl reminds me how I still can't shake the sensation of being watched. I hunch over the steering wheel and lean left to peer at the building's second-floor window across from me, expecting to find Stein's piercing eyes locked on mine, but the sun's merciless glare denies me confirmation.

I pull away from the curb and head home, Stein's words tumbling inside me. They oscillate between hope and madness. In this city, sometimes it's hard to tell the difference.

5

The next morning, I hear an insistent knocking at my door; it syncs perfectly with my pounding head like orchestral bass drums. I pry open my eyes to meet the harsh morning light that slices through the blinds. As I lift my heavy head from the kitchen table, puzzle tabs fall from my cheeks. They're irregularly shaped flat cardboard paratroopers descending into a battlefield of interlocked rice paddies. Empty bottles stand like giant glass ghosts, sentinels of last night's losing war.

The knocking persists like a woodpecker carving out his home. It's a jackhammer working my skull. I stumble to the door, yanking it open. The bright morning light blinds me until it reveals my partner, Mike Cordero. At thirty-five, he's slightly over six feet tall, clean-cut with a boyish face that makes him look ten years younger. His raven hair is slicked back, combed with the precision of a special forces sniper. A pressed brown suit, white shirt, and black tie with colorful oblong shapes hang on him like a painting at the Louvre. His shoes are black mirrors, revealing a distorted version of my face that reminds me of a depiction I once saw of Hamlet's father's ghost in a play that

Sarah took me to back when we were dating.

"Good morning, sunshine!" he says with a smirk that reveals two even dimples.

"What'd you want, kid?" I utter as he steps through the door. "We don't clock in till ten tonight."

"Dude, you look like bones wrapped in pig shit." He smirks again. "Bad night?"

"The usual," I reply as I shut the door. My eyes readjust to my somber habitat.

"Did you forget how to answer a phone? I called you eight times before heading over here," Cordero says as he strolls through my living room.

I gesture vaguely at the disconnected phone and landline on the floor by the kitchen entrance. "It's out of service."

He looks at my squalid home with disgust. He's like a choir boy in a whorehouse. "What the fuck happened to your phone? If Jacobs hadn't asked me to call you, you'd be in deep shit right now." His face is like a fucking mannequin.

"Stupid punk-head kids. Prank calling in the middle of the night. Two nights in a row. Made me lose my cool for a minute. I'll fix it later."

"Sure you will." He bends over, picks up the dinged phone, and begins installing it back on the wall mount. "You know, Sarge, this . . . this isn't healthy," he says softly. "You can't keep doing this shit to yourself."

He finishes with the phone. His eyes track around the room, taking in the giant glass ghosts, the fallen paratroopers, and the whiskey stains on the wooden table. His expression shifts from disgust to worry.

"I'm fine, kid. Just a rough night," I say with a smirk that's as annoying as his.

His eyes backtrack to the cardboard paratroopers. Picks one up and looks at it like a jeweler examining a diamond. "Working on a puzzle?" He looks at the dark irregular shape with curiosity and frowns. "What is it?" He tosses it back on the table. "They're all mostly black and red pieces. No picture box around here either. How'd you know what you're piecing together here?"

"Stein gave it to me a few months back. In that black shoe box that's on the chair. Said it would help me cope. It's supposed to be a cognitive exercise," I utter as I plop on my couch. "Damn thing just gives me a headache most of the time."

Cordero's face takes on an air of confusion. "You still seeing the shrink? I thought you said you weren't going to go anymore?"

"I wasn't going to go back. But I figured it helps to talk about it," I say, reluctantly. "Keeps Jacobs happy too. I think he follows up with Stein on my progress, they've been good friends for years. Since Jacobs was in I.A.D. Stein says all sessions are confidential. I say he's quacking to Jacobs. I don't give a rat's ass, anyways. Just glad it ain't official city requirement. Figured it's best I play along, you know?"

"Yeah, well, you sure as shit don't talk to me about it. That would save you from dealing with that bullshit. But you're a mute." This kid's a fucking smirking machine.

"We're working, kid, there's no time for that shit on the job," I growl as I lift my legs on top of my coffee table.

"You don't talk about it after work either. You come in, do the job, and then you ghost. You don't even call. What happened to us? We used to be so tight." Great, the kid's getting all sentimental on me.

"We are tight, kid. Don't sweat it. I'm just going through a rough patch," I say to shield the drama, it's like he's trying to peer into my soul. I don't want to deal with this bullshit now. My head's pounding like I just went twelve rounds with Rocky Marciano.

"Look, I didn't come here to bust your balls," Cordero says, sensing my discomfort.

"Let me guess." I cut him off before he swings another word at me. "We got another floating stiff shit-show that Jacobs wants me to take the lead on?"

"You're a psychic, bud. We've got a stiff, but it ain't floating. At least not on water." He smirks again. "The poor bastard was found in an old abandoned warehouse in Overtown. It's . . . weird, Tom. Real weird. Jacobs specifically asked for you."

"Fuck, couldn't Palermo take it?"

"He tried. Begged Jacobs actually. But you know he doesn't close cases like you do. This one's nasty. Jacobs wants you there. Pronto. So clean the fuck up and let's roll."

I nod, pulling myself together. "Okay, kid. Let's go see what all the fuss is about."

"That's the spirit, champ," he says, probably thinking I beat Rocky Marciano, when the reality is the referee is about to stop the fight to save my life.

I rise off the couch and stroll to my room. I find my black pants praying by the edge of the bed. I'm glad he still does, it's been a while for me. I apologize for interrupting and feed him my two legs. Figured he'd want breakfast. I know I do.

I open the closet to my pitiful wardrobe—four shirts hanging like condemned men. Light blue, faded as Sarah's dead eyes. Black, like the city's underbelly. Two whites, pits stained yellow. I'll need the cleaners soon. I choose blue—matching my mood— and yank it off the hanger, punching through the sleeves.

Buttoning up feels like sealing my own coffin. Each snap of the small plastic discs through the fabric makes me wonder about what'll be my shroud and who'll pick it for me. Will it be Cordero? Jacobs? Or just some underpaid mortician who's seen too many cops come through his door?

My tie's black and laying next to Loneliness. The bear's single glass eye stares at me, full of shame. I nab the tie quick before he can voice his complaints. I slide the knot down my now nearly bald head and immediately tighten the noose around my neck, wondering how many more pounds I've lost in the last two days.

I don my vacant shoulder holster, the leather creaking like old bones. On the nightstand, the gargoyles—my badge and .38— stand guard over Sarah and Emily's photo. They're stone-faced sentinels guarding a memory I can't bear to face and are ready to be relieved of their vigil.

The badge clips to my belt, its weight a constant reminder of promises I couldn't keep. The .38 slides into my holster with a soft whisper of steel on leather. Locked and loaded for another day in this sinful paradise. It's the unholy trinity—gun, badge, and grief, and it's mine to bear.

I take a look in the mirror, and dread stares back at me. My eyes are bloodshot, sunken into dark hollows. My skin's got a sickly pallor that screams I've got one foot in the grave already. Maybe I'll request my ashes to be scattered on the ocean. After all, I'm already drowning. Or maybe I just don't want to see the final picture. Maybe Stein's right after all, that old bastard.

I tread back to the living room and Cordero's entranced with the puzzle. He turns and gives me that damned smirk again.

"Ready, if you are, kid," I say hoping to drag him away from the kitchen table.

He moves to the counter and grabs two white disposable cups and strolls towards me. "I made some coffee." He hands me one. "Figured you'd need it."

"Good call. I do. Let's roll."

He opens the front door and gestures me to lead the way. "Age before beauty." His teeth are white pearls.

"Sure thing, kid." I stroll through the door, Miami's morning sun harsh on my bloodshot eyes.

"Gotta love Miami, huh Sarge? Fucking beautiful day isn't it?"

"A little too beautiful." I turn around and lock my door. My keys then dive into my left pocket.

Cordero opens the passenger side door of his unmarked white Diplomat. "I'll drive, Sarge. Drop you off back home later, so you can pick up your ride."

"Sounds good, kid." I plop inside and shut the door.

As Cordero drives, the silence between us grows thick like a fog. His mouth is loaded with unspoken words, ready to fire on command. I can feel his sidelong glances filled with concern and frustration is melting off on his face.

I stare out the window, the city's a blur. Miami in the morning is a totally different beast from the neon-drenched nightmare I usually work. Bright, shiny, and seemingly spotless on the surface, but I know better. The darkness is just hiding, waiting for nightfall to slither out again.

Cordero sighs, running a hand through his hair. "Look, Sarge, I don't mean to pry. But we've been partners for over seven years now. We're good friends. We're family. At least, I thought we were . . ." he pauses, mouth open like he's trying to reach for a thought lost in an abyss.

The hurt in his voice hits me like a bullet. Cordero's a good kid, a good cop. Maybe only one of the few left in this cesspool of a city. He deserves better than a decayed and dying partner who can't even keep his own demons at bay.

"We are, kid," I mutter. "We are . . . it's just . . . it's complicated."

"Then un-complicate it for me. Talk to me, Sarge. What's eating you?

"If it's about Sarah and Emily, I know it's tough, man. It's fucked up no matter how you slice it, but you gotta pull through this. It's been six months already. Nothing's gonna bring 'em back, and that hurts. It hurts real bad. I'm telling you, Sarge, because I went through it when my pops passed five years ago. I was a mess. But I remember him every day."

He nods at the small two-by-three-inch portrait of his father he's got tugged in by the corners on the dashboard. "I always remember what he used to tell me: 'Smile, son, and the world smiles with you.' That shit's true, man. It works, you should try it sometime.

We need you out here. All of you; mind and body. You're the best investigator the city's got. It's not just me that thinks that. Jacobs too. He's counting on you. Hell, I need you. I need you sharp and on top of your game, Sarge."

I pry open my mouth, then close it again. How do I even begin to explain? The guilt that gnaws at my insides, worse than my cancer. The nightmares that haunt me. Sarah drenched in blood screaming at me 'you killed us, Tom!' Emily's crimson-satined face whispering the question that always wakes me: 'Why did you kill me, daddy?' The unfinished puzzle that only seems to mock me from my kitchen table, a jumbled mess that feels too much like my life. Before I can find the words, the car radio crackles to life:

"Breaking news: A gruesome discovery in Overtown has police baffled. Sources close to the investigation describe the scene as 'ritualistic' and 'unlike anything seen before.' Stay tuned for—"

Cordero switches off the radio, glancing at me. "You ready for this, Sarge?"

I stare out the window, watching the city blur by. "Born ready, kid. Born ready."

6

We pull up to the crime scene. The rotating lights of multiple police cars paint everything in clashing shades of red and blue. Yellow crime scene tape flutters and twists in the breeze, setting up a "Do not cross" boundary as a garish barrier between the mundane world and whatever horror awaits us.

Cordero parks the car less than half a block away from the scene, behind one of the blue and whites that's barric ading the street. As we exit the Diplomat, I take the lead towards the yellow tape. Cordero follows me like a shadow.

The old abandoned warehouse is a faded lemon yellow. Sections of grey concrete are making their way through the paint like demons being exorcised. From the looks of it, the warehouse remains a graffitied playground for hookers, junkies, and homeless souls.

When I was a uniform it was common to get calls out here of overdosed victims. Many of them were just kids, barely eighteen years old. They'd try the needle or blow and get hooked on a deadly vice. Others were prostitutes or high-end call girls, all typical users, just like the destitute and vagabonds, many of which also found their deaths through needles, spoons, and pipes. Just one of the many curses that riddles Miami.

A short time later starting in the early eighties we had a few *Marielitos* also join the cocaine party. Many of them though, were staged to look like overdoses and were clearly gang hits. Just one of the many ways Cuban mafia enforcers employed taking out trash in a quiet way. Drowning was another favorite. The water takes care of a lot of the evidence we have to work with.

We flash our badges at the uniform on guard and as he nods an affirmation we duck under the crime scene tape. He points us in direction of the body. I can see crime scene technicians already working their way around the stiff. There's one throwing up just outside the main entrance.

The moderately obese man with the high-and-tight flat-top hair, bent over, spilling his guts all over the small section of greenery to the left of the building is Jesus Alvarez. He's a good guy with a heart as big as his belly. He loves his job as much as he loves Burger King, sodas, and sweets. Especially Twinkies. Big J always has Twinkies in his car. He's been with us for about twelve years. One of the best technicians we have. I've never seen him spilling chunks at a scene. Some mess this must be.

As we reach Jesus he's already straightening up and wiping the vomit residue from his mouth with the back of his left hand.

"Fucking craziest shit I've ever seen or fucking smelled, Tom," he says, gasping for air with his hands on his hips as if to balance himself.

"Take a breather, Big J. You'll be alright," I say, as I stroll by him towards the entrance.

Cordero's laughing. "Want me to get you a bottle of water from my car cooler, Big J?"

Jesus empties his nose onto the grass. "That's okay, Mike. Thanks. I've got water in my car. I'll get some now. Along with Vicks VapoRub for my nose. You want some? You're gonna need it!"

"No, I'm fine. It's not my first rodeo with a stinky stiff," Cordero says, as he turns his back to Jesus and catches up with me.

Cordero and I enter the warehouse. The smell hits me first—death has a particular odor, one you never quite get used to. But this is . . . different. Underneath the usual stench of decay, there's something else. Something . . . acidic. It's a sour note that makes my stomach churn. Like a sticky feeling that grabs you from your insides and doesn't let go. I take a few more steps and a stench of vomit and dried urine slams into me like a freight train.

As I lift my eyes to the giant concrete wall behind the body I see large streaks of red dried blood forming a message. There, scrawled onto the wall in crude, jagged letters is:

HOMO HOMINI VULTURIS

By its spelling, I definitely know it's Latin. But what does it mean?

My gaze drops to the victim who's sprawled in the center of the warehouse, rigid limbs contorted like a broken marionette.

The body is laying in a crimson pool that's slowly drying out.

The coppery tang lingering in the air is heavy and mixes with the large yellow-brown urine stains that surround the drying blood in a unique contrast, both in color and smell.

He's a middle-aged man with an advanced receding hairline. His face is a frozen mask of terrorizing fear. His brown eyes are open wide and purple lips decorate the mouth which is agape like a cave entrance. The chest is ripped open, the sternum and ribs splayed wide like some grotesque wildflower. And in that blood-adorned cavity, where a heart should be, is a void that makes my blood run cold.

The poor man's been emptied out; lungs, heart, and most of the intestines, gone. Telling by the victim's rigid hands, rigor mortis is still paying him a visit for at least another six to eight hours.

Cordero leans in close, his voice barely above a whisper. "Jesus, Tom. What kind of sick fuck are we dealing with here?"

I shake my head, trying to clear the fog of disgust. "It's a message, kid. That's all I know." I direct Cordero's attention to the inscription on the wall.

"Only a psychopath leaves a signature like that. He's proud of his work. Wanted to leave us a message. Which only means this is personal. And if not personal to this vic, it's personal to him, in which case, there'll be more of these, soon."

"You think we're dealing with a serial, Sarge?" Cordero asks, with a smirk that's a little inappropriate.

"Unfortunately that'll be determined if we get at least two more stiffs with the same M.O. within the next three or four weeks. But judging from what I see here, I'd bet my left eye we are. But, let's not jump to any conclusions just yet."

Alvarez taps me on the right shoulder from behind. I turn to see his pale face is regaining color. He's got a large glossy spread of Vicks VapoRub under his nose that looks like an invisible mustache. He hands me a pair of latex gloves.

"Thanks, Big J. Feeling better?" I say, as my fingers break in the gloves.

"Just a tad bit, Sarge," he says, trying to smile but only a face of disgust emerges.

"Got a pair for me?" Cordero asks Alvarez, his smirk bullying his disgust.

Alvarez digs into his left back pocket and pulls two crumpled latex gloves and shakes them in the air as if he's offering a fish treat to a seal. "Here you go," he says.

Cordero takes the pair like he's hungry. "Thanks!" he says, as he fingers the gloves.

I squat down by the body and dig into the man's right back pocket, where there's a bulge that appears to be a wallet. I'm looking for any form of identification. The dorsal aspect of my gloved right hand gets a slight smear of blood on it as I retrieve his wallet. I open it to find two five-dollar bills and his driver's license. Issued three years ago to one, Reyes, Miguel Jose. Born May 5, 1945. Male. 5 feet, 8 inches. His address is right off 15th Ave. and NW 8th Terrace. Little Havana district. Probably Cuban, maybe even a *Marielito*.

I stretch my arm out towards Cordero with the victim's driver's license in hand, and flop it up and down between my thumb and forefinger as a signal for him to grab it. "Run him and let me know what you get. ASAP."

"You got it, Sarge," he replies, as he snatches the driver's license and sprints to the car.

I stand back up, turn around, and face Alvarez. "Get me an evidence bag."

As he gets the bag from his van, the medical examiner pulls up to park next to his. Alvarez is already making his way back to me when Dr. Richard Horowitz, Medical Examiner, is gloving up and walking towards us. The white-haired Jew with a thick white walrus mustache is in his mid-sixties and looks like an Albert Einstein replica. He'd look fifteen years younger except for his tired bloodshot eyes and almost snow-white hair. His skin is taut and hardly shows any wrinkles. He has an elegant stride, almost militant.

"Here you go, Sarge," Alvarez says as he hands me the evidence bag, still looking unwell.

"Thanks. Listen, Big J, go take a seat in your van with the A/C on max. Have some more water. When you feel better, come on back. Don't want you croaking on me here," I say with a concerned smile.

"Okay, Sarge. Sorry about . . . you know. This ain't ever happened to me before," he says, almost as if ashamed of himself.

As he shuffles towards his van, I lift my voice so it reaches him. "I know. Don't worry about it. You're good." Without looking back, he lifts a hand in the air to signal he heard me.

I bag the wallet as Dr. Horowitz reaches me. He takes one look at the scene and lets out a low whistle.

"*Oy vey*," he mutters. "What kind of animal did this?"

"The two-legged kind, Doc," I reply, and extend my right hand in a fist towards him.

He makes a fist with his and bumps it to mine—it's our typical greeting when we have gloves on.

"How good's your Latin, Vogel?" he asks, with a smile that seems to imply a rhetorical question. His eyes are locked on the concrete wall with the blood-scrawled Latin phrase.

"Not good at all. You have any idea what it says?" My eyes are now fixated on the large bloody letters.

"Not a clue. But I do know someone who might be able to help you," the Doctor says with calm assurance.

"One of your colleagues, I presume?"

"Something like that, an old friend from yeshiva. Guy's a rabbinical genius. Studied ancient and Semitic languages. He's one of the greatest Kabbalists of the twentieth century, a mystical guru, if you will. Name's Ezra Goldstein. I can get you his contact info later."

"Yeshiva? You were in Rabbinical school?"

"Yeah," he says, his large blue glossy eyes showing strong nostalgia. "Back in New York. Many moons ago. I come from a long lineage of rabbis. But it just wasn't my calling. I've always loved the human body and medicine. My parents were heartbroken that I didn't follow through with the family tradition. But hey, our destiny chooses us, right?"

His beautiful but powerful words elicit a truth that makes my stomach churn, more than the smell of the rotting stiff. If our destiny chooses us, then my family got dealt a bad hand, and I picked up the most unlucky of them all—grief.

"Well, you're definitely in the right field, Doc. Let's get started." I move closer to the body, and Horowitz follows. He squats close to the stiff while I stand behind him and observe. He begins his examination.

"Well . . ." he pauses shortly, breathes in deeply, exhales, and then continues, "he was cannibalized. You see this here?" He points to a section of the lower torso—what's left of it—close to the pelvis. "This area has some toothmarks—not from an animal —and tears that seem to be made with hands. Doubt we can get any prints off the body. Lucky if we even get a partial. He was heavily urinated on and the uric acid's settled in quite well. You can see the difference in skin color from this area to this one." He points from one patch of dangling skin to the next one. It's a broken suspension bridge.

"What you see here . . ." He shifts his hand to point at a section between the ribs and the contorted limbs. "is vomit. Not likely to be the victim's, since what's left of his insides looks basically clean and his mouth shows no residue.

"Those raw chunks you see there lying on the spew are organ matter and skin. I'm assuming some of it's liver and spleen from their size and color. Would have to tell you for sure after I examine him back at the morgue."

"Oh, and this yellow stuff here," he says as he points to a small neon yellow pool that's hiding under an armpit, "is bile; might be from the victim's gallbladder or it belongs to the two-legged animal who's responsible for this mess. What happened here was he ate the guy—while he was still alive—then threw up some and finished by urinating on the corpse."

I feel an unease settling in my gut like a lead weight. "Looks like you've got your work cut out for you."

"It'll just take a bit longer to sort this mess out and give you a solid report," he says as he stands back up.

"Bag him and tag him. You know where to reach me as soon as you've got the report." I remind him because I'm at a loss for words.

I feel a presence behind me and turn to find Cordero. He's got the look of an amused seven-year-old who's found something cool in his backyard while playing in the dirt.

"Our vic's a *Marielito* and a repeat offender. His rap sheet's about a page and a half. Done time for everything from robbery to DUI manslaughter," he says as he hands me the license back.

Cordero's face retains that inappropriate amused smirk. "Also, Rodriguez—the initial responding officer—says the junkie that called it in saw a large black bird about six feet tall, walking out of the warehouse around 4 a. m. Says its head was bald and red—like a giant vulture."

"Damned crackheads, fucking hallucinating. Some witness that'll be." I toss the license in with the wallet in the evidence bag and seal it. "Anything else?"

"Yeah. He's got unpaid parking tickets up the yin-yang," he says, following it up with a laugh.

I don't find it amusing. "Sanchez point out any other witnesses?"

"Nope. Just the junkie. Patrol took him to the station for questioning. Palermo's team's already interviewing him."

"Looks like Jacobs gave him some crumbs to chew on, huh?" Now it's my turn to smile.

"Poor guy's gotta eat, Sarge," Cordero says, his dimples showing strong.

"We start digging, kid," I say, my voice rattling deeper than I intended. "This is just the beginning."

"Yes, sir," Cordero replies.

"Let's roll," I say, as I hand the evidence bag to a crime scene tech passing by.

I peel off the gloves and fold them into each other as they slip off my hands and toss them into an open black trash bag thats on the far left corner of the warehouse. Cordero follows my routine.

As we head out the entrance, I turn back to Horowitz, who's already zipped up the body bag and is loading it onto a trolley with the help of a couple of techs. "Catch you later, Horowitz." His blue eyes lock on mine like a bear trap. He nods once and continues his work.

The Miami sun beats down, harsh and unforgiving, as Cordero and I head back to the car. But I've never felt colder in my life.

7

My wife and daughter are buried in Memorial Cemetery off West Flagler Street and 55th Avenue. It's 7 a. m. on a Tuesday morning in September. I haven't been here in over three weeks; I miss them terribly.

The cemetery's black iron gates open before me; guardians of a dead city allowing my entrance. I loom the Diplomat in, treading slowly as if it's stepping through a minefield. I nod at Pedro, the security guard that's always on duty here. He's short, bald and fat, with a thick black mustache. His skin is dark from the sun and when he's sitting inside the small security cubicle, he looks like a Cuban version of those old genie machines with the automaton that gives out a card with a prediction of the future. I've never asked him for a prediction, although I'm sure he'll be right about where I'll end up soon. He's familiar with the territory.

The sky is bleeding black and threatens me with rain but I know it's just waiting to join in with my tears so it doesn't cry alone.

I reach the small bend where I always park, kill the engine and sit for a moment watching the thin mist that clings to the gravestones. The tick of cooling metal soothes my ears; it's the sound of the rest that I need and can't have. The cemetery is quiet but the ghosts are screaming; a reminder the clock's ticking for me on two fronts, and I'm losing on both.

Sarah and Emily are waiting for me. I grab the white roses laying on the passenger seat and step out the car, my shoes crunching on the gravel path. Old and weathered tombstones of varying shapes and sizes stretch out in neat rows in front of me. The scent of damp earth and wilting flowers enters my nostrils as I make my way through a labyrinth of markers until I reach their plot. Sarah and Emily Vogel. Beloved Wife and Daughter. The words are hard to read because they're true. They should have buried me. Statistically wives outlive their husbands and it's only natural for a daughter to bury their father, not the other way around.

I deserved to be where they are now more than they did. It's not fair. It's not just. My heart's wrapped in barbed wire. Each visit I make here etches another deep scar into my soul as deep as the engraving on their gravestone. The white roses I brought them almost a month ago are now withered husks, they might as well be a mirror I am staring into. I lean in and replace them with the fresh and vibrant white roses I bought from a street vendor on my way here. White roses are the closest representation of their innocence.

For the last five months or so I've managed to convince myself that I'm not just speaking to the slabs of granite. So, I lean in brush away some dead leaves and dust from the base of the headstones and follow through with my greetings.

"Hey, girls," I mutter, my voice striving to sound cheerful but only succeeds in sounding hollow.

"I'm sorry . . . I know it's been a while." My words slither out with guilt.

"It's been really difficult for me lately . . . I'm sure you know . . ." a tear begins to roll down my left cheek.

"You wouldn't be so proud of me . . . I've . . . been thinking of . . . ending things, again . . . . I just . . . miss you two so much . . ." I pause, swallowing hard.

"I don't know if I can do this anymore. Maybe it's time I join you . . . if you'd just give me your blessing . . . please . . ."

Sarah had always been contemptuous of those who took their own lives. Each time I'd mentioned closing another suicide case, she'd dismiss it as cowardice. So, my confession feels as if I'm letting her down.

"I'd just be speeding up the process a bit . . . you know . . . I'm due soon, anyway," I whisper, like bargaining with her ghost.

Inside my head, I swear I can hear Sarah's voice and I repeat her question with a chuckle as I wipe my nose and eyes with the palms of my hands. "What's my rush?"

"Well, for starters, I caught a case. It's bad. Real bad. The kind of bad that makes me question everything. At this point, I'm just asking myself 'what's the point, anyway?' Sometimes I feel I should just throw in the towel."

The wind picks up and the trees surrounding me are now rustling a strong whisper. Light drops of rain begin to slowly drizzle on me. Sarah's voice is stronger now, almost as strong as the wind. She's scolding me for even letting the thought of giving up enter my mind.

"Yeah, yeah, I know," I mutter, a faint smile now forces it way out, "I have to see it through."

Her voice grows serious. She wants me to promise that I'll see this through to the end, no matter how difficult it may get. She says I owe her that much. She didn't marry a coward, she reminds me.

"I'm not afraid," I reply with a serious tone, "I'm just so exhausted . . . the cancer . . . the sleepless nights . . . that fucking puzzle that Stein's got me doing . . . and to be honest . . . you and Emily are really doing a number on me . . ." I force a laugh so as to conceal my complaint but I feel terrible for expressing how tired I am of the nightmares they incite.

I can feel Sarah's disappointment lingering in the air. She says the nightmares are only there as a reminder.

"A reminder of what?" I ask her, perplexed.

Sarah stays silent for bit, her disappointment now feels more like resentment. When she finally breaks her silence she asks me to promise her I'll see this through. My deep love for her floats up to the surface and exits through my tear ducts, rolling down my cheek, uniting with hundreds of rain drops that are now picking up their pace.

"Yes, I promise." I say feeling a bit more confident. Sarah's always had this effect on me. She's always brought out the best in me. Always pushed me to do more and be the best I can be. She's my better half and she's gone; left me to face the horrors of grief and loneliness. At least, right now, I'm satisfied I'm not holding on to my life with the fear of death. I sometimes feared getting killed on the job, not because I was afraid of dying, but because I feared leaving Sarah and Emily alone—to fend for themselves. The fucking irony of it all.

Emily's voice now comes through and says, "Make this right, daddy. Only you can do this. You're my hero. Don't ever forget that. I love you."

"I will honey. I promise. I love you more." My voice is drowning as I wipe more tears and rain drops away.

"She's right you know," Sarah chimes in again, "There's no one left to finish this but you." Sarah's final words spiral away with the wind, losing itself in the ether.

The silence that follows is deafening. I'd give anything to hear Sarah's voice again, to feel Emily's small hand in mine. Instead, I've got my lymph nodes full of cancer and an unsolved case that's full of unspeakable horrors.

I spent the whole day yesterday going through the preliminary investigation process with Cordero. We followed our typical routines, canvassing the neighborhood of the crime; interviewing residents, merchants, and others who could possibly give us leads. No one except that single crackhead Palermo and his team interviewed—saw or heard anything. So all we have to go on is that junkie's tale of a six-foot-tall-vulture exiting the old warehouse around 4 a. m. yesterday. That and the fact the vic was a repeat offender. The only positive thing about this lead is the vic's body shows signs of cannibalism which coincides with the consumption of flesh associated with vulture behavior, which in turn gives the junkie's trippy testimony at least somewhat of a grounded resonance to it.

Vultures aren't taller than two-and-a-half feet and I've yet to see one that knows how to write, let alone one who knows Latin; so I doubt there's a six-foot-tall vulture who eats people and scribbles Latin phrases on walls with their blood—walking around Miami looking for victims. We're most likely dealing with some nut-job who either thinks he's a vulture or some other wild animal or who's obsessed with the occult. Maybe we're dealing with more than one nut-job. Maybe this whole thing might even be connected with those so-called "Satanic cults" disappearances and ritualistic sites found down south by the Everglades. What's for sure is we are probably going to see more bodies turn up in a similar fashion because this type of crime is not typically an isolated event. Dr. Horowitz is currently working on the autopsy, and we're waiting on his report for confirmation of any specific details that may aid our investigation. There's more behind this and I'll be damned if I don't get to the bottom if it, even if it's the last thing I do.

The sand that's left in my hourglass is picking up the pace almost as strong as the harsh rain that's now pouring on me. I turn towards my car, and as much as I want to, I don't turn back to view my family's gravestones. Heavy thunder now roars far away, a primal growl that matches the determination burning in my gut.

The Diplomat roars in unison with the thunder. It reminds me I've got a reason to keep breathing a little longer; a monster I need to catch. It's time to hunt.

8

The fluorescent lights in the Miami Police Homicide Department office hum with a dull but consistent buzz. If I weren't so used to them already, I'd be pulling out what little hair I have left. I've been scribbling circles on my yellow legal pad for over three hours now as I think about the case. Its eerie nature looms over me like a black cloud. Swarms of local press have settled outside the station like desperate creatures in famine. For the first time in my career, I feel lost. I've been told that I'm not a run-of-the-mill detective. My abilities are unmatched in all of South Florida —at least that's what Jacobs always says. Over the last eight years, I've closed more cases than most detectives have in their entire careers. But I just can't shake the bad feeling I have about this one.

Cordero and I have followed protocol—we've done all the preliminary investigation work there is to be done within the first forty-eight hours. Now, there's nothing else to do but to play the waiting game. We're still waiting for the autopsy report— Horowitz usually doesn't take this long, but it's understandable as he's working a complicated corpse—whatever's left of it anyway

—I can only imagine what a shit show his report will be. Sadly, at this point, we're also waiting for either a lead or a new body to pop up.

So here I am, three goddamned hours scribbling circles like an idiot, and no new leads have come up. The phone's been quiet except for a call I received earlier from Dr. Stein as I was sitting back down at my desk after refilling the white eight-ounce Styrofoam cup with the black battery acid the rest of the detectives audaciously call coffee. He'd called to check up on my progress with the puzzle. He mentioned he couldn't reach me at home, so he called the office. I told him I haven't been home for a minute—that I caught a tough case; that I might have to cancel our next session—that I'd keep him posted. He wasn't too conversational other than trying to convince me not to miss the session, as he'd like to start the hypnosis treatment as soon as possible.

Cordero excused himself to the restroom at least forty-five minutes ago—he's either shitting up a storm or is chit-chatting around the station—this younger generation of detectives lacks the fundamental discipline so common among the veterans. It's frankly quite concerning for the future of this city. I'll continue to embrace the discipline of what a real detective should be, with the hope that these young bucks decide to mirror my actions— but I don't have too much time left to do it.

I'm just about to stand up and go find Cordero when Jacobs opens his door and barks a command for me to enter his office. I don't have time to wonder what he wants because his office is less than ten feet from my desk and I'm still thinking about the case.

VULTURE

Like an automaton, I just march on through his door.

Jacobs's office still has the same chilling temperature of that terrible night he called me in. There hasn't been a time since then that I've entered this office without being transported—at least for a few seconds—to that most horrific moment of my life.

The acrid smell of stale coffee and bureaucratic despair lingers in the air and reminds me of the weight Jacobs carries. He sits behind his desk barricaded by a wall of case files. He's a budding bodybuilder, with thick blond hair combed back, and a thick blond chevron mustache. He reminds me of Chuck Norris, except he's twice the size. He wears a brick-red tie on a white long-sleeve shirt that's a bit too tight and only serves to accentuate his muscles. His brown suit's coat is resting on his chair's back.

"Sit down," Jacobs says, with a large pale open hand pointing at an empty chair in front of his desk; the same one I sat down on that cursed night of the accident. His hand withdraws back to the paperwork like a turtle's neck. He doesn't take his blue eyes off the file he's organizing but is still able to notice my apprehension.

"Down, Vogel," he commands again.

I don't want my body resting on it again, but denying his request would probably raise an unnecessary red flag, so I plop down on it without giving it another thought, like diving into cold water. The worn leather creaks a complaint beneath me, and I smile at Jacobs, attempting to set the tone.

He finally raises his head, his bloodshot eyes give me a stare that can melt metal. A knot forms in my gut. I breathe in and exhale my question as tame and friendly as possible. "What's on your mind, Lieutenant?"

He stares at me intently for a few seconds, but it feels like minutes. He exhales, "Have you seen the press outside?"

"Yeah, they're like rabid dogs."

"It's only going to get worse, Vogel." He rubs his temples. "I've got the chief so far up my ass he can tickle my uvula."

"Sounds uncomfortable."

"You think it's funny, Vogel? The mayor's chewing the chief out, and the chief's ripping me a new one. The press's got someone spilling beans, and the city's panicking. To top it off, you look like shit, and frankly, I'm concerned if you're fit to handle this one. How are you feeling? Are you still taking your meds?"

The question hangs in the air like cigar smoke. I lean forward, staring at the floor, searching for an answer that will satisfy Jacobs but that allows me to shift the conversation toward its conclusion. I finally raise my eyes to meet his.

"Yeah, oral chemo. I'm fine, really. Just some trouble sleeping. Typical side effects. Got some kids prank-calling me in the middle of the night too, almost every night, which hasn't helped. Thinking of tracing the call. Maybe give them a little scare in person, since they haven't taken my threats seriously."

"You let me know if I can do anything to help. Listen, you're the best I've got. I know what you were capable of—that's why I've got you on this case," he says, emphasizing the past tense. "But lately . . . and I hate to say this, but you've been looking off your game. You've been sitting at that desk, scribbling God knows what on that pad of yours."

"Yeah, I appreciate it a lot. Get me a copy of my phone records—I need to find out who's been calling me. About the scribbling . . . sometimes scribbling helps me think."

Jacobs sighs. He's irritated like an untreated hemorrhoid.

"I'll do that for you . . . maybe later this afternoon it'll be ready for you. I just want to know if I can really count on you. If you're not feeling well, it's okay—you take a break, handle your health, and I'll just pull you off the case and give it to Palermo. He's begged me for it more than once. There's no shame in taking care of yourself."

"Palermo?" I snap with a condescending smirk. Guess some of Cordero's habits are rubbing off on me. "Most of his cases are colder than Siberia. You might as well give the Chief your resignation letter, while you're at it."

"Don't push it, Vogel. We're friends above everything, but you've got to cut the crap. You know I want you on this case . . . need you on this case . . . which is why I told Cordero to get you. If I didn't want you on it, you'd be home sleeping right now."

"I told you, Lieutenant, I'm fine. I'll—"

Before I can finish the lie, the door opens and Cordero walks in. He carries an exaggerated smile like a child who's found a large rock in his backyard while playing pirate and thinks he's struck gold. His timing's finally improving.

"Ever heard of knocking?" Jacobs asks, directing a fierce look at Cordero.

"Sorry, Lieutenant. . . . Oh hey, Tom. . . ." His perfect dentures glisten under the fluorescent bulbs. "I just thought you'd like to know I saw Palermo talking to one of the reporters from channel 7. You know . . . the cute blonde petite with the bob cut. She's a knockout, but I'm pretty sure he wasn't asking her out, if you catch my drift."

"Goddammit!" Jacobs stands up and bolts through the door. We follow behind him.

Jacobs turns back to us momentarily before reaching the elevators.

"Palermo's our snitch," Jacobs says. "We'll continue this conversation later, Vogel. In the meantime, get off the desk and hit the streets. Proactive detective work."

I nod an affirmation, and he fingers the elevator's call button with the downward arrow. The elevator's door opens almost immediately, and he disappears into it. I feel a strong relief settle within my entrails, but I know it's only momentary unless I can catch this psychopath before my health takes me out of the game or before my breakdown's noticeable enough that Jacobs can't bypass taking me off the streets. Hell, I'd be lucky if I catch this freak show before the monster that's eating me from the inside finally takes me out.

"Palermo's fried chicken," Cordero says with a chuckle. "Jacobs's gonna tear him a new one."

"Yeah, that'll get him off our ass for a bit." I say and press my right ear's tragus as the high pitch that haunts my brain synchronizes with the hum of the fluorescent lights. Tinnitus is a bitch.

"Was he drilling you before I walked in?" Cordero asks.

"Your timing couldn't have been better, kid. He was

questioning my fitness for duty. Walk with me," I say as I head down the hallway to the stairs. "I'll head home for a shower and meet you later at the diner."

Cordero paces next to me. "I don't blame him. I'm concerned about you too."

"You'd be better concerned about yourself, kid."

I stroll through the large and heavy stairway door and down the old and pale yellow stairs, Cordero trailing right behind me. Chips of cracked paint peeling off the stairs remind me of the frailty of life.

"You're off your game, bud," Cordero replies. "It's the truth. Not picking on you; just looking after you. To be honest, my bathroom break was to get away from that solitary confinement you set up at your desk. I'm sorry, but I can't do that. I can't just sit there and loathe."

"Loathe? It's called thinking, kid," I reply as I push through the door that leads to the parking lot. "You should try it sometime."

The humid heat hits me harder than the scorching sun. I feel like a vampire—weak and melting under its powerful rays.

"I've never seen you 'think' like that before. It's like you're a prisoner of your mind," Cordero says with a floating air-quotes hand gesture.

"Now you 'see' how I think?" I respond by mocking him with air quotes. "That's a great talent. You should use it on our suspects from now on."

"I didn't mean it like that, Tom. Why are you being so defensive?"

"I'm not being defensive, kid. I'm simply reflecting your snot-nosed attitude back at you."

"I just think—"

"That's exactly my point . . . you don't think . . . you're so caught up in playing hot-shot detective that you get lost in the smoke. Just because you got a degree in psychology before becoming a cop doesn't mean you can jump to psychoanalytic mumbo jumbo."

Cordero stays silent. He's clearly offended. I can tell because he's not smiling.

"I'm going to solve this case, with or without your help, kid. We're done here. I'm gonna head home, shower, and meet you at the diner later in the evening," I say with a tone that masks just how irritated I am right now.

"I'll be there at seven sharp," he replies.

"Horowitz should be done with the autopsy soon. Give me a call if he gets in touch with you first."

We stop in front of the black Diplomat. I open the driver's side door. Before I can sit down, I see Pedro Sanchez walking toward us. Detective Sanchez is a thirteen-year veteran and has been in homicide for the last three. He's short, fat, bald, and sports a thick black mustache that completely covers his thin upper lip. He wears brown slacks, an olive tie, and a white shirt with buttons so tight that anyone within five feet of him should wear eye protection.

"What you ladies fussing about now?" He says with a chuckle. "Why don't you two just kiss and make up?"

"*Dímelo, Gordo*, how was your vacation?" Cordero asks as he leans over to shake his hand. The handshake morphs into a hug.

"Riquísimo, spent it fishing at the Keys; caught a bunch of Red Groupers. How's the family?"

"Todo tranquilo, hermano. My mom's still struggling a bit, but hanging in there. That last fall she had really did a number on her."

"Heard you guys caught a wild case. You let me know if I can help," Sanchez says, addressing both of us.

I've always admired Cubans for their brotherly natures, but these two sometimes just get on my nerves. Sanchez especially. I can't shake the bad feeling he's always given me. It's a feeling that there's more to him than meets the eye. Luckily for me, I haven't had to deal with him too often.

"I think we got it covered," I say with a raspy, clipped voice.

Sanchez raises his hands up. "Just offering to help." He begins to slowly walk backward toward the building. "Good luck with the case, gentlemen," he says as he turns around.

I turn to Cordero. "Listen, I gotta go, kid. We'll continue this later."

I lift my voice toward Sanchez. "Good seeing you, Sanchez."

Sanchez turns around and points his hands at me like a Wild West cowboy firing his pistols. "Likewise. See ya, Vogel."

Cordero shuffles over to his car, a few spots away from mine. He opens his door and tosses me a nod and a smirk before entering the vehicle.

I plop into the Diplomat, start the engine, and pull out of the parking lot. I'm focused on the case, and nothing's going to stop me from catching this freak show.

9

I've been lying on the couch since I left the shower. The fan above me whirs lazily; it reminds me of the progress of the case. It makes me dizzy. I close my eyes, and the crime scene spills across my mind like bleeding entrails. It fills my every lingering thought. I attempt to make sense of the madness, but all I can do is focus on the terrible flashes of torn flesh. My own mortality creeps in, its ugly face fills me with doubts, and I fear this might be a puzzle I won't be able to finish. Like the puzzle Stein gave me.

I sit up and stare across the room to the kitchen table. The unfinished puzzle mocks me. Each piece is a thorn ripping through my flesh. My head begins to throb. It's a dull ache that's as familiar as my grief. It's become a constant companion since the accident. Only whiskey seems to dim it down a bit. It's not like I want to drink. I've tried all the pills, even the doctor-prescribed ones, and they don't do half of what whiskey does.

I stand and shuffle over to the kitchen table. A sweet vanilla fragrance hits my nostrils when I open the half-empty bottle of whiskey. I take a sip. It runs down my throat like burning lava, cooling down by the time it reaches my gut. I don't want to overdo it, but I need clarity. I make a mental note to keep it light. I'm meeting Cordero later at the diner, and I don't want him smelling it on my breath.

My eyes move to the window across from me. Through the open blinds, I see the darkness seeping in. It hums a song—a nocturnal rhythm that infiltrates my veins. My heart mulishly pumps to the beat of this daunting dusk. A feeling of emptiness settles in my bowels and reminds me of all I have lost. I'm falling into an abyss.

For a moment, the room seems to turn upside down, and I lean on the table to stabilize myself. Puzzle pieces grip onto my palms as I instinctively find the chair behind me and guide my rear onto it. The dizziness passes within a few short minutes. I close my eyes once more only to see the images of blood, entrails, urine, and vomit swirling round and round like a carousel, taking me along for the ride. I can taste the coppery tang of blood and smell the rotting flesh.

I open and close my eyes again, hoping to clear my mind, but the images come flooding back again. This time I see the blood-scrawled Latin phrase on the wall.

HOMO HOMINI VULTURIS

Its obscure and occult nature haunts me. I'll have to pay a visit to the rabbi Horowitz referred to me—hopefully he'll be able to help decipher this cryptic message.

I open my eyes and begin scraping off the puzzle pieces from my palms when the phone rings. I let it ring once, twice, and three times before I pick up. Sharp, piercing static thrusts through my ear, forcing me to pull the receiver away. I lean my back onto the wall and gently guide the receiver back to my ear.

"Hello?" I say into the menacing silence on the other end.

There's no response, only what seems like a faint whisper.

"Hello?" I say again, only to hear the line go dead.

I hang up the receiver, and before I can sit back down on the chair, the phone rings again. I pick up and repeat my greeting.

A low and all-too-familiar menacing whisper builds to a crescendo. *"Hoooommmmooo . . . hoooomiiinnniii . . . vuuullltttuuurrrissss."*

Its dark and eerie tone causes my skin to shiver. It's the same voice I've heard this whole week. Calling me every night. I don't think about it twice. I slam the receiver down, my heart racing. I'm going to trace these sons of bitches as soon as I get down to the station. I've just about had it with this shit. I don't have time for games and childish pranks.

The phone rings again, and I pick up the receiver before it rings a second time. I open my mouth, but before I can curse this son of a bitch out, the eerie voice speaks again.

"Hello, Tom," the voice says. Its dark and muffled tone seems to mingle with the darkness outside.

"Yeah, can I help you?" I respond, hoping that somehow my question brings some clarity.

A haunting laugh pierces loudly through the receiver.

"Is something funny, asshole?" I say, hoping my insult will

provoke this bastard to reveal himself.

"You can't even help yourself, Tom. . ."

As much as I dislike this jackass, he's right. "What do you want?" I ask.

"I want you to believe, Tom."

"Believe what?" I ask.

"Believe in redemption. . ."

"Look, I've been more than patient with you. I could have traced your calls since that first night you called me, but I've let it slide. I've got a lot going on right now to waste my time with you, but I'm just about to reconsider, and since you haven't taken my warnings seriously, I guess I'll have to pay you a visit soon. That way you can tell me everything you want to tell me in person. How does that sound?"

"Oh, look at you, Tom," the voice says. "So tired, so weak," he says, with an undertone that implies he finds this whole thing amusing. I sense he almost feels sorry for me. "You won't find me that easy. You can't trace me. You can't even finish that puzzle. What's even more amusing is that you can't stop thinking about my work. It's beautiful, isn't it?"

The hair on my arms rises up. Could this be the psychopath I'm after?

"Yes, Tom, I am, but I'm not a psychopath. I'm an artist. A redeemer," the voice says, as if reading my thoughts. "I bring forth righteous judgments. I bring balance to the scales."

"Okay, you've got my attention," I say.

"I know, Tom. I know. Now, if you want to find me, listen very carefully. Firstly, you must believe in redemption. Every cause has an effect. Every action a reaction. There will be more of my work for you to enjoy. Each offering will be a reminder of redemption. Each one consumed for righteousness. Every body is a piece of the puzzle. Remember, only you can find me. If you believe. Now go forth and witness my work. *Hoooommmmooo . . . hoooomiiinnniii . . . vuuullllltttuuurrrissss*. Good-bye, Tom."

"No! Wait!. . ." I exclaim as a high-pitched static-filled hum pierces my brain.

"Fuck! Fuck! Fuck!" I wail as I slam the receiver on the wall three times before jamming it into the hook switch.

My frustration grows to a fever pitch. I grab the chair and hurl it into the living room. It knocks a vase and a frame onto the ground. The shatter of the frame's glass compels me to walk over to it. Sarah and Emily's faces are obscured by cracked glass. I pick up the frame and begin to remove the broken glass. Each piece I remove is accompanied by a tear that rolls down my face. How could I do this to them? My girls. My everything. Frustration turns to anger, and I grip one of the large shattered pieces in my left hand and squeeze hard, embracing the pain until I feel the warmth of my blood dripping down my forearm. I open my hand, and the blood-stained glass tumbles onto the floor. I hug the frame tightly against my chest. I haven't cried like this since the funeral.

My eyes burn as I lay the glass-less photo frame on the living room coffee table. I glance at the wall clock to my left. It's twenty to seven. That gives me about half an hour to make it to the diner before Cordero.

I head to the bathroom and use my first-aid kit to patch my

hand up. A thick white bloody gauze now decorates my left palm. After getting dressed, I call Cordero and tell him to stop by the station and pick up a copy of my phone records from Jacobs before heading to the diner. He confirms he'll pick them up and meet me at the diner around seven-fifteen.

I lock up and climb into my car, catching a glimpse of myself in the rearview mirror. I release a deep sigh and examine the hollow-eyed stranger staring back at me. Fear and desperation linger all around me, but I push it all down.

I crank up the engine, pull out of the driveway, and focus on the dark road ahead. There is no other choice for me because somewhere out there, a killer is watching—waiting. And I'm the only one who can stop him.

10

It's five past seven, and I've been waiting for Cordero in our usual booth at the diner for the last ten minutes. The joint's empty again tonight—not a soul has walked through the door since I got here. Fluorescent lights whisper a dull buzz, like dying insects reciting their own epitaph. The stench of burnt coffee and stale cigarettes has become my aromatherapy, reminding me to light up while I wait for him to arrive.

With my pack of smokes already out on the table, I pull the metal ashtray closer, palm a Camel, and let the flame of my Bic lighter welcome the nicotine into my bloodstream. I wonder how a stimulant like nicotine can bring me so much relaxation.

Marge brings me a cup of joe and tells me my burger's almost ready. As she's turning to head to the kitchen, Cordero walks in, smiling like a kid on Christmas morning.

"Sorry I'm late," he says, tossing a large sealed yellow folder onto the left side of my booth. "Your phone records. Jacobs says it's clean. No calls registered except those from the station and my home." He plops down on his side of the booth. "Those calls you mentioned? They're nonexistent."

"What the fuck? That can't be," I say, laying my cigarette on the ashtray.

I open the folder and pull out the copy of the records. I scan through the papers. Jacobs is right, but it doesn't make any sense.

"What the fuck happened to your hand?" Cordero asks, staring at my bandaged hand.

"Cut myself with glass from a broken picture frame." I say, still scanning through the papers. "Doesn't make any sense, " I say thinking out loud. I feel my frustration stirring like a cyclone in my gut.

"Maybe those bastards have some sort of anti-trace technology?" Cordero suggests.

"Could be," I respond, because there's no other logical explanation.

I take a sip of coffee. It's as bitter as I am right now. Tastes a bit like toasted copper.

"Your nose, bud. It's bleeding again," Cordero says, handing me a few napkins from the dispenser.

I look down at my coffee cup, now stained red. I lick my lips and realize he's right. The blood has contaminated my coffee and the booth's tabletop, missing my shirt by a stroke of luck.

"Fuck... thanks..." I mutter, taking the napkin from his hands and cleaning up the mess, leaving crimson flowers on white napkins. The copper tinge hangs heavy like my sorrow.

"You okay, bud?" Cordero asks.

"Fine, just side effects of the meds..."

"Right. So about these calls," Cordero says, leaning forward. "You're sure they started after the first murder?"

"Before. Just a few nights ago. At first, I thought it was just punk kids prank calling. But whoever it is, they... He knows some personal things about me. Mentioned my father, my mother, how they met. And today, right before I headed out of the house, he called me again. This time he claimed he's our guy."

"Our cannibal freak show? You've got to be kidding me?"

"Yeah. I wish I were. He seems infatuated with me. Knows about Sarah and Emily. About my illness. Said some weird shit about him being an artist and redeemer. That I should believe in redemption and witness his work."

"Sounds kinda religious... He could be involved in some kind of cult..."

I take another sip of coffee and nod. "Yeah, that's what I was thinking. He also chants some weird phrases every time he calls me. Sounds Latin. Wondering if it's the same message he left at the scene?"

"Probably... Fucking nut job... so what's next?"

"We wait. He'll be striking again soon. That's why he called me. He wants me to witness his work. That's how we'll catch him. He wants to be caught. He wouldn't have reached out to me otherwise. Psychopaths always want to be recognized for their work. They crave attention. He's trying to play some sick little game. The bodies... he sees them as some sort of 'redemptive artwork'."

"If he's an artist, then I'm Van Gogh," Cordero says with a chuckle—a failed attempt to lighten the mood.

"No wonder you have trouble listening," I retort.

Before he has a chance to reply, the images on the wall-mounted TV behind him catch my eye. Cordero notices and turns around to watch with me. A weatherman gestures at white swirling patterns over the Gulf. The captions announce another storm rolling in. Miami in September, when the rain is thicker than blood.

"Looks like we're gonna get pissed on for the next couple of weeks," Cordero says.

"Yeah, that'll be a problem for the integrity of any stiffs found outdoors," I respond.

"Rain water washes away evidence like Jesus washes away sins."

"I didn't know you had a religious kink."

"I don't... but you remember my father, right? He ingrained these sayings into me."

"God rest his soul, I remember him well. He was very religious indeed. You, on the other hand, always seemed like the black sheep of the family. I mean, I know your brother Andrew seemed to take after your father, with all that involvement in the church. Even though you were the one who ended up following his footsteps into Law Enforcement."

"Yeah, Andy's one of the deacons of our church. He was the youth leader for years before that. He was always Dad's favorite. But it's okay though, Dad was tight with me too. Between you and me, he's the one who convinced Jacobs to give me a chance."

"I figured... he was Jacobs's lieutenant for a while and really took him under his wing when we first started out. Jacobs is who he is thanks to your father."

As Cordero opens his mouth to respond, his radio crackles to life. Both of us stare at the black Motorola with concern. Dispatch requests our immediate presence at a crime scene—a new body found in Wynwood. Same possible signature. Blood-scrawled message on the wall in some cryptic language. Uniforms are already on scene.

I glance at Cordero. "Let's roll," I say as I stand up from the booth.

"Motherfucker wasn't joking," Cordero scolds. "Here, don't forget your phone records," he says, handing me the yellow folder.

"Thanks," I say, grabbing it and tucking it under my left arm.

I pull a twenty-dollar bill from my wallet, take a last sip of coffee, and lay the cup on top of Jackson's face. Marge is already heading over to us with the food.

"We're out of here, Marge," I say as she looks at me with a disjointed face and turns back into the kitchen. "Keep the change."

As we head to our vehicles, hard rain begins to fall. Inside the Diplomat, I turn the windshield wipers on—they're two falling lungs. Their wheezing reminds me of the many people I saw take their last breath when I was in uniform. Now all I see are stiff, lifeless corpses. There's a big difference; it takes a different toll on you when you see them go. Somehow it's easier when you just see the empty vessel.

I grip the steering wheel tight, white knuckles bubbling to the surface. I feel like I'm drowning. Lightning splits the sky, illuminating this nightmare-ridden city. For a moment, it looks like an ancient serpent swallowing the city whole.

VULTURE

We head into the neon-lit snake pit, our headlights, lights, and sirens cutting through the watery void until we reach the crime scene. Cordero pulls up right behind me. We kill the sirens. The red and blue rotating lights on top of our dashboard strobe through the rain, entwining with the lights of the patrol cars already on scene. We flash our badges to the uniforms behind the yellow tape and duck underneath it. Lightning cuts through the obsidian sky, illuminating our faces in harsh white before the darkness swallows us again.

Big J and the rest of the crime scene technicians are all here. They all wear dark blue raincoats that reflect the red and blue lights of the patrol cars. As I approach the entrance of what used to be a shoe store, but is now just another empty storefront in an abandoned strip mall, I notice Detective Palermo standing with some kid under the overhang—couldn't be more than twenty, having what seems to be a panic attack.

Palermo's large and heavy frame casts a shadow over the kid, whose dark skin is only being lit on his left by the old neon pink and blue sign that once invited large crowds of teenagers to this once-thriving strip mall. His black mustache moves like a salsa dancer as he taps the kid on the shoulder and tries to apply everything they've taught us at the academy about crisis intervention. This kid was probably the one to call it in.

About fifteen feet behind them, the body's laying in a pool of blood, bile, vomit, and urine. From what I can tell from here, its positioning is nearly identical to the first victim's.

The bitter stench of bile is just as strong and mixes with the coppery tang of drying blood that lingers in the air and makes my feet feel like they're stuck in quicksand. Behind the body, on the old peeling drywall, is the same cryptic message scrawled in blood:

HOMO HOMINI VULTURIS

It makes my skin crawl, and my head begins to throb.

My vision blurs as I attempt to lift my feet from the quicksand. For a moment, I feel like I'm about to collapse when Cordero grabs my shoulders from behind and says, "You okay, bud?"

I quickly regain my balance and adjust myself by grabbing onto his forearm. "I'm fine... just lost my footing for a second." I'm not fine. My headache is worsening, and there's a metallic taste lingering deep in the back of my throat which rises behind my nostrils. Another nosebleed is coming.

As soon as I straighten up and thank Cordero for his help, a river of blood gushes through my nostrils. The blood and rain dance to the beat of my darkest fears. I instinctively raise my left hand to my nose in a cupping motion and tilt my head backward as if my hands could stop the bleeding. Cordero signals one of the crime scene techs to bring us some paper towels. The tech rushes to his van as Cordero leans me against a wall that's under an overhang and guides me to sit down on the floor. I can feel the humidity of the wet concrete filtering through my pants.

"Easy now, bud. Paper towels are on their way. Just keep your head tilted back," Cordero says. I'm doing just that, but I'm swallowing my own blood. When I can't take it anymore, I turn my head to the left and spit out a chunk of red gelatin that splashes on the edge of a yellow parking block. It quickly begins to dissolve with the rain.

By the time the crime scene tech arrives with the paper towels, the nosebleed and dizziness have subsided. I wipe the blood off my hands and face, stand up, brushing the humid dust off my rear with my hands, and ask the crime scene tech for some gloves. He hands me a pair of off-white latex gloves while Cordero attempts to persuade me to take a break. I maintain that I'm fine and remind him that these are just side effects of the meds. Eventually, Cordero accepts my lies, and we glove up while we walk toward the body.

The victim is face-up, surrounded by blood, bile, urine and vomit. White male. Late thirties. His jaw is broken; his arms spread like broken wings. Rigor mortis. Most of the flesh and insides are gone. The rancid smell makes my blood freeze. A few times I turn away, fighting the urge to vomit.

I find his trifold leather wallet in his front left pocket. Ken Williamson. Thirty-seven. Resident of the Coconut Grove area. I jot down his info in my pocket notebook, rip the paper, and give it to Cordero to run.

I'm bagging the evidence when Horowitz arrives and examines the body. He confirms the wounds are consistent with the first victim's. He says he's almost done with the report we've been waiting on—he's just waiting on some pending lab and dental results that are taking a bit longer than usual. "I should have the results within a day... I'll be calling you soon," he says.

Horowitz proceeds to bag and transport the body to his van with the help of a few techs while Cordero returns with information. "Our vic's got priors just like the first victim. His rap sheet's long," Cordero says.

"We might have a vigilante on our hands," I respond.

"Nah, I don't think so. Maybe he's just targeting lowlifes because it's easier for him to create his artwork. Cheaper materials," Cordero says with a chuckle.

Before I can let him know how disappointed I am with his joke, he turns my attention to the cryptic message on the wall. We acknowledge its importance in the case and discuss some theories based on our previous conversation at the diner. We conclude once more that we need an expert in languages to assist us, or we won't make any progress.

As we exit, I'm able to catch Horowitz before he plops into his van. I lay my hand on his left shoulder and say, "We need to pay your friend, Rabbi Goldstein, a visit."

11

The occult book shop belonging to Rabbi Ezra Goldstein hunches like a forgotten tome on the corner of Douglas Road and 27th Street in the Coconut Grove District. Its narrow two-story façade, adorned with antique-style masonry plasterwork, mesmerizes passersby—as if King Arthur himself were paying Merlin a visit in a fever dream.

It's seven o'clock in the morning on the day after we left the second crime scene. Last night, Horowitz managed to give me Goldstein's address before he vanished into the morgue's fluorescent-lit bowels. He'd mentioned trying to reach the rabbi before starting the first victim's autopsy, to no avail.

Cordero and I had time to dump the white Diplomat at the station, update Jacobs, and knock back a cup of joe that tasted like liquid insomnia before arriving here. I wedge the black Diplomat parallel to the shop's main entrance, its government-issue frame a stark contrast to the mystical façade.

We step out into a morning as dark and brooding as my thoughts. The "CLOSED" sign leers at us from behind the front door's grimy glass, but we knock anyway. We lean into the large windows, peering through the cracks in the old, dark curtains like kids at a peep show.

Suddenly, one of the curtains jerks aside. A face appears—heavily wrinkled, framed by a beard as white and wild as a blizzard, with eyes like soft blue sapphires set in weathered stone. We flash our badges, the metal catching what little light dares to creep through the overcast sky.

"Police, Mr. Goldstein. We need to ask you a few questions," I growl, my voice rough as cheap whiskey.

The curtain falls back into place, and the face vanishes like a ghost at dawn. Locks click and groan, and the door swings open on hinges that cry out like violins in Berlioz's *Symphonie Fantastique*.

Cordero and I step inside, and the scent of old paper and incense assaults my nostrils like a prize fighter. My eyes water, whether from the smell or the dust, I couldn't say. The stale odor of cigarette smoke lingers in the air, a testament to late nights poring over ancient tomes.

The shop is a labyrinth of towering bookshelves. Ancient tomes lean against each other like drunks at closing time, whispering secrets from shadowy corners. Strange symbols adorn the walls, hieroglyphs from some forgotten tongue. The whole place feels like a tomb of lost knowledge, with dust motes dancing like restless spirits under the dim light filtering through windows caked with the grime of ages.

From a dark corner, the rabbi emerges, sifting through artifacts I can't make out. He places a small lit lantern on an antique mahogany desk, its light revealing his face once more.

"Now what could Miami's finest want with an old Jewish man and his books?" he asks, his voice as grave as a midnight funeral, his smile as enigmatic as the Sphinx.

"Dr. Horowitz suggested we come see you," I say, handing him a photo of the wall with its blood-scrawled Latin message. "He thinks you could provide us with some crucial information for our current case."

"Oh, Richard, yes," he says, taking the photograph. His eyes widen like a man who's seen his own ghost. "Where did you see this?" His voice tightens like a snare drum.

"That's confidential," I reply, my tone brooking no argument. "What can you tell us about it?"

Goldstein traces the writing with his fingers that seem to know more than they should. "It's Latin."

"We figured that much. Any idea what it means?"

"'Man is a vulture to man.' But its origins are much older. Much darker."

Cordero leans in, intrigue pouring from him like cheap cologne. "How so?"

"It's a pastiche of sorts," Goldstein begins, his voice taking on the cadence of a practiced storyteller.

"Taken from '*Homo Homini Lupus*'—'*Man is a wolf to man.*' It speaks of the cruel, predatory nature lurking in human hearts. This version, though . . . it hints at something worse. A transformation of human qualities into something inhuman. Both phrases whisper of cannibalism, of the beast that lurks beneath our civilized veneer."

Cordero and I exchange glances, words failing us like

witnesses in a lineup. My pulse quickens, a staccato beat of dread. "That's interesting," I finally manage. "We're dealing with something of that nature. Anything specific we should be looking for?"

Goldstein's gaze locks onto mine, blue eyes suddenly as hard and cold as glacier ice. "The vulture, Detective, is more than just a bird. It's a symbol—an archetypal representation of the beast within man. It speaks of nature's brutal cycle, the unconscious desire of nature consuming itself to birth something new. This is a Plutonian message, Detective. Think of the Ouroboros—death and rebirth, eternally entwined. This isn't random graffiti. It's an invocation."

His words settle on my shoulders like a lead overcoat.

"An invocation of what, exactly?" The question slithers out of my mouth, fear nipping at its heels.

"Of the darkness within, Detective," Goldstein murmurs, his voice as grim as a hangman's. "An invocation of man's evil inclination to prey upon his own kind. Whoever wrote this . . . they may be seeking redemption—for themselves or for all mankind—through the consumption of human flesh."

"What type of twisted crock shit is this?" Cordero growls, his usual cool cracking like thin ice.

Goldstein turns to him, his voice taking on a lecturing tone that seems wildly out of place in this den of occult whispers. "In Kabbalah, Detective, there's a concept—a lore, if you will—of the Nephilim. The children of fallen angels and mortal women. Some say they became cannibals, devouring human flesh to sustain their unholy immortality."

86

He pauses, letting the weight of his words sink in like a stone in a dark pond. "The person behind this message . . . they're either trying to imitate the Nephilim, invoke them, or—God help us—they might be possessed by one. At the very least, we're dealing with someone whose psyche has shattered like a mirror, leaving only the darkest reflections. They're unconsciously performing a ritual, guided by primal urges, trying to correct some cosmic imbalance in their personal universe."

The room begins to spin, reality blurring at the edges like a watercolor left in the rain. I stumble to the nearest bookshelf, grasping for support. Books tumble to the floor, their pages fluttering like startled birds. Blood rushes to my head, and before I can stop it, a crimson tide flows from my nose, staining my shirt, my hands, the floor.

A single drop of blood lands on an open page of one of the fallen books. The illustration there—a human-bird hybrid— seems to writhe before my eyes, man and beast merging and separating in a dizzying dance macabre.

"You okay, Tom?" Cordero's voice seems to come from miles away, echoing down some vast, dark tunnel.

"Fine," I manage to mutter, though I'm anything but. "Just . . . a bit . . . dizzy."

The rabbi studies me, his gaze a laser that seems to penetrate flesh and soul. It's both comforting and deeply unsettling, like a surgeon's touch before the anesthesia kicks in.

"Would you like a glass of water, Detective?" Goldstein asks, concern coloring his words.

I blink hard, willing the room to stop its nauseating carousel ride. "No, thank you. I'm fine, really."

"You're not well, Detective," Goldstein insists, his voice tinged with something that might be worry—or might be recognition.

I wave off his concern, straightening up and finally releasing my death grip on the bookshelf. Bending down, I retrieve the fallen book, my stomach churning as I focus on the hybrid creature illustrated on its pages. "What's this?" I ask, handing the tome to Goldstein.

"That's a ten-thousand-dollar book with a blood stain on it," he says with a chuckle that seems wildly out of place.

"I'm sorry about that," I mutter, embarrassment warring with the lingering dizziness. "I'll see if the city can do something about it. What can you tell me about this illustration?"

"No bother. I wasn't going to sell this one anyway," he says, chuckling again. "Pardon my Jewish humor."

He stares at the illustration for a long moment, silence stretching between us like a taut wire. Finally, his soft blue eyes find mine again. "There are forces at work here, Detective, that are much older and wiser than you may expect. It's not a coincidence that you knocked this precise book open to this page. Is this not revealing whom you seek?"

"It's revealing a bird man, and we are looking for a man, enacting vulture-like behavior. If that's what you mean, then yes, it's revealing it," I reply, my patience wearing thin. "But, with all due respect, Mr. Goldstein, we don't have time for metaphysical lessons. We're trying to catch a killer."

Goldstein's eyes smile, though his lips remain still. "You've been experiencing things, Detective, haven't you? Things you can't really explain?"

I feel Cordero's gaze boring into me, but I refuse to meet it. I won't let him see the truth of my strange vulnerability. "I don't know what you're talking about, Mr. Goldstein," I lie, the words tasting bitter on my tongue.

"I'm sorry rabbi, but my partner here, doesn't believe in hocus-pocus nor does he need it to solve cases." Cordero mutters with a forced chuckle.

I let out a small laugh, hoping it will dissipate the tension hanging in the air like smoke. "I'm a man of facts and evidence, Mr. Goldstein, not mystical mumbo-jumbo, no offense."

"None taken, Detective," Goldstein replies, his voice soft but insistent. "But you must understand that you have a terrible, wonderful gift. You're connected to this case in ways you don't yet understand, and I can help you understand if you let me. I can teach you to control your gift."

For a moment, I'm tempted. His words offer a lifeline, a chance to understand the mental plague that's been tormenting me. But then I remember who I am, what I've always been. A cop. Not a mystic.

"Thanks, rabbi," I say, extending my hand. "You've been of great help. We'll let you get back to work and if anything else comes up we'll contact you."

Goldstein's grip is surprisingly firm, betraying a vitality that puts my own to shame. "As you wish, Detective, my doors are always open for you. But please remember this—every action—every choice we make, creates ripples out into the universe, affecting things in ways we can't always consciously see or understand."

As he speaks, my vision blurs again. Flashes of bodies, blood, and bile assault me like strobe lights in hell. The coppery smell of blood fills my nostrils, and for a moment, I can taste metal on my tongue, making my stomach lurch.

I blink hard, pressing my thumb and forefinger into my eyelids, desperate to anchor myself in the present.

When I open my eyes, Cordero is looking at me strangely. "You okay, partner?" he asks, concern and suspicion warring in his voice.

I nod, managing a terse, "I'm fine."

Goldstein is still watching us, a kind smile playing on his lips, when Cordero's radio crackles to life. Another body has been found. Same MO as the other two. This one's in Little Havana.

"*Oy vey,*" Goldstein mutters, the Yiddish exclamation oddly fitting.

"Here we go again," Cordero says, his voice a mix of resignation and determination.

Cordero and I lock gazes. "Let's roll," I say. Then, turning to the rabbi: "Thank you, again for your time, Mr. Goldstein."

"Don't mention it. I'm always here if you need anything," the rabbi replies, his words carrying more weight than they should.

As we're exiting through the front door, Goldstein grabs my right shoulder from behind. I turn, our eyes meeting once more. "Be careful, Detective," he says, his voice low and urgent. "Those who look into the abyss might find it looking back." He presses a business card into my hand, his name and number embossed in gold. "Give me a call whenever you wish to expand on your gifts."

I don't know what to say, so I settle for a simple, "Thanks." Goldstein taps me twice on the shoulder, his face solemn, and I step out into the gray Miami morning.

As we walk to the Diplomat, I can't shake the feeling that something different—something fundamental—has been set into motion. Maybe this rabbi's right about everything, maybe I should come back to see him.

Before I slide into the driver's seat, I pause, looking back at the dim interior of the bookshop. Through the grimy front door window, I see the rabbi watching me. He nods once, a gesture of understanding that seems to span centuries.

I drop into the Diplomat, fire up the engine, and roll out towards our grim destination, Goldstein's words echoing in my mind like a prophecy I can't quite grasp.

12

The lights and sirens of the Diplomat cut through the overcast Miami morning like a knife on a fresh bruise. The engine chews through the thick air and rumbles with indigestion. As we arrive on the scene, I kill the sirens but leave the lights flashing, the red and blue swatches dance between the old rustic buildings and the yellow crime scene tape, transforming the area into a disco for the dead.

We exit the vehicle, heavy humidity lingering in the air like the dark clouds above signaling irrevocable rain. The stench of the city—a nauseating cocktail of rotting garbage, stale urine, and despair—assaults my nostrils. The dilapidated buildings are corpses with boarded windows for eyes. The old decrepit folks of the neighborhood are gathered in masses outside like macabre Halloween decorations. The reporters on scene are like zombies devouring the brains of the citizens. Their unified voices are ghostly murmurs, a cacophony of morbid curiosity and fear.

Patrol officers are backing the crowds up from the crime scene. Keeping the reporters in check as well. The place is in utter turmoil. Panic oozes from everyone's eyes. Crime scene technicians surround the body, placing yellow markers, photographing the scene, and collecting evidence.

"You ready for this?" Cordero asks, his voice tight.

"Ready as I can be," I growl. Truth is, I've never been ready for this. Each body adds more weight on my soul, burying me deeper in this nightmare-ridden reality. But I have no other choice, I must press on. This city needs me, even if it's slowly killing me. The irony isn't lost on me—I'm dying to keep others alive.

"Looks like we've got ourselves an official serial killer. . . this one's number three. . . all under two weeks," Cordero says as we duck under the crime scene tape and step into the front yard of this concrete jungle where the cannibalized body lies.

I nod in agreement. "He wanted this one to be seen. Completely unlike the previous two."

"Why the sudden exhibitionist behavior?"

"He wants to be in the spotlight. You see the crowds? This is what he wants. Panic. Fear. Reverence for his work."

"You think that's what he meant when he said he wanted you to believe in redemption?"

"Maybe. . . I think he wants me to believe in redemption through watching him inflict fear into the hearts of the citizens of this city. I mean, look at them. Between the media pushing the Satanic cults, the disappearances of those kids a few weeks ago, the supposed ritualistic paraphernalia found at that daycare in southwest 8th st, and now this body, right in the open, they're like rabbits being flushed out of their burrows."

"I guess we can also thank Palermo for running his mouth to

the media."

"That schmuck didn't do much, just probably gave that bunny reporter a few carrots to chew on, hoping he'd eventually get laid."

"We'll at least he got some from Jacobs," Cordero says with a chuckle, "he ripped him a new one."

I smirk at his joke but my face quickly frowns as the smell hits me—that sickly sweet odor of decaying flesh and coppery tang of blood drying. That smell I know all too well, one that clings to my clothes and follows me home like a stray dog. It's the perfume of death, and I wear it like a second skin.

The victim, a white Hispanic male—no more than fifty years old—lies with his arms spread open, as if crucified on an invisible cross. His face is frozen in a rictus of terror. His torso hollowed out. Most of his insides are completely gone. What's left are chunks of viscera. Like the previous two victims, he's surrounded by blood and large amounts of vomit. The yellowing concrete ground speaks of drying urine. The smell confirms it.

I swallow hard, pushing down the bile that's bubbling up. Cordero mutters a curse under his breath.

"Jesus Christ," he says, his face pale, "This one's worse than the others."

"It's getting worse," I mutter. "He's picking up the pace. Notice the rigor mortis. He must have done this one right before sunrise."

"How do you even open ribs like that? That requires some abnormal brute strength."

"Maybe he used some sort of apparatus to splay them open

like that."

"I doubt it," Cordero replies, "there would be some sort of damage on the ribs. . . it's. . . just way too clean."

I nod, he's right. The ribs are intact, just spread open, seemingly by fierce hand strength. My eyes proceed to scan the rest of the scene. That's when I see it—the writing on the old weathered plywood of one of the boarded windows. There for everyone to see; blood-red letters, dripping like tears:

HOMO HOMINI VULTURIS

I stare at the gruesome message. Same as the others. Now, it's expected, this will be in every scene. It's his calling card. The thought of knowing more victims will be found, that this psychopath is picking up his pace, makes my heart race. Nausea bubbles from my insides. My head's pounding. My vision blurs. For a moment I'm not here anymore. I'm somewhere else, somewhere dark, somewhere I can't fully describe. Everything is filtered in red. I feel the heaviness of death lingering all around me. I can smell blood, I can taste the fear. It isn't my fear though, it belongs to someone else. I can hear someone screaming. Everything around me begins to spin.

"He's way too proud of his work," Cordero says, his voice feels distorted, like he's speaking through glass. I want to respond but I feel like we're not in the same space. Deep within me I know he's just a few feet away from me. I'm trying to follow his voice, trying to keep my balance in this spinning red chaos.

"Tom?. . . Tom!" Cordero's voice progressively takes on a concerning tone.

"Tom!" Cordero grabs my shoulders and shakes me, "Hello? Earth to Tom!" Within seconds, his voice and violent shaking finally snaps me back to reality. I blink, realizing I'm on my knees, one hand pressed against the cold concrete ground.

"You okay, partner?" Cordero asks, I can see his concern etched on his face.

I nod, pushing myself to my feet. "Yeah, just. . . just. . . a little lightheaded." My feet feel like I'm standing on marshmallow clouds. The world tilts and sways, like I'm on a ship in choppy waters. Part of me wonders if I'm losing my mind, if this case is finally pushing me over the edge I've been teetering on for years.

"That was weird," he says.

"I'm fine, kid. Going to have to cut the dose of the meds, they're doing a number on me." The lie tastes bitter on my tongue, but it's easier than admitting the truth—that this case is eating me alive from the inside out.

Cordero doesn't look convinced. I know he's worried, I can see it in his eyes. For some reason he doesn't question me further. Instead he turns back to the scene.

I force myself to focus, to push past these symptoms. I've got to catch this son-of-a-bitch. Even if it's the last thing I do. And at this rate, it just might be.

By the time I'm feeling back to normal, Cordero's already gloved up and searching through the victim's pants for identification.

Cordero stands up and turns to me, his focus is on the license in his hands, "Santiago Jesus Villaverde," Cordero reads the victim's name out loud. "Forty-nine years old. Local. His apartment is about two blocks down that way," He says as he points east. "I'll run it when we're done here. I think we should head back to the office. You need a break, before you have a breakdown."

I nod, though reluctantly, but he's right. If I want to catch this asshole, I need to get my shit together. A break, at least for a couple of hours, would help. Maybe I'll contact Dr. Stein, maybe it's time for that hypnosis session he's been pushing me for. Worst case scenario, I'll just take a nice nap and regroup. But deep down, I know sleep won't come easy. Not with the faces of the victims haunting my dreams.

I stare back at the body. It tells a story of an insatiable violent hunger. The killer's getting bolder. His viciousness is growing. This one's an escalation, a step further into the abyss. There's no stopping this maniac, unless we understand his mind. And to do that, I might have to venture into places I'm not sure I can come back from.

Something catches my eye. A tiny white tip of something is in the vic's shirt pocket. I turn to one of the crime scene techs and ask for some gloves. After he hands me a pair. I crouch next to the body, reaching for it, my hand trembles slightly.

It's a business card. Dr. Gerald Stein's business card. Was this one of his private clients? My blood runs cold. I glance around, everyone, including Cordero is occupied with something or someone. Swallowing hard, I palm the card, and slip it into my left pocket without anyone noticing. I don't know why, but something tells me this needs to stay between me and Dr. Stein. At least for now. The weight of the card in my pocket feels like a ticking time bomb.

"Find something?" Cordero asks, coming up behind me.

I remain calm and composed. "Nothing important. Just getting a better look at the vic."

He raises an eyebrow and smirks, but doesn't comment. Instead he nods with his chin towards our left. I turn halfway to see Horowitz walking our way.

"Bet he's got some info for us," Cordero mutters.

"Hope so," I reply, though part of me dreads what new horror we might uncover.

Horowitz's finally in front of us. He extends a gloved fist bump to both of us. We pound in return. "Gentlemen," he greets us. "I'm still working on the full reports. . . but at least I've got those lab results of the first victim, you've been waiting for."

"And?" Cordero prompts, impatient.

Horowitz sighs. "It's. . . unusual. The saliva samples found on the first victim. . . they're human. . . but altered somehow. . . the DNA is scrambled, unlike anything we've seen before. Some sort of hybrid mutation. The guys down in the lab are going to run some other tests and compare it to the second victim. They'll have this one's samples to work on as well," he says nodding at the body on the cold concrete. "And there's something else."

He pauses, sighs and says, "You're not going to believe this. . ."

"Try me," I growl, my patience wearing thin.

"We found. . ." he continues, "we found trace amounts of a strange substance in the vomit. We don't know exactly what it can be but we're guessing it's some kind of hallucinogen, but there's nothing in our database like it. It's almost as if. . ."

"As if what?" Cordero asks.

Horowitz shakes his head, as if not wanting to believe what he's about to say, "as if it's not from this world."

His words make my stomach churn and for a moment the image of the hybrid bird-man illustration pops into my mind, the rabbi's words echoing in my head. *"There are forces at work here, Detective, that are much older and wiser, than you might expect."* The boundaries between reality and nightmare are blurring, and I'm not sure which side I'm on anymore.

Horowitz's still talking, his words are muffled, scientific terms exiting his mouth that mean nothing to me. The more he speaks the more I feel reality bending at the edges. I can't seem to process this information. All I can think about is the gruesome flashes of torn flesh, blood and viscera, the blood-scrawled words on the plywood, the card in my pocket, and how little time I have left on this earth. I need to catch this son-of-a-bitch, whatever it takes. Even if it means crossing lines I've sworn never to cross. I feel a rush of energy fill me from the top of my head to the tip of my toes.

I turn to Cordero "Let's roll," I say, interrupting Horowitz, "I'm sorry to cut you off, but we're on a tight schedule here, we still need to run this guy, and follow up on some leads.

Cordero catches my drift. I can tell Horowitz isn't fully buying it, but he plays it off, offering a goodbye fist bump to us before we leave.

We climb into the Diplomat, my hands shaking as I start the

engine. The familiar rumble of the car is oddly comforting in this sea of uncertainty.

"Want me to drive?" Cordero asks, his voice still creaking with concern.

"I'm fine, kid," I respond with a grin that feels more like a grimace. "Just had to cut him off. . . all that scientific talk had my head spinning. How about that break?"

"Yeah, we need to regroup," he says, nodding in agreement.

As I pull away from the crime scene, I notice the fear in the eyes of the crowd. Rain drops begin to fall, as if the city is crying. For a moment, the Latin phrase flashes in my mind once more:

HOMO HOMINI VULTURIS

Man is a vulture to man.

A vulture haunts this city. He's circling above, threatening to catch its next meal. And if I can't catch him, I might as well be his next meal. The way I see it, I'm already dead. The only question is whether I'll take this bastard down with me.

13

I'm standing outside headquarters, watching the building across the street. My eyes are set on the window of Dr. Gabriel Stein's office. A Camel dangles from my lips, its smoke a dragon rising to the heavens and washing down with the torrential downpour that turns Miami into a watery hellscape.

The city's drowning, and so am I—in doubt, grief, and frustration. This case is eating me alive. I take a final drag, letting the dragon uncurl itself and exit from my nostrils. I watch it rise and wash down with the rain one last time before crushing the butt under my heel. It's time I face my doubts, my fears, my inhibitions, and see if this hypnosis crap the good doctor's been pushing for is the real deal, or some pseudo-scientific mumbo-jumbo.

I jog across the street, the cold rain hitting my trenchcoat like hail. My shoes splashing through ankle-deep water, send grimy waves against the curb. I make my way into the building, through the large hall, up the stairs, and into the smaller hall that leads straight to Dr. Stein's office.

The halls are silent. The entire building is nearly empty,

except for a few guards on duty and a couple of city employees waiting outside an office for their respective appointments.

Most of the offices are dark. But at the end of the corridor, a sliver of light spills from beneath the door with the frosted glass and clean golden letters proclaiming "Dr. Gabriel Stein, PsyD, M.D." For a moment I pause, about eighteen feet away from the door, fighting my doubts. I snort, thinking the sign should say "Dr. Frankenstein," as he's about to experiment with a walking dead man. I sigh, walking up to the door.

I wrap my knuckles into a fist and knock. The three sharp taps echo in the empty hallway. A few seconds later Dr. Stein opens the door, the hinges crying out like agonizing souls. "What a pleasant surprise, Detective," Stein says as soon as he sees me. "Please, come in," he continues as he steps aside, his head slightly bowing while his right hand sweeps in a semiarc from the ground and toward his back horizontally, pointing into his office as if gesturing a welcome to royalty.

I stroll inside. My feet dragging across the red carpet. I watch the shadows of the embalmed birds dance across the room, turning the bookshelves and plants into twisted, reaching things. The entire place feels like a decompression chamber.

"I thought you'd decided to cancel our session," he says. "Please, have a seat." He gestures to the large couch next to me.

I remain standing, my doubts manifesting as rebellion. "I've been thinking about what you said, and maybe it's time we give that hypnosis thing a try."

"Well, you're in luck. I don't have any clients for the rest of the day—the rain's got everyone immobilized."

"Everyone except that maniac that's cannibalizing the city," I say as I shrug off my sodden trenchcoat and plop it on the edge of the empty wooden chair, right across from the couch.

"I heard about that. What a terrible, terrible act. How's the case treating you?"

"Off the record?"

"Off the record," Stein replies.

"Everything about this case is fucked. We have no suspects. No leads. I mean, for all intents and purposes, this guy's a ghost. We basically have a psychopath—who's clearly obsessed with the occult—murdering and then eating his victims. For what reason? Who knows?"

"I'm sorry, Detective. If there's anything I can do, please let me know."

"Yeah, buy me a bottle of Jack," I say, hoping we're still off the record.

He chuckles, gesturing me to lay down on the large leather couch beside me. "Shall we begin?"

I lower myself onto the couch, my doubts following me like a shadow. As I lay my body on the cold leather, my bones creak like they're about to reveal secrets. "Let's get this show on the road, Doc." I lay face up, staring at the ceiling.

Stein settles into an armchair across from me, his yellow pad resting on his knee. "Before we begin, I want to reassure you that there's absolutely nothing to fear about this process, Detective. Hypnosis is just that, a process. It's a natural process. In fact, I can assure you that you've already experienced some form of hypnosis on a daily basis.

"You see, Detective, hypnosis is a state of trance, and human beings go through many different trances throughout the day. Each trance is unique and each one serves a specific purpose. Some trances concentrate on a high level of awareness, such as when you're working and feel 'in the zone' and other trances function more like daydreaming and feel more unproductive.

"Today, however, in order to willingly produce a state of hypnosis, and to use it therapeutically with you, I will be inducing a hypnotic trance for you as a simple step-by-step process. It's a process of slowing the mind down until it reaches a subconscious state of awareness. You'll feel very relaxed throughout the whole process, and will probably feel much better when we're done.

"At the very least you'll feel very relaxed, and at the very best, we may discover the root cause of your situation. I want you to know that throughout this whole process you are in control. I will simply be your guide. Do you have any questions before we begin?"

"I'm fine, Doc. Let's get this over with. I've got a serial killer to catch."

"Right... Now, Tom, go ahead and take a deep breath through your nose and as you exhale, close your eyes all the way down."

I do as he says. Feeling like a goddamn fool.

"That's right. You're doing great, Tom. Now, I want you to relax your eyelids. Relax all the muscles around your eyes. Relax your eyelids to the point where they just won't work. Relax them so much, that even if I told you to open them, you wouldn't be able to. When you know you've got them so relaxed that they just won't work, go ahead and try to open them and notice how you rather just keep them closed and relaxed. In fact, the more you try to open them, the more they relax."

I keep on following his instructions. My eyes are so relaxed they feel glued down. Shut tight. I can't open them. I try and I try, but the more I try the heavier they get. What kind of witchcraft is this? I ignore my thoughts, and allow the sensation of relaxation to wash over me like a warm wave.

"That's right Tom, you're doing great," Stein continues. I don't know why, but every time he repeats, "that's right" I seem to relax even more. I feel the tension start to ebb from my muscles.

"Now, Tom, I'm going to count down from ten down to one, and with each and every number I count, I want you to imagine yourself going down a staircase. With each step you descend, you'll drift deeper into hypnosis, feeling more relaxed with each step. Wherever you go, and whatever you experience, Tom, my voice will go with you and it will be your guide... Simply follow my voice, and you'll be safe... remember Tom, my voice will always help you go deeper relaxed... my voice is your guide... you can already see the staircase, Tom, am I right?"

I nod a yes, feeling so relaxed, my tongue is useless in my mouth.

"That's right Tom, you're doing great. Start descending. Ten... nine... eight..."

As Stein counts down, I feel myself sinking deeper into the couch, deeper into my own mind.

The room begins to fade, leaving only darkness and the faint, drifting sound of my heartbeat. With each and every staircase, the world around me dissolves, replaced by swirling colors and half-formed shapes. Stein's voice seems to get farther away with each number.

"Three... two... one... good... now, Tom, can you hear me?"

"Yes," I mumble, my voice sounding distant to my own ears.

"Where are you, Tom? Can you describe your surroundings?"

For a moment I pause, trying to understand where I am. I see flashes of red. I'm stepping on broken glass as I walk through this place. It's dark. Humid. Cold. There's a strong stench of copper. A stench of death and decay hits my nostrils. My stomach churns.

"I don't know..." I say, my voice trembling. "It stinks in here. It smells like death."

"Look at your hands, at your feet, at your clothes, can you tell me what you're wearing? Can you tell how old you are?"

"I'm forty-two, I'm wearing my shirt, tie, my everyday shoes. I'm stepping on broken glass. My hands... they're... wet... red... bloody... I must've broken a window or something..."

"That's good Tom, what happens next?"

"I see... I don't know... it's too dark... I'm in a warehouse or something... it just feels too empty."

"Look around, do you see anyone else?" Stein asks.

I keep walking forward, until I see it—the body, on the ground, about fifteen feet away from me. But something's not right. A portion of it seems to be cut off by darkness.

"There's a body... on the ground... I'm walking towards it."

"Good... What else do you see?"

I keep walking forward slowly. It's alive, writhing in agony... shaking violently... the darkness surrounding it is moving. It looks like two large wings. I can hear them rustle... something's tearing into the body's flesh. I can hear the wet sounds of flesh ripping. The victim's screaming in agony. There's blood everywhere. I feel like I can't move.

"Oh God," I cry out. "It's... eating him... the fucking vulture... it's eating him alive!"

My heart's pounding, cold sweat dripping down my face. I feel weak, like I'm going to faint. The vulture is hunched over the body, its face buried in the victim's chest cavity.

"Stay with it, Tom, my voice is with you... you're not alone," Stein says.

I force myself to focus on the scene. The vulture turns his bald head to me, his eyes are a black, deep void. His entire face is red, dripping with blood. Pieces of torn flesh and viscera hanging from his mouth. But his face... isn't that of a bird... It's a man... it seems to find pleasure in knowing I'm watching him feast. It turns back to the body, digging its face deeper into the intestines, its hands, like claws, now joining in, splaying the ribs open. The sound of the ribs separating from the sternum is like nails on a chalkboard. The victim lets out a final scream before going completely silent, his body no longer withstanding the pain.

"No!" I gasp, my body's shaking violently in the couch. "No, no, no!"

"Tom... listen to my voice... in a moment, I'm going to count to three and you're going to come back to me, you'll be back here safe and sound in my office."

I can hear Stein's voice surrounding me. The acoustics like that of an empty theater.

"One... two... three..." Stein counts.

When I hear "three" my body jerks upright on the couch. I'm still shaking, albeit a lot less intensely. I shake my head, trying to make sense of what I just lived through.

"Tom, what did you see?"

Stein's speaking, but I'm now trying to clear the images from my mind. They cling like cobwebs, suffocating me. The room feels like it's spinning.

"Tom, are you okay?" Stein's concerned voice is now coming through a lot clearer.

"Yeah... I'm fine... just a bit overwhelmed," I mutter.

"That was an intense moment. Give yourself some time to adjust. Just relax there while I get you a cup of water."

Stein gets up, goes to his desk and takes one of the two glass cups he has upside down on a silver platter, and fills it halfway with water from a copper water jar. He brings me the cup.

"Thanks, Doc," I take a sip. Then another. Then another until I empty the glass.

I hand him the cup. "I've got to go, Doc, I've got work to do. Cordero, my partner, he's waiting for me."

"Wait. We need to talk about what you experienced. It isn't a good idea for you to just leave without processing everything that occurred in this session," Stein says.

"Look, Doc, I appreciate you, this session, all your efforts, but honestly, I've had enough for today. I'm exhausted and I still have to get back to work."

"I understand, Tom, but you need to take the time to process this before you leave. What you experienced isn't a normal hypnotic trance. You didn't experience a regression, which is what I was guiding you to. You experienced some sort of psychic phenomenon... some sort of psychic revelation. You were there with the killer you're searching for. This is beyond ordinary. You have a gift."

"What? Now I'm psychic, Doc? Really?" I say, surging to my feet. For a moment the room spins around me, and I struggle to maintain my balance. I sit back down.

"Tom, listen to me, there are forces at work in this world that science can't explain. I'm not just a psychologist, I'm a trained psychiatrist, and I've seen things throughout my career that have no scientific explanation. Your connection to this case... it's more than just professional. It's spiritual. You must understand this and I strongly suggest you think about working with me until you solve this case. Off the record. Just you and me. No one else needs to know."

I think about the business card I found on the last victim. I might want to take him up on his offer.

Maybe, there's something more to this. "I'll think about it."

"You can bring justice to the victims, Tom, remember that," Stein says.

I stand up again, slower this time, my legs heavy like lead. "Thanks for the session, Doc. I'll follow up with you soon. I just really got to get back to work."

As I reach for my coat, Stein's words cut through the air like arrows. "Tom, if there's something you aren't telling me, remember, that suppressing things isn't healthy. If you need someone to talk to, just reach out. You've got my number."

I nod in agreement. "Thanks, Doc."

I step out into the dark, empty hallway and before I take my fifth step, Stein's voice reaches for me.

"Detective," he says.

I turn around and face him.

"Remember, the monsters we chase are sometimes closer than we think."

I nod, smiling. "Let's hope this one doesn't get close enough to bite me."

"Talk soon." Stein smiles, waves, and shuts the door.

I continue down the hallway, down the stairs, through the large hallway until I reach the main entrance. Through the reflection of the door's glass, I swear I see the vulture standing behind me. My heart pounds fast. I turn only to see an empty hallway. I turn back to the door. The reflection is gone. I blink hard and check again. I turn back and forth three times. Nothing. I must be losing my goddamn mind.

I push through the door and descend down the outside stairs. The rain's pouring down hard on me as I cross the street and head over to headquarters.

Before I enter the building, I light another cigarette, the flame flickering in the heavy downpour. My head's pounding. I feel my stomach churning again. This case's tearing into me like a starving vulture devouring a carcass. But I won't stop until I catch him.

14

I'm staring at the case files spread across my desk. They might as well be large tarot cards, each one painting a grim, hellish picture of what is to come if I don't catch this son of a bitch before he strikes again. I can't seem to make anything out of this god-damn information. The rabbi and the shrink have both implied that I'm psychic, that I have an innate spiritual gift. But the only gift I seem to have is confusion. Maybe I'm just slowly losing my mind.

The fluorescent lights drone overhead at 5:30 a. m., their sickly glow transforming the crime scene photographs into ghostly mirrors. The cannibalized bodies of the victims stare back at me, hollow-eyed and accusing. I can't stand looking at them, but somewhere in these images, the truth lurks just beyond my grasp, taunting me like carrion drawing circles in the sky.

Cordero slumps across from me, his boyish features withering under three days of stubble. His bloodshot eyes sink into dark hollows, and his tie dangles like a hangman's rope. Coffee stains snake across his sleeve cuffs like dried blood. Together, we've been sifting through the carnage, trying to impose order on chaos.

"Look at this," I mutter, sliding several photographs across the scarred desktop. "All the bodies are positioned identically. Staged like some twisted theater."

Cordero's head bobs wearily. "They're actors... or more like unwilling mannequins."

"And he's directing them." Pain thunders behind my eyes, a symphony of agony conducting its own private performance.

"The whole thing's a movie," he rasps, voice rough as sandpaper.

"But what does it mean?" The exhaustion in my voice betrays our desperate state—running on toxic fumes and false hopes.

"I don't know," he admits, "but there's definitely something we're not seeing."

Frustration bubbles up inside me like magma seeking release. The chief keeps bearing down on Jacobs, who in turn circles our desks hourly, demanding updates we can't provide. Outside, Miami broils under a mercenary sun while panic spreads through the streets like wildfire. The press hovers overhead—vultures waiting for the next corpse to drop—knowing it will. It's only a matter of time before that dreaded call pierces our fog of exhaustion.

An intense pressure builds behind my nose. Before blood can baptize the files in crimson, I lurch toward the corner coffee station, hands cupped beneath my face.

"You should really get that checked out," Cordero croaks, watching me stumble past.

My bloody fingers fumble for napkins. Each crimson smear I

wipe away echoes the doctor's words: "The lymphoma's spreading, Tom, faster than we anticipated." But I press on, ignoring death's inexorable descent.

"The nosebleeds are side effects of the meds," I growl back at Cordero. "Nothing to do but ride it out. Resignation's the name of the game."

Cordero holds his tongue, then releases a bitter chuckle that morphs into a sigh. The kid can't decide whether to worry more about me or the case. There's no hope for me—he might as well choose the case. I know I am.

Detective Sanchez materializes beside me, his bulk casting a shadow across my peripheral vision.

"You ladies look like death warmed over," Sanchez drawls, punctuating with a wheezing laugh.

"The case's a real cluster fuck, isn't it?"

"The master of cluster fucks," Cordero mutters, his trademark smirk struggling to surface.

Sanchez lurches toward the coffee pot, his thick fingers bleaching white as they strangle the sugar dispenser. He dumps what looks like thirty grams into the black liquid, then taps the powdered milk twice with incongruous delicacy. After a cursory stir, he hurls the wooden stick toward the trash and gulps deeply. "Perfection," he grunts, tongue darting out to collect the drops clinging to his mustache.

"We're racking our brains here, Sanchez. This guy's a ghost. We've got nothing," I confess.

Sanchez looms over Cordero's shoulder, scrutinizing the photographs. "Your guy really thinks he's a vulture." He snatches one photo, squinting at it. "That's urine, isn't it?" His finger jabs at dark stains marring the concrete.

"Yeah, the sick fuck's peeing on the victims," Cordero confirms.

"No, he's not." Sanchez's voice drops an octave. "He's peeing on himself. That's what vultures do. It's called *urohydrosis.* They urinate on themselves after feasting. Kills bacteria from the carcass, helps them cool down."

Warning bells shriek in my skull. Since when did this guy become an ornithologist?

"And this," Sanchez continues, trading photos like playing cards, pointing at chunks of vomit, "Another vulture trait. They vomit when threatened. Self-defense."

"How do you know so much about vultures?" I demand.

"I read, Vogel," Sanchez sneers. "Majored in zoology before the badge. Wanted to be a vet like my old man."

"But you ended up a cop," Cordero interjects, words hanging between statement and question.

The phone's shrill cry cuts through the tension. I snatch it before the third ring. "Vogel."

Horowitz's voice from the morgue sends an incongruous wave of relief coursing through me. The reports are done. He needs us there immediately. "We're on our way," I bark, slamming down the receiver and reaching for my jacket. "Time to roll, kid."

"New lead?" Sanchez inquires, dropping the photo like a dead thing.

I shrug into my jacket. "Maybe. Horowitz wants us at the

morgue. Says he's found something."

"God willing," Cordero murmurs, straightening his noose of a tie and rolling up his stained sleeves.

"Thanks for the ornithology lesson, Sanchez," I offer, watching him chase another coffee drop across his mustache.

"Yeah, good shit, Pedro. Maybe Jacobs can throw you onto this case," Cordero adds with a forced smile.

I silence him with a glare that withers his grin. I work alone for a reason. Sanchez's methods and mine mix like oil and water.

As we push through the door, Sanchez's voice pursues us: "Hey ladies!"

We pause, Cordero propping the door, turning back.

Sanchez's mustache rides up on a predatory smile. "Watch yourselves out there. Remember—vultures are the most patient predators. They wait for their prey to start dying before they descend."

I match his smile, retorting, "This one won't have to wait long for me. Bet he's circling already."

Sanchez hoists his coffee in mock salute. "Vogel, you're a sack of bones. What's that poor buzzard going to eat off you?"

"My ass," I fire back.

Cordero's face tightens with concern. "You worry me, you know that?"

As we exit, Sanchez's gaze bores into my back like talons. Something about his insights feels too precise—like he's playing a game whose rules only he knows. Still, his words help sketch a clearer picture of our killer. This psycho's transforming, becoming something inhuman.

Profiling him will take work, but we're closing in. We just need to crack his code before more bodies stack up.

We descend the stairs into the parking garage as the first drops of rain begin to fall, a cold drizzle that whispers promises of storms to come. Sanchez's words circle overhead like carrion birds, diving down to peck at the dying questions in my mind.

The Diplomat welcomes us with a roar that sounds almost protective. I throw her into drive and pull out into Miami's rain-slicked streets, the wipers dragging across the windshield like a mourner's hands wiping away tears. Somewhere in this decaying city, a vulture circles, hunting its next feast.

We're about to get a closer look at his handiwork. Understanding him is the first step to finding him—before I become nothing more than another photograph on my own desk, another tarot card predicting someone else's future.

15

The morgue's fluorescent lights are dying fireflies, buzzing louder than the ones at the office; their sterile glow hovers over three sheet-covered bodies. Formaldehyde thickens the air, strangling the secrets the bodies are whispering.

Horowitz stands across from me at the head of a large stainless-steel table; one of the bodies lies on it. To his right is a medium-sized tray upon which sharp medical instruments of precision cutting rest horizontally like soldiers after a war. His latex gloves are stained with things I cannot name, but whose smell infiltrates my nostrils unapologetically.

"Show me," I growl, fighting back a wave of nausea. The pressure in my skull and the swirling sensation in my solar plexus makes me notice just how much I've deteriorated; even the familiar smell of the morgue is now a punch to the gut.

Horowitz pulls back the sheet on the latest victim, and Cordero inhales sharply next to me. I've seen my share of horror shows, but this one threatens to become a tenant in the suburbs of my mind.

"Look at the precision of these marks," Horowitz says,

pointing at the remaining viscera.

"These... I assume, are ritualistic markings. They have to be. We haven't seen anything like this before." His voice carries the tremor of lingering fear. "You see, this killer didn't just eat the victims. He... prepared them... the stomach contents of all three victims showed traces of their own flesh. He made them participate."

The pressure inside my skull intensifies and cues me to an upcoming nosebleed. I walk over to the large service station behind Horowitz. Reaching for the large brown roll of paper towel, I feel the warmth of blood trickling from my nose. I'm able to wrap a substantial amount around my hand and wipe my nose before the blood hits my shirt.

"What do you mean, prepared them?" I ask, wiping my nose completely; Cordero and Horowitz follow me with their eyes until I arrive at my original spot.

Horowitz continues, his warm blue eyes revealing he's pushing back the desire to ask me about my health. "The cuts are methodical, surgical even. But that's not why I called you here... you see, it gets weird. Real weird." He moves to a small steel table, picking up an evidence bag. Inside are dozens of small corroded metal objects that catch the light. "I found these embedded in each one of the victims' large intestines, well... what was left of them, anyway. Dozens of these inside each victim. They're entirely unrelated to the wounds on their bodies."

I take the bag, studying the objects. "What exactly am I looking at, Doc?"

"They're beer caps. Well, the majority of them are fragments.

You see the corrosion? That's caused by a very strong acid," Horowitz says, his face frowning with doubt as much as mine. "We also found large amounts of *Clostridia, Fusobacterium,* and *Acinetobacter calcoaceticus."*

Cordero's face twitches with confusion etching itself deeper into the creases around his eyes. "Clostri—what?"

"The first two are forms of anaerobic bacteria—bacteria that don't need oxygen to survive. *Acinetobacter calcoaceticus* is aerobic and produces phenol, a chemical that is commonly used to disinfect things."

"What are you getting at, Doc?" Cordero interrupts.

"There's someone walking around with deadly bacteria not compatible with living humans," Horowitz responds.

"What are you implying?" I ask.

"What I'm trying to imply is that your killer isn't choosing random victims. These people were chosen. They were forced to ingest their own flesh and the beer caps—"

"That doesn't imply they were chosen, Doc, that just indicates the way this guy works," I say, interrupting.

"Yes, it does, Detective. All three victims had *hepatic steatosis*."

"English, Doc," Cordero says.

"Fatty liver," Horowitz replies. "They were all heavy drinkers."

"Okay?" Cordero asks, his face drawing blank.

My head spins, my gut churns, and not just from the cancer eating at my bones. Heavy drinkers. The words echo in my skull like an empty bottle rolling down an alley. I may have to cross-reference their histories; there's definitely a trail to follow.

"There's more," Horowitz says, moving to another body and

pulling back the sheets, revealing the first victim's upper torso. For a moment, I'm back at the scene. Flashes of when I first laid eyes on him. I blink hard, seeking to focus on the present moment. Horowitz continues, "The digestive enzymes found in their wounds... they're not... entirely human. They're mixed with something else. Something highly acidic that accelerates decomposition."

My head throbs, and the room tilts slightly. I lean against the cold steel table, steadying myself. "Like what?"

"I haven't been able to figure it out yet. I sent a few more samples to the lab to confirm the doubts I have. But this kind of acidity isn't found anywhere except in the stomach of vultures." Horowitz's words linger in the air like poison. "The killer is either somehow collecting and using carrion bird digestive enzymes to make his victims decay faster—even while they're still alive—or he's literally becoming one."

I grip the edge of the steel table. Cordero notices, takes a step forward, but I wave him off.

"The writing on the walls," I mutter. "*Homo Homini Vulturis. Man is a vulture to man.* He's not just killing them to eat them. He's sending us a message of his transformation."

"What's up with the beer caps? I still don't get it," Cordero asks.

Horowitz turns to him, his face growing grimmer. "The connection, Detective, and the reason I called you here, is that the victims were heavy drinkers, so much so they had advanced stages of fatty liver, and they were forced to consume beer caps. There's a clear correlation. He's obviously targeting alcoholics."

"Oh," Cordero says.

The wall-mounted phone in the morgue rings, its shrill cry cutting through the heavy air. After three rings Horowitz answers. "Horowitz." After a pause, he locks his eyes on me, holding out the receiver. "It's for you, Detective," he says. "They found another one."

I stroll over, taking the phone, already knowing what I'll hear. "Vogel."

The young officer's voice sounds distraught. Confused. Fear is taunting him, testing his breaking point. He notifies me they've found a fourth victim. Same M.O. They need us on scene, immediately.

"Secure the scene. No one touches anything until we get there." I hang up, turning to Cordero.

"We've got number four waiting for us. Allapattah."

"Fuck," Cordero mutters, running a hand through his hair. "This guy won't fucking stop."

"He's working faster. He's taunting us," I say, moving toward the door.

"He's running out of time," Horowitz says. I pause at the doorway, looking back at him.

Horowitz continues, "No one can walk around with those kinds of bacteria in their system, Detective. My guess is that he doesn't have much time left. Even if you don't catch him, he's a dead man."

"As am I, Doc. Guess we've both got one-way tickets to the big sleep."

"I'm sorry, Detective," he says, his blue eyes revealing

compassion.

"Don't be," I say. "Catch you later at the scene." I turn away, letting the door close behind me.

We ride the elevator up from the morgue's depths. My reflection in the steel doors reveals the lymphoma's effect. My eyes are hollow, my face gaunt. The cancer's eating me like those vulture enzymes are decaying the victims.

Cordero notices me dabbing at my nose again. "You okay?"

"No," for the first time I answer honestly. "But neither is our killer. Right now, it's a race to see who drops first. And by God I swear it won't be me."

"That's the spirit, soldier," Cordero says.

The elevator door opens to the parking garage, and we step out into the dark and nearly empty concrete jungle.

I turn to Cordero. "Let's roll," I say, striding to the Diplomat.

Frustration continues to bubble in my gut, knowing we're too late, again. Another body is waiting for us. Another victim we couldn't save. Its flesh already beginning to decay. And somewhere in this city, the killer is watching us, taunting us. Each new body is carrion, an offering—a sacrifice to his cause. He's always one step ahead of us. As we head to each new crime scene, he's already selecting his next victim from a list that suddenly feels far too specific for comfort. I just hope I can catch him before my own body betrays me completely or before I become carrion on his concrete plate. I can feel the vulture circling, his eyes on me and on this city. Miami's nights are about to get a lot darker.

16

Rain falls from the obsidian sky onto the Diplomat. They're Sumi ink drops that hit like hail. They contrast the rhythmic sound of the dangling keys in the ignition and the sirens outside. Together they're an atonal fragment of Schoenberg's *Verklärte Nacht*.

Cordero hasn't said a word since we left the morgue, his eyes transfixed on the road and on the rain. The silence between us is as thick as the morgue air we left behind. The rain persists like the cancer that runs through me, but the music stops when we reach the scene.

The old and worn concrete home looms against the dark clouds like a twisted graffiti cathedral. Pink and orange neon light bleeds through the broken windows. Large abstract patterns of light emerge on the wooden floor, sticky with something gelatinous, darker than the sky. The roving lights of seven police patrol cars paint the crowd of bystanders standing behind the yellow crime scene tape with red and blue faces. Crime scene technicians are slithering in and out of the home like snakes. Everything pulses before me, making my head throb to its deadly beat.

"Jesus Christ," Cordero whispers beside me.

The body, just like the previous three, sprawls beneath a wall. The white middle-aged male's torso is a hollow cave, exposing ribs and missing viscera. The limbs are arranged in a grotesque imitation of Da Vinci's Vitruvian Man, floating in a nauseating pool of blood, vomit, and urine.

Above it, dark crimson letters drip down, attempting to reach the body and whisper secrets only it knows. Its message repeats the same terrible three words we've seen before:

HOMO HOMINI VULTURIS

"Same as the others," Cordero says, kneeling besides the corpse. His latex gloves gleam a wet red under the lights. "Massive trauma to the abdominal cavity. Most of his organs have been removed."

"You smell that?" I ask, my gloved hands covering my nose and mouth with a handkerchief.

"Of course, blood, piss and vomit, like the rest," Cordero mutters.

"No, it's . . . something else . . ."

"It's the high concentration of stomach acid," a familiar voice says from behind. I turn to see Horowitz striding towards us. "I can smell it from here," he continues.

I move closer to the body, the copper and bile penetrating my nostrils, reminding me of the diner's dumpster on a hot Miami day. I kneel down and dig through the victim's pockets, searching for identification. The worn leather wallet is dripping wet with blood, staining my gloves with the color of Mars.

"Roman Sokolov," I read his name out loud for Cordero to hear as I continue going through the wallet.

"Guessing he was a heavy drinker as well," Horowitz says. "Look at all the beer bottles in this place."

I stand up, looking around the room to see dozens of beer bottles on the floor, some empty, some still unopened, most of them upright, standing like valiant sentinels guarding the body of their fallen king.

"He's right," I say. "Look what I found." I lift high an Alcoholics Anonymous card I pulled from one of the inner pockets in the wallet, so Cordero and Horowitz can see it.

Cordero takes the card. "Faith & Hope AA Center . . . Maria Suarez . . . maybe she's his sponsor . . . the address is Little Havana area, we should pay her a visit."

I nod in agreement. "As soon as we're done here, she's our first stop. Write down the address. I need to bag this up."

Cordero writes the address down in his pocket notebook, and I place the wallet, license, and card in an evidence bag and hand it over to one of the crime scene technicians. As soon as I'm done taking off my gloves and disposing of them in the trash, I feel an intense pressure behind my eyes. I find the nearest wall and place a hand on it to stabilize myself. My head begins to spin. I feel the world shifting. I'm sinking into darkness, moving through what seems to be a home. A red filter descends. I hear agonizing screams, but the sound is muted, distant, underwater. A sharp beak tears flesh before me. Above me, I hear wings beating against hot air. The smell of copper floods my insides.

"You okay, Detective?" I hear Horowitz's voice coming through, albeit distant.

I feel a hand patting my back and I snap back. I turn to see Cordero staring straight into my eyes, like he's looking for something he's lost in them. "Hey buddy, you okay?" he says. "Focus on my voice. That's good. You're good. Keep your eyes on me."

"I'm . . . okay . . . I'm okay," I growl. Now I notice I'm holding on to him. My feet feel firmly grounded. "Just got really dizzy all of a sudden." I'm feeling better. I'm breathing better. "Thanks, kid."

"Maybe his sugar's low . . . might be time for lunch," a voice says, followed by a chuckle.

We turn facing the door to see Detective Sanchez standing in the doorway, silhouetted against the weak light from outside. Something about his posture triggers a memory, but it slips away before I can grab it.

"Sanchez, what are you doing here?" Cordero asks.

"Heard the call. Asked Jacobs if I could join in. Thought you could use an extra pair of eyes." Sanchez steps inside, his heavy frame pressuring the black Florsheims enough to make the wooden floor creak.

"Four bodies now," he continues as he walks the perimeter with a practiced ease. "Their insides—the killer's dinner. Reminds me of the stories my *abuelita* used to tell me. About the monsters who fed on the guilty."

Something doesn't fit. The way he says it—something's not

right.

"Found something," Horowitz calls from behind a sofa in the large family room. "It's a sobriety chip. Five years sober."

The red filter threatens to descend again but I squeeze my fists hard, managing to stay present. Something doesn't feel right. I feel the vulture's presence, like he's here, taunting us, watching us.

"Bag it," Cordero tells him.

"Reminds me of a case back in '72 when I was a rookie. Some junkie was torn apart, downtown. As if by a wild animal. Never got solved." Sanchez says, kneeling by the body, examining it with peculiar intensity. "I remember the media pushing a werewolf story." He giggles and coughs as he stands back up.

That detail isn't in any of the cold case files I've read. But I focus on what's before me. I turn to Cordero. "We've got Maria Suarez to visit, kid. I think it's time to roll out."

Cordero looks at me and nods in agreement. His face reveals he's ready to leave this slaughterhouse. "Ready when you are," he finally squawks.

As we walk to the Diplomat, I hear wings beating overhead. I look up to see dozens of black crows slashing through the dark mid-morning sky like broken paint bristles on a rough cotton canvas. For a moment I think about Dr. Stein and all the dead birds that decorate it.

"You think this lady will be a good lead?" Cordero asks, as soon as we enter the vehicle.

I start the engine, but I don't pull out yet. I watch through my rearview mirror as Sanchez emerges from the house. His chubby body jiggling as he takes each step down the porch into the front yard and all the way down until he reaches his car. "I don't know kid, but between what Horowitz found and now all the bottles in this scene . . . we have no choice but to check it out."

As I put the car in drive and pull out into the street, a vicious downpour of rain begins. Miami's neon lights strive to shine but are blurry through the windshield. The fast-moving wipers clean the blur momentarily but their efforts are immediately washed out, as if their work were in vain. It reminds me of our progress with this case. But my efforts won't cease.

Although grief and frustration continue to accompany me, I focus on the road ahead. If we can't catch this monster through the little evidence he leaves behind, we'll have to catch him through the sins he feeds on.

17

We emerge from the Diplomat into a baptism of Miami tears. Our shoes splash through puddles, crunching the drowning broken glass beneath them. We make our way to the entrance of Faith and Hope AA center. The center's a blind python; its beige paint peeling like dead skin, its windows clouded with grime. A neon cross flickers through the rain like a dying heartbeat.

I pull the heavy metal door open and gallantly gesture Cordero to walk through. "Ladies first," I say with a smirk.

"Funny," he says, stepping through the door, his leather soles squeaking against the linoleum.

We shuffle down the narrow hallway and turn right onto chameleon green double doors. We push through them and enter a large spacious room with a ten-foot stage all the way at the end. An ancient AC unit growls a static dirge for the damned. About fifteen aluminum folding chairs form a circle. Each face that turns to see us enter has seen better days. In the center of the circle stands a woman. She's in her late forties, about five feet four, honey-skinned and stocky. Her hair's jet black. The fluorescent lights create bright white streaks on it that creates the illusion of poliosis. She closes her mouth, drops her scarred hands that conducted as she spoke, and smiles.

"Welcome," she says. "Grab a chair and join us."

"Police, ma'am," Cordero says, flashing his badge. "We're looking for Maria Suarez. Just need to ask her a few questions."

"That's me," she says. "I'll be right over."

She excuses herself from the group, weaves between two chairs, and when she finally reaches us, she extends her hand to each of us and greets us with a charming smile and thick Cuban accent.

"Maria Suarez. What can I do for you, Detectives?"

"Do you know Roman Sokolov?" I ask, not wasting any time.

She smiles again. "Yes, I do. I'm his sponsor. Is he in some sort of trouble?" Her smile drops right after the question. She's quite intuitive, I'd say.

"He's dead. We're investigating his murder," Cordero says.

"Oh my God," she mutters. "Who would do such a terrible thing to such a kind soul?"

"That's what we're looking into. Do you have any meaningful information you'd like to share with us?" I ask.

"Well—" she says, and after a small pause, she continues, "all I can think of is his troubled past. He was a heavy drinker for many years. I recall his stories of being arrested many times for driving under the influence. He struggled quite a bit to go through the program. But for the last five years he's been holding strong—was holding strong." Her lips tremble a bit and she wipes a tear that tumbles from her left eye.

"Is there anything else?" Cordero asks.

She gazes upward, as if waiting for some angelic figure to whisper guidance. "Well, I'm not sure if it has anything to do with your case, but I've had a few guys who haven't shown up in the last two weeks. I mean, in this world, it's normal to have guys drop off and come back, and disappear again. But maybe it helps. Who knows?"

"Any information you'd like to share, we're open to listen," I growl, pressing her to spill the beans.

"Which guys are you missing?" Cordero interjects.

"Well—there's Miguel," she says, pausing, her eyes rolling back into her skull searching for his last name. "Miguel Reyes. There's Ken Williamson. And then there's Santi—Santiago Villaverde. They haven't shown up in about two weeks, maybe less. Like I said, unfortunately, it's a normal occurrence."

Cordero pivots toward me. "That makes four out of four."

I nod. "Horowitz was right. There is definitely a connection."

"Excuse me," Maria says, her face contorting with a weary frown. "What do you mean four out of four? What's going on?"

My eyes lock onto hers. "That's confidential information, ma'am. All we can disclose right now is that your group here may be in danger."

Her face blanches. "You're scaring me right now."

"No need to be. Just stay vigilant, and you'll be fine. Here's my card," I say, handing her one of our contact cards. "If you find anything suspicious around here or your home, call nine-one-one and then call this number. It's a direct line to us."

"You can also share the number with your folks down there," Cordero says, nodding his chin toward the circle of people sitting on the chairs. "If anyone sees anything, hears anything, tell them to please not hesitate to call us."

I face Maria. "Thank you for your time, Ms. Suarez."

Cordero thanks her as well, and we exit through the chameleon green doors, down the narrow hall, and through the heavy metal front entrance door into a powerful downpour that feels more like a deluge.

The Diplomat then navigates us through the heavily flooded streets like a ship at high seas until we reach the station. Maria's information still echoes in my head.

It's about three o'clock when we're having a word with Jacobs, updating him about our current findings when my desk phone rings. It's Leland Callahan, former medical examiner for Miami-Dade County, retired in '62. Says he heard about the murders, that he wants to help with the case.

"I taught Horowitz everything he knows," Callahan says, reminiscing. "Well, almost everything." He follows up that last remark with a chuckle and then a cough that's quite concerning.

"Patterns," he continues, "are everything. They tend to repeat themselves. We just have to be aware of them."

My hand shakes as I jot down his address in my pocket notebook. For the last seventy-two hours I've been running on less than three hours of sleep and about ten cups of coffee. I've skipped my last three chemo doses, and it's barely detained my nosebleeds. Maybe it's time I drop the meds altogether and just let nature take its course. At the end of the day, I'm not getting out of this alive.

I notice the address is in Coconut Grove, quite close to Ken

Williamson's place, I'd say less than twenty minutes from here. Maybe Cordero and I can make it later this afternoon before heading home. I need to rest.

I agree to visit him soon with Cordero, thank him and hang up when I hear the voice of a ghost from my past floating right above my head, one that I know wears an FBI badge. "Hello, Tom," Special Agent Lisa Chen says, materializing beside me. "It's been what? Three years?"

Her smile's bright and full of joy, kind of like Sarah's. The only women besides my mother who ever looked at me that way.

I look up at her and smile. It's the first time I've felt even a slight moment of genuine happiness since the accident. For a brief few seconds, I think about her question. She's right. Three years have passed since our last case together. She hasn't aged a bit. Her suit's federal-agent crisp, as it's always been, but her eyes are pure street cop. "That's right. Three years—going on four now. Good to see you, Chen."

"Good to see you too," she says, perching on the edge of my desk. "I've been meaning to call you. I need to apologize."

I look at her dumbfounded. "For?"

"Not being able to attend the funeral. I was up in Quantico, Behavioral Science Department—special training—couldn't get out of it."

"Don't worry about it," I say. "It is what it is."

Her eyes lock onto mine. They are two drops of sweet honey. "How you holding up?"

"I'm not," I say, feeling my emotions stirring in my gut. "But work keeps me busy. Thank God."

"I'm sorry, Tom. Listen, if you ever need to talk or go for a drink. You've got my number."

I smile at her again. But I'm spinning inside. Hoping the conversation takes a different direction. "Thanks, Chen."

Chen stares curiously at my bandaged hand. "What happened to you here?" she asks, pointing at it.

I stare at it again, almost enthralled by it. "Broken glass. Frame fell."

"Ouch," she says, looking at me like she knows I want to change the topic. "Hey... I've been following your case since it started."

I feel a sense of relief wash over me. "I'm glad," I say, with a smile that syncs with hers. "I could use your expertise," I add, enticing her to give me a new perspective, a new angle to the case. At the very least I need some real hope.

"He's methodical. Precise. And is seriously mentally ill," she says, her voice taking on a serious tone.

"Tell me something I don't know."

"Well, he's got a behavioral profile similar to Lawson. Remember our last case in 'eighty-one?" she asks.

"How could I forget?" I say, trying to avoid focusing on the flashes of mutilated bodies flooding into my mind.

"He's got an agenda, just like Lawson. He won't stop until he completes it. After he's done, catching him will be nearly impossible. Lawson nearly got away with it."

"Well, Lawson screwed up on his last one. Left us a trail of bread crumbs to follow. I think he just wanted to be caught, like all of these nut-jobs do," I say.

"No, he didn't. He didn't want to be caught. We studied him in-depth after the trial. He didn't screw up. It was you. Your intuition. That's what cracked the case wide open. Face it, Tom, you knew things... things you couldn't have known... it's like you were inside his head."

"I got lucky, Chen. I made a few good guesses. That's all."

Chen laughs, as if she can't really believe I think this way. "Are you making lucky guesses with this case as well?" She leans in closer, her voice dropping to a whisper. "You're doing it again, aren't you? Seeing things?"

Before I can answer, the room begins to spin violently. I grab onto my desk, seeking stability. I blink my eyes, striving with every ounce of power within me to avoid focusing on the red-filtered patterns forming before me—pieces of torn flesh tumble across a dark room.

Screams fill the empty space around me. I see seven points laid out across a map of Miami, almost like a compass. Something about the geometry feels important but I can't seem to grasp it; it slips away like smoke through my fingers.

"You okay, Tom?" I hear Chen asking me, her voice distant and muffled. "Tom? Can you hear me?"

I focus on her voice, attempting to follow it like a thread back to reality. As I do, I begin to feel the pressure building up behind my eyes. By the time I make it back to my desk, blood is already making its way out of my nose. I quickly reach for my pocket and pull out my already stained handkerchief and use it to hold off the bleeding until I can make it to the coffee station a few feet across from my desk.

After wiping my nose and hands clean with the napkins from the coffee station, I notice Chen and Cordero staring at me, both their faces screaming with concern. I find it amusing but don't really understand why.

I attempt to let out a laugh but succeed in releasing a sound that can only be likened to a death rattle. "I'm fine, guys. No need to worry. It's just a little blood. No big deal."

Chen straightens herself out, smoothing her jacket. "I'll be around, Tom." Her face still carries the weight of worry. She makes her way over to me before heading out the door, lays her hand on my shoulder and whispers, "You're not alone on this. I'm here for you. If you need resources, Tom, count on me. You've got my number and you know where to find me."

Cordero clears his throat. "Lunch time?"

I turn to him, still thinking about Chen. "Grab a snack from the vending machine—we're going to check up on this new lead that came in. Former M.E. Leland Callahan. He's over in the Grove."

"You okay to drive?" Cordero asks with a smirk, jingling the car keys he took from my desk.

I fold my handkerchief into a neat little crimson square while I think about it. "Give me my keys, kid. I'm fine."

Cordero hands me the keys with the face of a saddened child who's just been denied recess. I look at him and smile. "Let's roll," I say as I walk over to my desk, peel my trenchcoat from the chair it's on, and don it as I head out through the door. "We've got a bird to catch."

Cordero treads right beside me until we reach the Diplomat.

VULTURE

The whole ride I'm thinking about the case, the visions, and my inevitable end. The way I see it, everyone's a suspect right now. Maybe this old Doc will give us something to chew on before this maniac takes his next meal.

18

I steer the Diplomat through the nearly inundated streets in the heart of Coconut Grove. Wet Spanish moss hangs from ancient oaks like dangling arteries masquerading as cobwebs. They fail in their imitation and only succeed in making the oaks look like giant ghosts trying to cross the road. The rain momentarily dissipates, and I turn down the speed of the windshield wipers, making the ghosts stop dead in their tracks.

We're almost at Callahan's place, and Cordero hasn't shut up since we left the station. He's a fucking yapping machine with no plug to pull. He's talked about the case, about Chen, and now he's saying something about his mom. All I've done is nod my head, occasionally turning to him, lifting my eyebrows and dropping them back down before nodding again and then looking back at the road, as to pretend I'm listening to him and being responsible enough to keep us safe while driving under this storm; when in reality, all I've done is replay the words of Goldstein, Sanchez, and Chen like an old broken record, alternating them with intermission breaks where Dr. Stein interjects his wise words of counsel like a carousel run by an automaton.

VULTURE

We finally pull up to Callahan's place, a weathered two-story Spanish colonial that's twice as old as he is. Two large ghosts frame the house on either side. I park right behind a cherry-red '54 Ford Thunderbird in pristine condition. The rain blurs the windshield as I kill the engine, making the ghosts wave a greeting at us. Instead of waving back, I turn to Cordero, interrupt him, and say, "Look, this guy says he's a former County M.E. He claims to have trained Horowitz when he first started out. Says he's got something that might be of help to us. He was mentioning something about patterns. I want you to shut up and take notes. Let me do most of the talking. *Capiche?*"

Cordero looks at me with confusion but nods his head up and down like a bobblehead. Something about how he looks at me lets me know he trusts my judgment. "Yeah," he murmurs, "you take the lead. I'll just blend in with the background."

We step out of the Diplomat, our shoes sinking into the wet mushy ground until we reach the steps leading to the porch. Our shoes leave muddy prints on each of the white-painted steps. I curl my hand into a fist and let the tip of my phalangeal joints make a rhythmic knock.

Before Callahan can open the door, Cordero taps me on the shoulder. When I turn to him, he puckers his lips while wiggling his index finger under his nose, signaling me a nosebleed. I dab two fingers under my nose and they come back the color of the Thunderbird.

"Thanks," I say, quickly pulling my now nearly useless handkerchief and catching the rest of the blood before it lands on my shirt.

It's not long after I've folded the handkerchief and stuffed it in my pocket again when Leland Callahan opens the door. He looks like he's in his late eighties, with skin cracked like old leather and sunken eyes that seem to have witnessed years of unspeakable horrors. We flash our badges and announce, "Miami Homicide, Mr. Callahan."

"Yes, Detective Vogel," he rasps, shifting with baby steps to one side. "Welcome."

"This is my partner, Detective Cordero," I say, right before we enter.

He smiles at Cordero. "Yes, that's fine. Come on in."

He closes the door, locks it, and guides us down a long and narrow hallway lined with framed medical degrees, newspaper clippings yellowed with age, and mostly black-and-white photographs with what seem like old Miami politicians.

"Glad you were able to make it down here so quickly," he says, followed by two very dry coughs. "I've got a lot to show you," he continues, leading us into a large study that looks like an ancient Victorian library. "Sorry about the mess. Ever since my wife Patty passed away three years ago, it's been a bit difficult for me to clean up as well as she did. I just don't have the energy."

All of the walls are covered by bookshelves, except one which serves as a decor wall filled from top to bottom with glass frames containing collections of taxidermy moths and butterflies. In the center of the room there's a large pure Rosewood Chesterfield leather love seat facing a large and dark antique mahogany desk. The place feels like a fortress of secrets.

"I started pulling the files as soon as I saw the news," he says as he pulls out a massive leather-bound volume, the size of an encyclopedia Britannica. Its spine cracks like old bones as he opens it on his desk. He beckons us with his hand. "Come. Miami's got secrets. They run as deep as the roots of these oak trees surrounding my home."

Callahan flips through the old yellowed pages of the historical Miami book. It's filled with a mix of black-and-white and sepia-toned photos dating back to the early 1900s. As he turns the pages, I catch a few titles covering everything from political stories to sociological, legal, agricultural, medical, and criminal. He finally settles on a section filled with several pages of crime scene photos depicting mutilated bodies in various states of consumption. They remind me of our victims—their positioning and state of decay are nearly identical.

"See?" Callahan asks, pointing to one of the graphic images. "1902. Notice the body." He flips the page, pointing to another photograph. "Now, look at this one. 1905." He drags his finger to the photograph underneath that one. "1908." Continuing to the page across, his finger tracing the torn pieces of flesh, "1910. See the pattern?"

I do. My stomach churns as I notice the familiar markings, the positioning of the bodies resembling occult ritualistic behavior. Each scene has blood-scrawled phrases in some foreign language. "Is that Greek?"

"Yes, it is, Detective," Callahan whispers hoarsely. "The words you see here are *Harpyia*, *Zeus*, and *Aetos Dios.*" His fingers underline each word as he translates. "*Harpyia* refers to human-bird hybrids, traditionally depicted with pale faces and long claws on their hands in Greek and Roman mythology.

"*Zeus* refers to the chief of the Greek pantheon of Gods, Lord of the sky, father of Apollo and Artemis, and associated with the planet Jupiter. *Aetos Dios* is what unifies the message, you see. *Aetos Dios* is the epithet of *Zeus*. It literally translates to 'the eagle of *Zeus*' but refers to vultures in particular. The vulture was believed to be a messenger of the gods and a symbol of divine power."

"There was a cult," Callahan continues, "known to have arrived from Europe in the late 1800s." His voice drops lower. "They were known as 'The Children of *Cathartidae*.'"

Cordero can't help himself and opens his mouth. "*Cathartidae?*"

Callahan turns to him. "Yes, *Cathartidae*, Detective. It refers to the 'new world vulture.'"

"The Children of the new world vulture," I say, attempting to make sense of all this.

"Yes, exactly. They came to the new world to worship their carrion bird-god. The cult adopted various sacred texts and symbols," Callahan continues, "The guilty were purified through the consumption of their flesh by the righteous members of the sect." Callahan's voice drops even lower as he pulls a weathered leather-bound book from his desk drawer. The binding creaks like an old gallows as he opens it.

"All of this was steeped in ancient mysticism," he continues, his liver-spotted fingers tracing strange characters on a yellowed page. "They drew from various sacred texts, but this Sanskrit verse from the *Bhagavad Gita* was central to their beliefs:

'मृत्युः सर्वहरश्चाहम्."

My blood turns to ice. Those symbols—I've seen them before, carved into that wooden plaque in Stein's office, mounted between those damned falcons. Every session, those alien characters seemed to mock me, whispering secrets I couldn't decipher. Now Callahan's translation crashes through me like a wave of ice water:

"I am all-devouring death."

"The Children of *Cathartidae* saw themselves as agents of death itself," Callahan continues, oblivious to my internal struggle. "This verse embodied their divine purpose—consuming sin through the flesh of the guilty. Each member would incorporate these Sanskrit characters into their ritualistic markings, their ceremonial objects. It was required that every member display this verse somewhere in their home or place of work—a reminder of their sacred duty."

My mind races back to those birds in Stein's office, their razor-sharp beaks forever frozen in attack position. Were they more than just macabre decoration? A trophy collection perhaps? Or something worse—a perverse shrine to this twisted legacy?

"All of this was legend, of course," Callahan rasps, "as there was never any solid evidence found that linked the murders to the group. There were a lot of religious groups and cults fighting for territory back then. Law enforcement could never pin anything on the Children of *Cathartidae*, and there was suspicion that it may have been a setup to destroy the cult. There were also rumors that the mayor was secretly part of the group. There's just no way of distinguishing the truth from the lies."

My pulse intensifies as Callahan flips through pages of masked cult members. Their masks, crafted from what looks like red-dyed pig skin, are sewn to a large black beak imitating a turkey vulture's head. He stops on a page showing a group photograph of the members. This time their faces are unmasked. I scan each face carefully until I see him, and my blood turns to ice. There, staring back at me from the sepia-toned image, is a face I know too well. "That's impossible," I say, leaning in to take a better look.

I read the name beneath it aloud. "Adolf Steinburger."

"The resemblance is striking, isn't it, Detective?" Callahan's eyes narrow. "To your department's psychiatrist?"

I turn to him. "How did you—"

"Because," Callahan interrupts, "that's his grandfather. Grand Master of the Lodge of the Children of *Cathartidae*. Practiced psychiatry too. Graduated in 1881 from University of Vienna Medical School, along with his fellow alumni Sigmund Freud. Came to Miami shortly after completing his residency at General Hospital in Vienna. However, his dedication to the cult took prevalence over his career. His private practice quickly became more of a recruitment office for the cult than a psychiatry clinic."

My head begins to throb, the pressure behind my nose intensifying as I attempt to piece this all together. Dr. Stein's unusual deviation into the metaphysical, his intense interest in the case, his probing questions during our sessions, the business card I found at the scene, and the birds . . . oh those damn fucking birds that decorate his office.

Callahan shambles over to a large metal file cabinet next to his desk and pulls out a file, this one looks more recent. "Here's where it gets interesting. In 1954, there were a few murders resembling these, but the city kept it quiet, well, as quiet as they could. They made a little task force to find the killer and eventually pinned it on someone. The guy had priors, but honestly, I didn't think he was the guy. The strength required to do what was done to those victims just wasn't possible by a hundred-and-seventy-five-pound man. The lead investigator was one Lieutenant Detective Manuel Cordero."

Beside me, Cordero goes rigid, his eyes widening. "My father," he says softly. He turns to me, his face heavy with confusion.

"Your father," Callahan nods, "disappeared three days after getting too close to solving the case. He was found unconscious in a trunk of an abandoned vehicle near the Miami River. His task force eventually took in the vehicle's registered owner for questioning and pinned it all on him while he was still hospitalized over in Jackson Memorial. Your father never agreed with what they did. He always held a heavy weight of guilt over that—we talked about it for many years. He eventually gave up looking for the killer as no other similar murders ever occurred. I retired back in '62, and I remember him being quiet about that for a couple of years before I left."

I feel the room closing in, the air becoming thick. I look at Cordero, the color draining from his face as he attempts to process all of this.

His father's disappearance was one of the darkest moments of his childhood. He's expressed this many times since we first began working together. Part of his pain lay in his father never revealing to him what had happened back then. Manuel Cordero took that event to the grave with him.

"The cult believed in signs," Callahan continues, oblivious to our discomfort. This man wants to speak his mind before he croaks. "Legend says they sought out those guilty of crimes but who managed to escape earthly punishment for their crimes. Some of these were people in power; others were deemed lucky individuals whose charges were dropped, or simply weren't prosecuted for one reason or another. But the cult was firm in their appointment as 'eaters of sin,' as they were alternatively called by the locals.

"Many of the members eventually died or left the city. It was rumored they relocated to expand the cult. I haven't heard anything about them ever since, and I've searched far and wide. I even hired a private detective once, and he couldn't find anything. If they're still around, they are truly invisible."

The implications hit me like a death blow. From my nose, a scarlet river breaks out. I cup my hands underneath my nose, catching the red liquid, but some of it lands on the desk, barely missing Callahan's large old book. I reach for my handkerchief, but it can't hold any more blood.

"Are you okay, Detective?" Callahan asks, quickly reaching under his desk, grabbing a roll of paper towels, and handing me a large batch. He closes the book and slides it to the right and wipes my blood clean from the desk.

"It's just some side effects from my meds," I say, tired of repeating the same old shit.

"What's the diagnosis?"

"Stage four *Waldenstrom's*."

Callahan's eyes widen. "I'm sorry, Detective. I commend you for your strength and determination. Not many people could work with that diagnosis, let alone a job like yours."

"What am I going to do, Doc? Wait for the grim reaper at home? No thanks, I'd rather go out fulfilling my purpose."

Callahan nods, his eyes are two blue large fish tanks. Cordero breaks my rules and cuts in, grabbing my arm. "It's getting late. We should go."

I nod, agreeing with him. "You're right, kid. We've got a lot to work on."

We shake Callahan's hand, thanking him for his time and effort. He walks us out and offers us his help, stating his door is always open to us, both personally and professionally.

Outside, Miami's still crying. The Grove's streets now black with night, the ghosts whistling a song of fear.

We make it to the Diplomat completely drenched. The engine roars a bass line accompanying the ghosts. The wipers dancing to the beat of this dreadful song. Cordero's eyes are fixed on them. He finally opens his mouth and says, "Tomorrow," nodding his head. "We'll figure this out tomorrow. Take me to the station so I can pick up my ride. I need to get my shit together."

I can't shake the feeling that tomorrow might be too late, but I lie to him and say, "Tomorrow's another day."

As I drive out of Callahan's driveway and into the night threatening to swallow us whole, my mind races with the images of the mutilated bodies, the face of Adolf Steinburger, and the red-dyed pig-skin vulture masks. They circle my mind like vultures, lingering there, as patient as death.

The city's neon lights cut through the darkness and the rain. Somewhere between a slash of the wipers, I catch a glimpse of my reflection in the car's windshield. I can barely recognize myself anymore, except for the tint of dried blood on my nose— my totem between this world and the next.

19

The desperate ghosts of Miami's sea moss-filled oaks follow me home. They're hungry souls that chase me, hovering outside the Diplomat, extending their soaked hands toward me, screaming my name. As much as they beg me to let them in, I ignore their keening voices, focusing my eyes upon the slick road that slithers before me like a black snake, leading me into its abyss.

I've managed to lose the ghosts of the oaks by the time I make it home. The heavy rain pelts me as I dash from the Diplomat to my front door. My home still grieves with me every time I walk inside. Mozart's *Lacrimosa* echoes off the walls, lifting every hair on my body like thousands of tiny cobras mesmerized by a Hindu snake charmer posing as an orchestra conductor. I drop the case files on my living room couch and head into my room. Loneliness is there, waiting for me, watching me with its single eye. I hear the living room television droning somewhere in the background—some late-night news report about a fatal hit-and-run on the causeway. I imagine Jacobs will put Sanchez on it, or maybe Palermo.

Something's been gnawing at me since leaving Callahan's

home. A connection hovers just beyond my reach. It taunts me with floating images that take turns projecting themselves inside the theater of my mind: faces of the victims, torn flesh, bodies buoyed in their own blood, vomited viscera merging with drying urine. And in the background, I hear the awful agonizing screams. Then the red-dyed pigskin vulture masks. The cult. The Children of *Carthatidae*. The red filter becomes the intermezzo. All the images begin to circle like vultures focused on their prey. They begin their descent toward me and merge with the memories of my wife and daughter.

When my pulse increases and the pressure begins to build in my head, I make my way into the kitchen looking for my bottle of Jack. It's there, half-empty—a faithful guardian of the puzzle Stein gave me. It greets me with the affection of an old caring friend and invites me to catch up. Pulling up the chair at the table, I tilt my friend over, his old stories pouring into the glass with laughter, like dark, syrupy medicine for the soul.

The scotch burns going down, but the images don't fade away. They search my cavernous skull for places to hide. I search for them and drag them out, set them ablaze in a fire pit and watch them burn. But they come back—like ghosts—haunting me and dragging me into the darkness. Making me their prisoner. Making me watch them dance against the setting sun, their silhouettes twisting and turning like living marionettes. They sing songs of death and corruption.

I take another drink and the room spins. I'm not sure if it's the scotch or another vision creeping in. I grip the table, my eyes blurring the unfinished puzzle before me. I know there's something else, something I'm not seeing. And then I hear her laugh. I follow the laugh, turning my head to the left, and she's there. Sarah. She sits across from me in the living room couch. She's in her usual spot. She's as beautiful as the day I first saw her. Emily's on the floor, doodling in her sketchbook, her box of crayons lying next to her whispering choices of colors like a muse. They're both bathed in a silvery light I know doesn't exist. At least not in this world I'm still stuck in.

I pour myself another glass of magma and gulp it down, wondering if it's burning through the line of memory and madness.

"You look tired, Tom," Sarah says, her voice heavy with concern. It reminds me of how she used to make everything better. Now seeing her pierces my soul like shattered glass, each shard a memory that bleeds me dry.

I don't answer her. I can't answer her.

I stand and reach for the files on the couch, snatching them from beside Sarah before she can go through them. Turning my back to her, I spread the files on the living room floor. The files fan out before me, and suddenly my eyes catch sight of Dr. Stein's business card among them. The Sanskrit characters from his office plaque flash through my mind:

मृत्युः सर्वहरश्चाहम्

"*I am all-devouring death,*" as Callahan had translated. The phrase pounds in my skull like a death knell. Those ancient symbols I've stared at through countless sessions, mounted between those damned falcons, their meaning now a whisper of accusation.

Each photograph is a horror show, a window into a world few dare to visit. A world that devours the soul like a vulture consumes the entrails of its deceased prey.

Nothing makes sense anymore. Nothing helps. I feel lost and weighted with grief that crushes like a mountain of iron. I'm tired. I'm so fucking tired.

I collapse to the ground, my body landing on some of the case files. My face feels cold against the floor that collects my salty tears. After a moment, I press myself onto my knees, breathing deep. Making a decision I should have made months ago.

My service weapon feels heavier than usual as I pull it from my shoulder holster. The .38 Colt Cobra Detective Special catches what little moonlight filters through the rain-slicked windows, its black steel promising an end to all this—the cancer, the pain, the confusion, the guilt that sits in my gut like a block of ice that refuses to melt.

I press the barrel to my temple, the cold metal somehow feels more right than anything else in my life right now. My finger tightens on the trigger and I shut my eyes, the darkness enveloping me like a shroud, singing a promise I know it won't keep, telling me to squeeze hard for the ticket to freedom.

"Don't you dare, Thomas Vogel." Sarah's voice cuts through the room like lightning. Her hand—impossibly real, impossibly there—grips my wrist, lowering the gun. "You have work to do, honey."

"I can't," I whisper, each word splintering like broken glass. "I can't do it anymore."

Sarah takes my face into her soft hands, cradling it with love. "Oh, honey. We've been through this before. You know we'll be together again soon, but you can't go now. Not like this."

"I miss you. I miss Emily. I miss you girls so much," I say, tears slithering down my face and into her hands.

"You'll be with us soon enough," she says, her perfume penetrating my nostrils, hints of jasmine triggering memories of times long gone. "Promise me you'll finish this."

The .38 is heavy like lead in my hand, so I holster it. "I promise."

Sarah smiles, the gentle curve of her lips fills me with hope. A hope of our reunion. "Good. Now go solve the puzzle."

Sarah picks Emily up and they vanish into the silvery light surrounding them. I'm left with an empty feeling, a void that only expands. I cannot live like this.

I stumble back to the kitchen, fighting my mind to leave my ghosts behind. The puzzle Stein gave me sits on the table, halfway finished. Its pieces are scattered like the fragments of my sanity. I pour myself another drink, my mind wandering back to Stein's office as I add a few pieces to the puzzle. The whole damn place is a bird cage. The taxidermy birds staring at me with their glass eyes. His grandfather, Adolf Steinburger, Grand Master of the Children of *Cathartidae*. The business card I found in the third victim's shirt pocket. His questions probing my subconscious with intentions far beyond my current understanding. My experience in the hypnosis session—there's something there. I know it. He's always steering me, pushing me toward redemption, toward justice, toward punishment.

The room spins again, this time I'm falling, circling down into an abyss I don't know I can escape. I taste the warm coppery tang, a nosebleed I don't care to stanch. I'm falling fast, but the visions move faster, flooding my mind with crime scenes. *Case files. Photos of the mutilated victims. That hideous blood-scrawled message.* And then, something clicks. *DUI charges. All of them. Every victim. The fatty livers. The beer caps.* The Alcoholics Anonymous group. All had DUI charges. Some did jail time. The rest dropped or dismissed. And there, in the stack of files flooding my mind, his last name jumps out at me. *Reyes.* The same last name as the drunk driver responsible for Dr. Stein's son's death. It's him. I remember him now. *Miguel Reyes.* That son of a bitch who just got out of the can four months ago.

The revelation hits me like a physical blow, my head still spinning, doubling me over the kitchen table. Blood drips onto the puzzle pieces, staining them scarlet. The first victim is the drunk driver who killed Dr. Stein's son. That's it. That's the connection.

The pattern's clear now: *Dr. Stein, the Children of Cathartidae. The late-night phone calls—pushing me to believe in redemption. The caller's knowledge of my family history in detail—of Sarah and Emily's death. Dr. Stein's business card in the third victim's shirt pocket. His son's death. All the victims with DUI pasts. His fucking obsession with those goddamn birds.* Each kill is another turn of his cycle—the vulture cleanses, death redeems. Over and over until he's satisfied.

Outside, dawn is breaking through, the first weak streak of

gray morning light struggling to push back the darkness. I check my watch: 5:33 a. m. It's early enough to get to the station and share what I've discovered about Stein with Cordero and Jacobs.

I head into my bedroom, undress, looking at my deteriorating body in the full-length mirror. There's a large bulge, the size of a tennis ball, in my pelvic area. My ribs are starting to show, my sternum peaking through underneath another large bulge in my chest.

When I step on the scale, it reveals a four-pound drop. I'm withering away, the cancer and the chemo devouring me from the inside out.

Before I can step inside the shower, my stomach churns and I feel the acidic bile rising through my esophagus. I open the toilet seat, tilting my head and letting the magma-like chunks spew out. The burning sensation lingers well after the retching stops.

In the shower, more of my thinning hair clings to my hands, like lint on an old sweater. I shave the remaining hair off. After all, what's the use of holding on to these lifeless strands?

I slide into my black suit, then shrug on the trenchcoat. Check the .38's cylinder, brass gleaming back from each chamber in the dim light. The leather shoulder holster creaks as the two-inch snub-nose finds its home, hammer shroud snug against my ribs, the walnut grips jutting out like a mocking tongue.

It's 6:11 a. m. when I collapse into the Diplomat; the engine's roar scaring the ghosts of Miami's oaks away. I catch a glimpse of myself in the rearview mirror, my eyes reflecting the haunting fear that lingers inside me like the scent of Sarah's gardenias that decorate my front yard. I pull out into the wet road, tires screaming, racing toward what feels like the truth. Dr. Stein has some explaining to do. And I'm going to make sure this bird freak sings his song into the tape recorder, confessing his sins to me.

20

The rain breaks through weak silvery light that skulks behind the clouds of what's left of this overcast morning. It's building to a *crescendo*, hammering down like nature's judgment. I'm almost at the station, the Diplomat cutting through the streets like a guillotine. Last night's revelation tumbles through my mind like a loaded die.

I park the Diplomat outside the station, parallel to the sidewalk, the passenger-side door facing the building that houses Dr. Stein's office. The rain continues to intensify, threatening me with thunder and lightning. I tighten my trenchcoat, exit the vehicle, and scurry through the rain until I reach the station's main entrance.

I stride through the station, up the stairs until I reach the third floor, pushing through the double doors marked Homicide Bureau.

The office buzzes with early morning activity, challenging the droning of those damned flickering overhead fluorescent lights. Everyone looks pale and sickly under the stark white light they cast.

The phones ring off the hooks in an offbeat percussion of bureaucracy to the mechanical rhythm of typewriter keys. Detectives hunch over their desks, stacks of thick manila folders rising like miniature towers of Babel—some resembling the leaning tower of Pisa more than others.

Uniforms guide cuffed suspects out of interrogation rooms toward county jail. The scent of their cheap colognes and cheaper aftershaves lingers like bad habits as they pass through.

Through the frosted glass of Jacob's office, I make out his silhouette—his hands waving overhead revealing he's knee-deep in what looks like another call with the chief.

Cordero pins crime scene photos to the bulletin board, each black-and-white snapshot a gruesome reminder—more like a warning—of what we're dealing with. He fixes the last photo in place and intercepts me before I reach my desk, coffee sloshing in his Miami Dolphins mug. The aroma of dark roast, three sugars, and a hint of half-and-half hits me like a lifeline.

"Good morning, sunshine," he drawls, sipping his coffee with his usual smirk. "Nice haircut," he says, swiping his hand over his hair, as if combing the air. "Hey guess what? I just got off the phone with Maria Suarez, maybe twenty minutes ago." His eyes gleam with a rookie eagerness I can't help but envy. "Said we might want to talk to Dr. Stein. Apparently, he's been a guest speaker at her AA meetings, for a couple of months now. He's even been seeing one of the guys from the group—*pro bono*."

The synchronicity hits me like a kick to the groin. Stein's business card in the pocket of the third vic flashes in my mind's eye. "Villaverde," I mutter, stalking over to the coffee station.

"Santigo Villaverde. The third vic."

"Yeah, how'd you—"

I pour myself a cup of joe, my back to Cordero. "Get Jacobs," I growl. "You both need to hear this."

I turn to watch Cordero knock and enter Jacob's office while I sip the dark acidic liquid that raises my pulse and awareness. My ears pick up on the quartet of strings struggling to come through the humming air conditioner. Sounds like Mussorgsky's *Night on Bald Mountain*, but I might be wrong.

By the time the horns enter, Cordero opens the door and gestures me in. Jacobs hunches at his desk, stress hovering over him like a thundercloud.

"Take a seat, Vogel," Jacobs says, motioning to one of the chairs. "Cordero already briefed me this morning on what you guys learned from Callahan. What's up? You've got something new?"

I rest my cup on his desk, next to a framed photo of his smiling, gap-toothed kids in soccer uniforms. Then I lay out the cold truth like an old stiff in the morgue. "Reyes. Our first vic. He's the guy responsible for Dr. Stein's son's death eight years ago—"

"Holy shit. Talk about a fucking coincidence," Cordero interjects.

"No coincidence," I say. "Stein's responsible for the killings."

"What?" Jacobs bolts upright, hands gripping the armrests of his chair. His squinting eyes reveal he can't believe what he's hearing.

"I know it's a tough one to swallow, Lieutenant," I continue.

"But he's our guy. Look, for starters he's got motive. This guy killed his kid. The son of a bitch only did eight years. Got out early on good behavior, four months ago. His grandfather Adolf Steinburger was the leader of the Children of *Cathartidae*. All the victims—their DUI pasts. All of them connected to Faith and Hope AA Center. Now I find out he's been a guest speaker at their AA meetings for about two months—that he's been seeing one of the guys—Santiago Villaverde—pro bono—that's how he's gotten close to them."

"Tom." Cordero's voice drops soft and careful. "Maria mentioned him because she thought he might help us understand the victims better since he's been helping them at the center. She wasn't suggesting—"

"Listen to me, goddammit!" I slam my hands on Jacob's desk, the coffee cup trembling. "Stein's our guy. I know it. Have you seen his office? Guy's obsessed with birds. He's got birds all over the fucking place."

Cordero nods. "Makes sense. He's also been working with the guys from the AA center pro bono."

"He's seeking redemption for his son's death," I say.

"You really think our department psychiatrist is the Vulture?" Jacobs asks, glancing between us.

"I don't think. I know," I insist. "He has to be. The motive is clear. Plus, it explains how the mysterious caller knows everything about me. He's been my shrink since the accident."

"Makes fucking sense to me," Cordero murmurs, his smirk wavering under Jacob's gaze.

Jacobs studies me for a long moment, his face a perfect poker mask. He sighs, dragging a hand over his face. "Hell," he growls. "I've known this guy for years. I don't think he's capable of these atrocities."

Blood trickles down my nose, but I ignore it. "Please, Lieutenant. Check his schedule against the murders. Check his patient records. Something will match. It has to."

Cordero hands me a tissue from Jacob's desk, concern etched on his face. Then he turns to Jacobs. "Let me pull his records," he says. "If—and only if—we find something concrete, then we bring him in. What do you say, Lieutenant?"

"Fine," Jacobs concedes, his face heavy with frustration. "But you better be right. Stein's a huge asset to the department. He's got a lot of political connections, and if you're wrong about this, it's going to blow back on the department. The chief will rip me a new one, and I'll be forced to take extreme disciplinary measures on both of you."

"Understood," Cordero says.

I nod my silent agreement and dab the blood from my nose with the tissue, tossing it in Jacob's trash bin on the left side of his desk before hauling myself to my feet and trudging my tired bones to the door. Cordero trails close behind me. "First stop, employee records," he says, voice tinged with excitement.

Before we can exit his office, Jacob's voice slices through the air. "Wait. Before you two go digging through personnel files, let's try the direct approach." He rifles through his Rolodex, finds Stein's card. "Man's been with the department for years. Maybe there's a simple explanation for all this."

I can tell Jacobs is trying to avoid another face-off with the chief. He's got bureaucracy and politics clashing with his desire to continue doing real police work. I know deep down he's not really willing to risk it. As much as I want to protest, I hold my tongue. Jacobs is right—we need to do this by the book.

Without hesitation, Jacobs picks up the phone on his desk, his fingers rotating the dial with intense precision. After thirty-five seconds, Jacobs hangs up and says, "Didn't pick up, got the machine." He frowns, the usual certainty of Stein answering now replaced with confusion. He immediately redials and gets the same result. His confusion morphs into concern. "Let me try him at home," he says, dialing Stein's home number. After getting the machine twice, he swallows hard. "You two go ahead. Handle your business. I'll try again in a few. If I get hold of him, I'll send for you. Otherwise, proceed as planned."

We exit Jacob's office and five minutes later make it to employee records. We spend about two hours going through Stein's records and psychiatric schedules, seeking patterns, date alignments, and any information that could tie him to the victims.

The sparse paperwork we find spreads across our large conference table in an empty office two doors down from the Homicide Bureau's entrance, reserved for this type of occasion. The files look like tea leaves waiting to be read when Jacobs says, "None of this makes sense. It's like he deliberately didn't report anything connected to the AA meetings he attended."

I turn to him. "Maybe because it was pro bono. Technically speaking, it doesn't fall under department procedure. He's not required to report anything. Looks like we're running cold."

"Wait." Cordero pulls out a copy of an appointment log sheet from under a stack of files. "Look at this."

His finger traces down the page. "Every victim except Reyes had an appointment with him within forty-eight hours before their death. Including Santigo Villaverde."

My heart rate quickens. "Son of a bitch."

"We should take this to Jacobs," Cordero says.

"Later," I say. "Let's check his office first."

We hurry down the hall, out the station's main entrance, and across the street to the building housing Stein's office. The short, chubby elderly security guard with a thick white mustache—Nelson Martinez, who's been here longer than most of the doctors—greets us with a puzzled look and scratches his bald head when we ask about Stein. "He mentioned something about a conference in Orlando," he says with his heavy Cuban accent. "Been gone two days now. Never seen him miss appointments before."

We thank Martinez and make it back to the office, sharing our findings with Jacobs, who confirms he hasn't been able to contact him either.

"Cordero," Jacobs orders, "call dispatch. We need a BOLO out on Stein and his vehicle immediately."

My eyes lock onto Jacobs. "We should check his house." Jacobs agrees, running his hand through his hair and letting out a deep sigh. "Get going. I'll send a couple of units to catch up with you guys right now."

Cordero calls in the BOLO as we drive to Stein's place in Coral Gables. When we arrive, the house is dark, his car nowhere in sight. No answer to our knocks. Through the windows, we can see taxidermy birds everywhere, watching us with glass eyes.

"Motherfucker!" Cordero wails.

I turn to him standing on Stein's manicured lawn, feeling frozen in time. I can't help but stare at the dark house, knowing we've finally identified our killer—and knowing he's already slipped through our fingers. "He's running," I say, the words bitter in my mouth. "The son of a bitch is running."

The distant rumble of thunder echoes my frustration as Miami's afternoon storm clouds gather overhead, raindrops picking up their pace, synchronizing with my heartbeat. The hunt is on, and this time, there's no doubt in my mind: Dr. Gabriel Stein is the Vulture.

21

It's 4:47 p. m. The weak sunlight struggles to creep through the blackened clouds and somehow still manages to bleed through the Venetian blinds, painting prison-bar shadows across my desk. It's been about eighteen hours since Cordero put out the BOLO on Stein, and my radio lies silent like a useless paperweight, its long antenna a black tongue sticking out, mocking me.

A half cup of coffee—my fifth since I got back to the office—sits beside me, dark rings staining its inside, mimicking the circles under my eyes. My hands shake as I light a Camel, watching Miami's thunderclouds gather through the Homicide Bureau's windows. My empty hand's fingers drum against a stack of closed case files; these clean, simple, like surgical incisions. This case has been hideous, complex, like a gaping stab wound that refuses to close.

I want to pee, but my mind continues circling back and forth from those glass-eyed birds in Stein's office to the ones in his house. Their beaks point to something ancient, a sorcery or wisdom I can't quite grasp. I'm sure my bladder will pop before they find this son of a bitch.

Within a blink of an eye, Cordero materializes at my desk, coffee sloshing in his Dolphins mug. He's a bit winded. "They got him," he says. His eyes are wide, and in them I can tell he sees the cynical doubt in mine, swimming like a hungry shark just beneath the surface. "Patrol stopped him on I-95 southbound, just before the exit of NW 62nd Street. Says he's returning from Orlando. They're on their way here with him. Should be just a few minutes away."

I blow out smoke through my nostrils like an angry dragon. I force myself to believe Cordero's words as I stub out the cigarette in my round glass ashtray. The ash is as dark as the clouds outside, but I'm afraid my thoughts are darker.

Taking a final gulp of the cold, stale coffee, I stand up, lowering my shirt sleeve cuffs and buttoning them tight again. I peel off my jacket from my chair and punch my hands through the sleeves.

"Going to drain the snake before wrapping this case up. Be right back," I say, scuttling toward the restroom just three doors down the hall. Before I can push through the bathroom door, I hear Cordero say, "See you in Interview Room B." I give him a nod and a wave and then enter.

By the time I exit the restroom, I see Stein being escorted into the Interview Room. He walks with the measured pace of a man attending a routine appointment, his hair as white as his long-sleeve shirt, which is crisp and pressed despite having quite a few raindrops drying on it. His wire-rimmed glasses catch the fluorescent glare as he enters the room. Nothing about him suggests he's a savage cannibal-freak-show.

I let out a deep sigh and make my way to the Interview Room. Once I'm inside, my chest tightens, along with my skull; it feels smaller today, the walls pressing in with the weight of accumulated sins. Stein's sitting on the right side of the long whitewashed table, opposite Cordero and the empty chair beside him, waiting for me to sit. Our chairs are a bit off-centered to his left. We do this on purpose; it engages the less critically judgmental side of the brain. Allows for confessions to slip out easier. Knowledge and patience is the name of the game. Stein's briefcase is on the floor to the right next to Cordero.

"Have a seat, Detective," Stein says, seeking control of the situation. "Where are your manners?" He smiles calmly, pauses, and then speaks again. "I must say this is quite unprecedented."

For a moment I remain standing, fighting his suggestion to sit, letting the silence stretch like a garrote wire. But then I remember that building rapport precedes my ego—if I want him to confess—so I give in and sit down. Once I settle in, he smiles at me again.

I break my silence, my eyes locked on his. "Where have you been the last seventy-two hours, Doctor?"

He meets my face with stone-cold psychiatric neutrality. "I was presenting at the Southeastern Psychiatric Association's annual conference in Orlando. A two-day certification course on Hypnosis for trauma and psychosomatic disorders. I gave Jacobs one of the brochures from the conference before he brought me into this room. I have a couple more in my briefcase if you'd like me to show you."

"Convenient timing," I say with a crafted smile as I turn to my partner. "Don't you think, Detective Cordero?"

Cordero snorts. "I most certainly do, Detective Vogel."

A slight furrow appears between his brows that looks more like concern than guilt. I can tell he doesn't enjoy our sarcasm. But I do.

After a brief pause he says, "Not particularly convenient for my patients whose sessions I had to reschedule." He leans forward slightly, his hands folded neatly on top of the table. "Tom, I sense you're under tremendous strain, but that's something we can address later. First, can you tell me why exactly I am here?"

His words hit me differently, as if bricks were flying out of his mouth. My temples throb with the beginning of another headache. Blood starts sneaking through my nose; I dab at it with tissues from the box we keep in the room. Confessions usually come with heavy tears.

I attempt to imitate his cold stare. "Four murders. Each one torn apart. Cannibalized. At each scene, written in blood: *Homo Homini Vulturis*. Ring any bells, Doctor?"

Something flickers across Stein's face—grief, recognition, or maybe subconscious admission—but it's gone before I can name it. "That's a rather dramatic variation on an old Latin phrase. Though I suspect you already know that, Detective."

Outside, thunder rolls across the city. I don't know if it's the humidity or the cancer, but my teeth ache, the dull pain droning to the beat of the annoying hum of the light above us. I'd give anything to hear Mussorgsky's *Pictures at an Exhibition* right now to tune this all out. Instead, I pull the file on the table toward me and spread the crime scene photos across the table, watching his reaction. He studies them with clinical detachment.

After a long pause, he finally speaks. "These are quite disturbing. I don't see how this pertains to me in any way."

"Miguel Reyes. Does the name ring a bell?"

"Yes. He's the man who killed my son while intoxicated," Stein says.

Cordero cuts in. "You were aware of his recent release, weren't you?"

Stein frowns. "Yes. I'm aware he was released. What does this have to do with me?"

"Were you aware that he was a member of Faith and Hope AA Center?" I ask, looking for any signs of guilt to emerge from his face. But he's stone cold.

"Yes, Detective, I was well aware of it. I've spoken several times at Faith and Hope. I've made my peace with him. I've forgiven him. Helped him forgive himself."

"Are you aware he's dead?" Cordero asks.

Stein turns to Cordero, his face shows no signs of empathy. "Dead? No, I wasn't aware of his passing. I'm sorry to hear that." I sense relief washing over him from head to toe. "Although," he continues, "I was concerned about his suicidal tendencies."

As typical of the guilty, he's already dissociating from the murder. My job is to remind him. "He was murdered. Cannibalized."

"Oh my God," he says, "is he one of those recent murders featured on the news? I don't recall the media releasing any names. They've been saying something about Satanic rituals. Is that true?"

I've just about had it with his innocent façade. "Cut the shit, Doc. We know everything. It's better you come clean and save us the ring around the rosie bullshit."

"Excuse me, Detective?" Stein's smile is a scalpel—precise, clinical, cutting through my certainty. He's wielding those psychiatric powers, trying to slice apart my interrogation.

"What about Santiago Villaverde?" I lean forward, the metal chair cold against my back.

"Santiago Villaverde." Stein repeats the name like he's tasting it. "Another member of Faith and Hope. I've been seeing him pro bono for a couple of months. Making remarkable progress in therapy."

"Remarkable progress?" My laugh comes out like crushed glass. "That include getting gutted and pissed on?"

A flicker across his face—there and gone. "I'm afraid I don't follow, Detective."

"He's dead too. Carved up just like Reyes."

"How unfortunate to hear." His voice carries the warmth of a morgue slab.

Cordero shifts beside me. "Roman Sokolov. Ken Williamson. Those names mean anything to you, Doctor?"

Stein's eyes drift up and left, a calculated pause hanging in the air like cigarette smoke. "Yes, of course. More members of Faith and Hope. Has something happened to them as well?"

"Same song, different verse," Cordero says, his voice hardening.

I press my palms flat against the table, leaning into his space.

"Four victims, Doctor. All recovering alcoholics. All faithful members of Faith and Hope. Every single one with a DUI in their jacket. Just like Reyes, they all walked away clean after doing minimal time."

Stein preserves his decrepit smile. He removes his glasses, polishing them with a handkerchief he pulls from his shirt pocket. "Oh, I see, Detective, you're trying to pin this on me. Make me some sort of avenging angel... aren't you?" His voice drops to a softer register, almost paternal. "Well, I'd hate to be the one to add to your distress, but my work at Faith and Hope is motivated by personal suffering. What alcoholism did to Miguel Reyes had a direct effect on my life—on my son's life. If I can help just one person heal from that disease, then I'd be satisfied knowing I'm indirectly helping others avoid the pain I've endured."

He pauses, sliding his glasses back on, the fluorescent light catching the lenses. "Karma, Detective, is something we can't run away from, but we can make a conscious decision to help repair the world from the karma it's already living with." His smile returns, sharper now. "I'm sure you and your colleagues can get hold of the security cameras from the Marriott hotel I stayed at. Along with that, you should find credit card receipts and dozens of witnesses that can confirm my presence; I started my seminar at 7:30 p. m. two days ago."

My temples throb and I can feel another nosebleed circling around me like vultures surrounding their prey. "Don't fucking pretend like you haven't been playing me since day one, Doc," I say, frustration morphing into anger. "The birds in your office, you think I haven't noticed the connection? I know all about your grandfather. Adolf Steinburger." My eyes are fixed on his as I expose him. "I know about his little cult too: the Children of *Cathartidae*. When did you drop the 'burger'? Before you got into college? Thought it'd be wise not to be linked to him, huh?"

Before I can keep drilling the Doctor, the door behind me opens. Jacobs steps in, his face a thundercloud. "Detective Vogel. A word."

I ignore him, pressing my palms against the table. "What is it, Doc? Revenge? Or are you continuing the work your grandfather started?"

"Detective!" Jacobs barks.

I use my hands to push myself up, almost hovering above Stein, his eyes looking up at me. "Are you the new leader of the Children of *Cathartidae*?"

"That's enough, Detective!" Jacobs barks louder this time, grabbing my left shoulder firmly and pulling me toward himself.

Stein's face is a mask of concern. "I'm happy to continue cooperating, Lieutenant," he says, his façade still lingering there, like a nightmare I can't wake from.

"That's okay, Doctor," Jacobs says. "If you'll excuse us for a moment, we'll be back shortly." He turns to Cordero. "Outside. Now."

In the hallway, reality comes crashing down like that 1947 UFO in Roswell. In less than an hour—using the brochure Stein gave him—Jacobs was able to get conference organizers confirming Stein's alibi.

Twenty minutes later we're in Jacobs's office. He's telling us of the video footage that shows Stein lecturing, answering questions —provided and confirmed to Jacobs directly by Orlando Police.

The walls close in on me like a coffin lid as Jacobs shows me hotel key card logs, copies of faxed restaurant receipts—all of it forming an impenetrable wall between me and the truth I can't prove.

"Cut him loose," Jacobs says, his tone confirms it's not a suggestion.

"Lieutenant—"

"This isn't up for debate, Vogel. We've got nothing to hold him on, and the way you handled that interrogation is, frankly, quite unprofessional and will probably get us a harassment complaint. Look, the mayor's office has the chief on his toes. The chief is stepping on mines and the press has the city in a spiral of panic. And you bring in a politically connected psychiatrist, who's friends with me, the chief, and the mayor, on what? A gut feeling? Look, I know there seems to be motive but you can't prove it. You've got nothing, Vogel."

"I know it's him," I insist, my words raspy and hollow. "I know it's him, Lieutenant."

Cordero cuts in. "It's true. We've got nothing."

I turn to Cordero. "But the connections. You can't say it doesn't make sense."

Jacobs's voice softens. "Look, Vogel, you're a great Detective, the best I've got, and I know your intuition's always been on point in the past. But right now all you've got is a string of conspiracy theories. We can't hold him any longer, not without this biting us in the ass."

"Fuck!" I growl.

Jacobs's eyes lock with mine. There's a fire there that burns with the intensity of hell itself. "Get your head straight, or I'll have to take you off this case. Understood? This is your last chance, Vogel. Now go home, get some rest. Tomorrow's another day. And listen up real good: let this go before you destroy what's left of your career."

I watch through the two-way mirror as they release Stein. He glances at the mirror—straight at me—even though he can't possibly see through it—and gives me a smile that I can only categorize as evil.

He straightens his tie and adjusts his glasses before gathering his belongings and chatting with Jacobs for a few minutes. They finally shake hands. His posture reveals he's obviously apologizing.

I stumble out of the office, through the hall, down the stairs, and through the main entrance into the gathering dusk. The air is thick, humid, and I can smell the sulfur in the rain.

As I plop into the Diplomat, I stare into the rearview mirror, noticing my sunken eyes and the dark circles that surround them like an abyss. Then for a moment I swear I can see the eerie red bald head of a human-sized turkey vulture behind me, blood dripping from its beak. I turn back as soon as I see it, my hand on the butt of my .38, but it's gone. The empty back seat echoes a mocking laughter, one that hums deep in my bones, eliciting the certainty I feel about Stein.

The downpour begins once more. Turning back to face the front, I grip the wheel tight, a feeble attempt to ground myself in reality. After hearing the engine roar, I turn the windshield wipers on max and pull out into the dark night illuminated only by warm dying streetlamps and flashes of lightning.

The drive home is a blur through never-ending sheets of rain. My windshield wipers are vulture wings wiping away the doubts that seek to drown me. The evidence says I'm wrong about Stein. Every accusation I made is a witness of my failure, reminding me in conspiratorial whispers that I'm only chasing shadows.

But as I park outside my home, I can still feel it—the copper taste of truth on my tongue. I look in the rearview mirror again, this time I only see my frail reflection, accompanied by long streaks of crimson that flow like a river from my nose to my mouth, down my chin and into my shirt. I don't know what's worse—the possibility that I'm wrong about Stein or the fear that I'm right. All I know is that the truth is darker than anyone is ready to believe.

22

The Diplomat's tires swerve through the wet asphalt that looks more like a narrow river of blood than a road under this darkened morning sky. The rain drums feverishly against the windshield as Cordero and I pull up to Rabbi Goldstein's occult bookshop.

The store's front entrance is a blur through the storm's assault and the struggling wipers. After yesterday's disaster with Stein's alibi, and Jacobs's warning to leave the doctor alone, I'm back to square one, forced to find something that really ties Stein to the murders or find a new lead that reveals the real killer. But I've got neither one nor the other. I've got nothing but straws.

"You sure about this?" Cordero asks, unbuckling his seatbelt.

"I've got no other choice," I say, already exiting the car, my shoes ankle-deep in the puddles, the rain soaking through my trenchcoat. My bones ache with failure since Stein slipped through my fingers, but I tell myself it's just the moisture seeping through.

Cordero and I stand under the small awning that covers the front entrance, our refuge from the deluge. I knock on the door and wait until Goldstein pulls the curtains, revealing his blue sapphire eyes and snow-white beard followed by a gentle smile. He disappears momentarily and after a short pause we hear the rhythmic clicking sounds of locks being opened. When the clicking stops, the antique door creaks backward slowly with a sound that reminds me of the fact that violin strings were traditionally made from cat guts.

We stroll inside the bookstore. My eyes can't help but follow the stirring dust motes that are still dancing since the last time I was here. They're like lost souls, disincarnate entities that have chosen to stay behind seeking the ancient knowledge that hides under this dim light.

The heavy tomes with cracked spines tower around us, forming an ancient maze. Arcane symbols decorate the walls and seem to writhe when you look at them too long. The frankincense incense makes the air thick with something exotic and spicy that makes me think about the cancer being consumed by the smell. For a moment I laugh at the irrational thought, but only manage a weak death rattle.

"Detectives," Goldstein says, his voice soft but piercing, breaking my trance. "To what do I owe this honor?"

Following the sound of his voice, I turn to see him looming between two towering bookshelves. Under these light conditions his white beard looks silver and glows orange at the edges, picking up the light from the small lantern that stands on his antique mahogany desk behind him. His eyes are like two cold fires, piercing right through me.

"The pieces aren't fitting," I say, the words coming out heavy with guilt.

"The guilt weighs heavy on you today, Detective," Goldstein says, as if tapping into the energy of my words. He follows up with a gentle smile.

I stay silent, not wanting to confirm his perception. Flashes of yesterday's failure take turns mocking me.

"Sometimes guilt manifests in ways we don't understand at first," Goldstein continues, gliding behind his desk. "But it can lead us, subconsciously, to where we need to go." He crouches beneath his desk. "I've been following the news carefully and I've noticed some ancient patterns emerging." He rises, pulling out what looks like an antique map of South Florida, the heavy stock paper as yellow as old teeth, its edges crisp with age. "Perhaps that's why you're here. Your subconscious mind leading you to this revelation."

I remain silent, lost within the words he speaks.

He spreads the map open across the desktop's surface. Some of the neighborhoods and street names are different, buildings that no longer exist marked in black fading ink. He takes a red marker, uncapping it with deliberate delicacy. One by one, he marks four points, each one a precise little dot. "If you have eyes to see, Detective, you will find that guilt has its own language, and subconsciously, language can be expressed geometrically."

"I'm not sure I follow," Cordero says.

"Do you recognize these locations?" Goldstein asks, pointing at the four red dots.

Cordero leans in, carefully analyzing the map. After a short pause he says, "Holy shit, these are the murder locations, aren't they?"

"Correct, Detective," Goldstein says, crouching under his desk again, this time pulling out a long metal ruler. He lays the ruler on the map.

My head begins to throb as I watch Goldstein connect all four dots with the ruler. The lines tight and straight as judgment.

"Four points," he says, his finger tracing the pattern. "Each one's part of a greater whole. A septagram."

"A septagram is seven points, am I right?" Cordero asks, leaning in even closer, his eyes entranced with the map.

"Precisely. Seven points." Goldstein intones. "It's following the Chaldean order of the seven visible planets—Saturn, Jupiter, Mars, Sun, Venus, Mercury, Moon. Seven days of creation. Seven seals of Solomon. Seven energy centers in the human body—the Chakras as they are known in the East. Seven musical notes that created the universe." His right index finger traces the incomplete pattern. "Three sacrifices are left to complete the ritual."

Thunder crashes outside, rattling the shop's windows. It conceals the churning sound of my guts.

"All ancient spiritual traditions understood this," Goldstein continues, pulling out another map of South Florida, this one looking even older. It has more open spaces—half of the roads and streets the previous one contained. All four corners are decorated with pen and ink illustrations of large black birds that look like vultures. In the middle bottom it contains the word *Cathartidae* written in ancient calligraphy. "Some of them dared to use this sacred geometry to amplify the power of their sacrifices."

He compares the points he drew on the previous one with their placements on this one; they match closely with locations already marked on this map. "Their personal redemption putting the redemption of others at stake. The children of *Cathartidae* were one of the groups that ushered dark entities into this land. And this land remembers. Your killer, Detective—this vulture— he knows these patterns. Consciously or subconsciously. But he knows them." Goldstein looks up at me, his eyes dark with warning. "Do not be deceived. He will complete his mission. Seven victims total. No more, no less."

The room tilts slightly. I grasp one of the corners of the desk, taking a deep breath, a feeble attempt to lower my racing pulse.

Goldstein grabs the previous map and lays it on top of this one and proceeds to mark three more red dots. "The next three murders will be in or very close to these locations." The dots mark the areas of Coconut Grove, Flagami, and the Florida Everglades.

"Very fitting symbolism," Cordero says, pointing to the dot furthest south. "The Everglades is filled with vultures."

"Indeed, it is, and you shall see him picking up the pace with his work."

"How do you know that?" I ask.

Goldstein smiles, wisdom oozing from his weathered face. "There's a solar eclipse happening in less than a week. He will want to complete his work by then."

"At least we're approaching the end of this shit," Cordero says, raking a hand through his hair. "I've just about had it with this case."

"We're running out of time," I growl. "We need to nail this son-of-a-bitch."

Goldstein turns to me, his piercing eyes locked on mine like a bull's. "Perhaps you will consider utilizing your gift, Detective. I'd be glad to help you see with better clarity." He rests his right hand on my shoulder. "Perhaps together we can see what your gift is trying to show you."

"What do you have in mind?"

"Hypnosis," Goldstein says.

"Thanks," I say with a raspy chuckle. "But I think I'll pass. I've already done hypnosis with Dr. Stein. He proposed it for therapeutic purposes, but all I experienced was torturous images of death. I saw the killer, but I could not identify him."

Something shifts in Goldstein's expression. "Gabriel," he says, the name exits his mouth with the weight of lead. "He was my student many years ago. Before he walked away from the mystical path. Turned away from it all. Or so I thought."

The air feels heavy, thick, like grave dirt. Cordero straightens beside me, suddenly alert. His hand rests on his hip.

"You taught him?" I press.

Goldstein's voice drops lower. "The ancient ways. The sacred geometries. The tree of life. The power of life and death. He came to me as a young boy, seeking redemption from his family history. His parents and grandparents came from a lineage that immersed itself in the forbidden teachings of the occult. You see, Detective, the occult is not evil—they're just hidden teachings, but within it, there are things we have to avoid if we wish to live in the Light of the Creator. Gabriel was a boy who came to me in search of redemption. In search of truth. He fought bravely against his own family's corrupt path. But eventually he abandoned the mystical path he was—is—supposed to be living in. He externally chose science over spirituality. But inside, he will forever be yoked to the spiritual path. I'd be wary of seeking therapy from a man with this kind of internal battle."

"Don't worry about that because I won't be getting any more therapy from him. We've gone our separate ways since—"

"Let me help you see," Goldstein cuts me off, his voice carrying an urgency I haven't heard before. He guides me down a narrow hall, past several bookshelves into a small office, Cordero trailing closely behind us. Goldstein has me sit down on a leather couch. He turns on a lantern that's on top of a small table in a corner, revealing strange symbols and glyphs scrawled on the wall. One of them is composed of ten spheres interconnected by lines. Three of them are horizontal. Seven are vertical. And twelve are diagonal. Each of the spheres has a Hebrew word accompanied by a glyph inside them. Each one of the lines has a Hebrew letter imposed on it.

Goldstein catches me staring at it. "That's called the *etz hayim*. The tree of life. It's the most powerful and accurate representation of the power of God."

I remain silent, mesmerized by the design.

"Now please lay down and close your eyes," Goldstein says, his voice dropping into a rhythmic cadence. "Listen to the sound of my voice, and wherever you go and whatever you experience my voice will go with you and it will be your guide, it will keep you safe." He guides me down a staircase, each number taking me deeper, making the room fade away. The staircase morphs, coiling like a snake, and I lose my footing, dropping through an abyss, spiraling down, faster and faster each second. In the void, vultures circle all around me, threatening to consume my body and the cancer that gnaws at my lymph nodes.

I land softly on the ground but struggle to pick myself up. It's dark all around me. I can see nothing until the darkness is replaced by flashing images: Blood-soaked concrete. Torn flesh. Long fast flutters of black wings. Then I'm there, watching through the killer's eyes as he stands over a victim. He descends upon the torso, tearing the flesh like sheets of confetti. He digs his face deep inside the bowels, yanking the viscera with his beak. He turns back to me, chewing. But the face—it's not a vulture anymore—it's human—it's Stein. His features are twisted in a rictus of pleasure.

My nose starts bleeding, but I can't do anything about it. All I can do is taste the copper. The strong metallic tang lingers in my mouth like a bag of old pennies. I know I'm on the couch but I can't move my body. In my mind, I'm in real time with the killer. With Stein. With the vulture.

"No! No! No!" I bark. Swinging at him only to see him vanish into black smoke. It circles all around me, mocking me. Then the black smoke gathers a few feet in front of me materializing again into the vulture. Stein laughs and I force myself onto him, swinging with all my strength. I want to destroy him. But he dissolves underneath me. "Goddamn you," I yell. "I know it's you... you son of a bitch. I'm going to nail you."

My body begins to shake violently, shattering the vision. I bolt upright, gasping.

"Easy now, Detective," Goldstein says, steadying me. "Your abilities are growing stronger, but they're consuming you. You must learn to control this gift, to direct it, instead of being overcome by it."

"How?" I manage to ask, winded, dabbing my nose with my handkerchief.

"Through daily meditation. You can track the killer's pattern, foreseeing his next move. This and the geometry can guide you to him before he can take another life. But you are running out of time, Detective. I'm afraid that unless you start now, you won't catch him before he finishes his work."

The words hang heavy in the incense-thick air. Thunder rolls outside like a distant warning. Before I can respond, the radio on Cordero's belt crackles to life, its static cutting through the mystical atmosphere like a cold blade. A request for our assistance pierces the silence. The dispatcher's voice is steady, professional, but we both recognize the particular combination of location and description. It matches the Vulture's MO.

"That's number five," Cordero says grimly, already moving. His footsteps echo down the hall as he heads back to the main room. Goldstein follows him, his shoes whispering against the worn floorboards. My stomach lurches, but I force myself up, trailing them back to where the maps still lie spread across the ancient desk like prophecies written in blood.

Cordero and Goldstein stand over the map, their faces illuminated by the wan light of the storm-dark morning. I take a deep breath, exhale, and join them.

"It matches," Cordero says, his finger on one of the last three dots Goldstein drew. "Coconut Grove. It's exactly where the call is coming from."

"Jesus Christ," I whisper.

"The pattern demands completion," Goldstein says grimly. "Your killer is following the ancient ways, whether he knows it or not. Each point corresponds to a celestial body, a spiritual meaning. You've got two more victims before he completes his ritual. He won't stop until the seventh point is marked in blood."

"We need to move, partner," I say, already striding toward the door. The room spins like a carousel, but I force myself forward. Stein's bloody face flashes in my mind again, and something cold settles in my gut. "Thank you, Mr. Goldstein. We appreciate your help. We'll be in touch."

Cordero thanks him too and follows me out the entrance into the downpour, the rain hitting our faces like tiny bullets. Lightning splits the sky, the luminous veins scattering across the dark clouds revealing an outline that looks like vulture wings spread from horizon to horizon.

I slide behind the wheel, turn the engine over, and before I pull away from the curb, I catch a glimpse of Goldstein in the shop window, watching us leave. In my mind's eye I can see the map spread out before me, its red points glowing like wounds in the lightning flashes.

There are two more deaths waiting to fulfill this killer's septagram prophecy. His fifth victim's already waiting for us, while he maps his twisted vision of blood upon my city, drawing scarlet lines of death across its streets.

I wipe the last of blood from my nose and focus on the road ahead. Each stroke of the wipers brings a new vision between my eyes. Red filter. Torn flesh. Raw slimy viscera dripping crimson drops of fear. Stein's terrible twisted smile morphing into that hideous red vulture face. I feel weak and consumed. Fear and loathing fill my bones. My brain throbs hard between my eyes. I can feel my lymph nodes swelling in time with the rolling thunder, and all I can do is wonder if I'll live long enough to stop this freak show before the cancer wipes me out.

23

The rain looks black. Almost as black as the clouds from which it falls. It hammers down with the strength of a herd of elephants. The alternating red and blue lights of the squad cars make it look like blood. Yellow crime scene tape whips in the wind, dancing to lightning's brutal poetry—nature's own confession written in electric ink.

My hands shake as I open the Diplomat's door. The rain passes judgment with brass-knuckled drops, turning my trenchcoat into a lead shroud. My shoes splash through puddles black as morgue coffee at midnight, the asphalt beneath them drowning in borrowed guilt. I make my way to the house— looming against the clouds like a mausoleum where nightmares keep their promises.

The sharp angles of the concrete masonry home remind me of an old cathedral decaying in rust and shadows. Crime scene technicians have set up industrial lights, their harsh glare ironically creating more darkness than they dispel.

The victim lies spread across the floor of the living room, his mouth open in a silent scream. His open eyes reveal shock, as if he died seeking God's mercy. His insides are completely scooped out like a jack-o'-lantern carved by the devil's own hand. It's a memorial to gutted confessionals where sins once lived.

"Single male, William Parker, age fifty-five," Horowitz says, looking up from a wallet he's bagged as evidence. "Neighbor called it in about an hour ago - said the front door was standing wide open." He hands me a plastic evidence bag containing a wrinkled membership card. "Faith and Hope AA Center, just like the four previous victims. Place is a shrine to Jack Daniels though - kitchen's full of empties, recycling bin's overflowing with beer cans." He gestures toward the coffee table where a half-empty bottle sits next to a knocked-over glass.

Alvarez looks up from photographing the doorframe. "No signs of forced entry. Either he knew his killer, or the bastard found another way in."

Horowitz crouches over what's left of the victim, his latex gloves catching flashes of lightning that creep in through the large window that faces the victim. The chest cavity gapes open to the ceiling like a shattered cathedral dome.

My nose starts leaking copper pennies, mixing with rain that crawls down my face. I whip out my handkerchief, catching the scarlet drops, and they become crimson flowers.

The world shifts sideways, and suddenly the scene doubles, then triples, reality unraveling like old wallpaper. Past and present bleed together—every detail matching my vision under Goldstein's hypnosis, down to the last broken rib splayed open like a broken birdcage.

My eyes move to the wall. There gleaming in fairly fresh

blood is:

HOMO HOMINI VULTURIS

But there's something else beneath it—symbols and glyphs—I recognize from Goldstein's bookshop's walls, drawn with the same methodical precision, blood substituting ink.

"Jesus," Cordero whispers next to me. "The Rabbi was right about the septagram. Those are planetary glyphs."

I nod. "Five of them. Two are missing."

"He's taunting us," Cordero growls. "He wants us to know that he knows that we know."

Cordero's right. I let the goosebumps rise and allow the churning in my gut to morph into words. "He's fucking with us, kid. He wants us to know he's always two steps ahead of us."

Horowitz looks up at me, his face grim behind his fogged glasses. "You're not gonna like this," he says, his face heavy with concern, or fear, I can't really tell. "Same MO. But there's something different this time."

He's right. I don't like it. The body's been arranged with geometric precision, unlike the previous ones. Arms and legs stretched to form a perfect X. The chest cavity is splayed open with surgical care, not as barbaric as his friends.

"X marks the spot," I say, wiping the last of the blood from my nose.

As I move closer to the body, I notice the floor around it has been marked by twelve other symbols, enclosing it in a perfect circle. They're glyphs I've seen before, not just in Goldstein's bookshop but in the paper. Then it hits me. Horoscopes. These are the signs of the Zodiac. Sarah used to read her horoscope in the morning paper every day. I can still remember her smile as she read aloud the daily predictions for her sign. Aries. The ram.

She spent quite a few dollars on astrology books. She studied her sign diligently. She told me the ram was representative of the Fallopian tubes, which is why the sign of the ram was identical to their shape. She said she was ruled by Mars. The fierce warrior of the zodiac. The God of war. He represented and ruled weapons, sharp objects, things that cut, harm, penetrate the body in any shape or form. He even ruled surgeons, she said.

At first, I couldn't understand how my sweetheart was ruled by a planet that seemed to bring such harm and destruction until I saw a lady disrespectfully cut her off in a line at our local supermarket.

I could see the Martian influence palpate through her as she verbally caused the lady to cry for her insulting behavior. To be fair, the lady had rudely skipped in front of her, and when my wife confronted her she lashed out with verbal insults. She started it, she said later when we recounted the situation on our drive home.

The thunder outside drags me back here, where my head throbs and my lymph nodes continue swelling.

"Notice the symbols surrounding him, kid?" I ask, turning to Cordero.

"Yeah," he smirks. "This guy likes finger painting."

"Too bad he leaves no prints behind," Horowitz interjects.

"Not even a partial. It's like this guy's invisible."

Alvarez is photographing the scene when Horowitz says that and he chimes in. "Seriously. The fucking invisible man. Or more like the fucking boogeyman. I personally triple-checked all the prints we pulled at every scene. So far, the only ones that matched our databases were the victim's. The writings on the walls and floors—didn't have a single print. And I assure you that they were written with human fingers. Let's see if we get lucky on this one. But I doubt it. If he leaves us a print, it will be intentional. We're dealing with a fucking ghost."

"Ghosts don't eat people," I say, looking at Alvarez's huge gut and thinking he could probably swallow a midget. "Only animals eat people. Wild animals."

"And don't forget people who think they're a fucking animal," Cordero says, as if making an enlightened observation.

"In that case, they are a fucking animal, and should be caught and treated as such."

Cordero looks at me, his face showing both hatred and disgust at the whole situation. He's uncomfortable. I can tell. He wants to leave. To end this case. To quit. His eyes scream a primal fear that can only be connected to the thought that he'll end up like his father or worse.

"Time of death?" Cordero asks, shifting the attention to Horowitz.

"Based on liver temperature, between two and four a. m.," Horowitz says. "Keep in mind I'm working with a piece of what's left of the liver," he gestures to a piece of viscera in the nearly empty space on the victim's right torso. "Also, the wound patterns are consistent with the others, but..." he gestures to the chest cavity again, waving his hand in a circular fashion. "This was done with more...let's call it...dedication."

I feel a blow to my chest, like a train going through me. Dropping to my knees in pain, the world shifts. Suddenly I'm watching it happen, seeing the vulture as he works. The precision. The purpose. The terrible joy that fuels through him. He's ecstatic. His hands aren't hands—they're sharp elongated talons. He moves them with precision like a veteran pathologist. Carving the torso of the victim like a Halloween pumpkin. As he lifts himself from the pool of blood I see his face. The facial features morph from vulture to human.

Anger erupts through my insides as I realize it's Dr. Stein. His features are twisted in that same rictus grin from my vision at Goldstein's bookshop. I want to lash out at him but I'm paralyzed, knee-deep in what feels like concrete quicksand.

"Tom!" I hear Cordero's muffled voice calling me through the abyss. I hold on to it like a lifeline, following it back, marching through the darkness, my feet immersed in puddles of blood. The splashing sounds and metallic scent overwhelm my senses, twisting my stomach. The pain stops me cold, bending me over. Hot burning bile exits my mouth. Wiping my mouth with my forearm, I continue following Cordero's voice. I'm lost in the darkness, I can't find the exit. The vulture's mocking laugh surrounds me, echoing in the dark, resonating inside me. The red filter drops and all I can feel is the pressure building up again behind my eyes.

My body begins to shake violently, but this time it's not

autonomous like at Goldstein's bookshop—it's external. It's Cordero, shaking me, his voice repeating my name, calling me back to reality. Finally he snaps me back. He's pulling me up, back on my feet, to my right is Horowitz.

"Jesus, bud. Let's get you some air," Cordero says, his body straightening with mine. He attempts to guide me to the door but I hold my place.

"I'm fine, kid," I growl. "Thanks."

The copper taste dances across my lips, my tongue's the orchestra baton. As I regain my balance, my mind attempts to make sense of the experience. It feels like it's all finally making sense.

As Horowitz begins getting the body wrapped, a strange luminescence catches my eye, emanating from the victim's left forearm. I lean in closer, ignoring the concerned glances from the technicians. There, pulsing beneath the skin like living firelight, is what appears to be some sort of branded sigil—an ancient haunting emblem of death. I glove up, lean over the body before the technicians zip it up and take a good close look at the forearm.

As my gloved fingers stretch the forearm skin for a better look, the mark seems to writhe and shift, as if burned into the flesh from the inside out. Seven interlocking circles, each containing what I recognize as ancient *Carthaginian* glyphs—the same ones Callahan showed me in those crumbling texts. But there's something else, something that makes my blood run cold: at the center of the design is a perfect rendering of a turkey vulture head—like the red-dyed pig skin vulture masks in

Callahan's book. Below it, written in what looks like molten gold, are the words "मृत्युः सर्वहरश्चाहम्."—the same Sanskrit verse from the *Bhagavad Gita* that Stein has in his office, the one Callahan translated: "*I am all-devouring death.*" My heart hammers against my ribs. Finally—proof.

I reach to point it out, but when Horowitz glances over, he continues working as if he doesn't see it. None of them can see it. Even Cordero missed it. But I know what I'm looking at—this is how Stein mocks me. This is his signature slap to my face. He knows that only I know. He knows I can't pin this on him—at least not like this—not without getting myself baker acted.

I memorize every detail, every curve and line. They may not be able to see it, but soon I'll make them understand. Soon I'll make them all see the truth.

"Cordero," Sanchez's voice cuts through my focus. "Jacobs wants to see you. Now. Come on. You ride with me."

I straighten up, trying to hide the trembling in my hands as I take the gloves and crumble them up. Cordero turns to me, confusion's a loud symphony in his eyes. I nod, giving him a nonverbal 'it's okay, you can go' and add, "I need to swing by home, get my meds. Been off them for a few days."

Cordero nods back. "Catch you back at the station."

"Yeah, sounds good. I'll ring your desk later."

I dump the gloves in the black trash bag before exiting with Cordero and Sanchez. They get in Sanchez's car and pull out while I'm still lingering inside the Diplomat, the raindrops helping me make sense of it all. The sigil. The Sanskrit verse. My visions. It's all coming together. But I'm running out of time. I need to get permanent eyes on Stein. Follow him. Take pictures of him in the act. It's the only way they'll believe me.

I pull out into the road, heading home. The rain has turned the streets of Miami into obsidian mirrors that reflect the city's neon wounds. Desperation lingers in every corner. Death haunts every street. I'm just the dying witness seeking justice and peace.

I'm three blocks from home when I see it—a figure standing in the middle of the street, silhouetted against storm clouds. Not human. Not bird. It's something in between.

Wings unfurl like sheets of night, spanning the width of the narrow street. Its elongated beak drips something dark. Its head snaps toward my windshield and it leaps, too fast, too sharp. Threatening to pierce right through and devour me.

I slam on the brakes, the Diplomat's tires screaming. I can't see it before me. It's gone. I turn to my left then my right before turning back behind me. That's when I see it. The thing's on all fours, rising up—stretching, morphing. The beak recedes into a face I almost recognize, it's Stein but the eyes—they remain black, ancient, and hungry—the eyes of a vulture.

I gun the engine, peeling a u-turn, giving chase as it lopes ahead with impossible speed. Its movements are wrong, bones shifting beneath skin as it ripples between flesh and feathers. Lightning flashes making it look electric as it shifts from man to monster and back to man.

It leads me down streets and alleys until suddenly—nothing. It vanishes into black smoke, just like in my vision at Goldstein's bookshop. I exit the Diplomat, my .38 drawn, ready to put six bullets into its center mass.

Darkness grows as I search for him on foot, down the alley and circling back until I reach the Diplomat. I sink back in. It's gone. Like a ghost. But I'm getting closer to him. I can feel it. I can feel him. Haunting me. Hunting me. The molten gold Sanskrit characters etch into my mind as I pull up in my driveway, where shadows dance like vultures waiting for their next meal.

24

The words won't leave my mind—मृत्युः सर्वहरश्चाहम्—"*I am all-devouring death.*" The molten gold Sanskrit verse from the victim's arm burns behind my eyes, carving itself into my soul like the words carved on Stein's office plaque. The words are not just similar—they're identical. Callahan's revelation tumbles in my mind: photos of death, cults, and ancient rites take turns projecting inside my skull, hammering convictions about Stein deep inside my marrow.

I need to go back. I know something's there, something I somehow missed. By now the crime scene technicians are gone. The house sealed off. Horowitz has already hauled the body to the morgue and is probably halfway through the autopsy. Now is my chance to go back there. To patiently search and dig up a clue. There has to be something I can find. All I can think about is that cursed mark on the victim's arm—the seven interlocking circles, the Carthaginian glyphs, the vulture head—it all means something. Stein's the vulture. I know it. I just need some goddamn proof—proof the others can see.

My hands shake as I grab my phone, punch in Cordero's office number. It's almost midnight, he must be there.

His voice drags like wet cement when he answers. "Miami Homicide. Detective Cordero speaking."

"Kid, it's me. Something's not right. Meet me at the scene—Parker's place—Coconut Grove."

"Just reviewing the neighbors' statements." Even through the phone, I can taste his concern.

"You want me to head over there now?"

"Yes. Now. Trust me on this one."

"Okay. Give me twenty minutes."

I hang up, lock up and make it to the Diplomat, plopping into it quick enough to avoid getting soaked. The moon's light shines through my windshield and I remember Goldstein's comment about an upcoming eclipse. I breathe in and exhale a long-winded breath; for a moment I think I'm expiring, but I do my best to focus my mind on the task ahead. Entering Parker's place and finding solid evidence I can link Stein to. Turning the engine over, I pull out of my driveway and into the dark road ahead.

The city bleeds rain. I grip the steering wheel, my knuckles foam white against black leather. The windshield wipers paint an arc across my field of vision, each violent sweep revealing another blurry sheet of rain-slicked asphalt and twisting shadows that threaten to wrap their long fingers around my throat and squeeze whatever little life is left in me. Miami at night is a different creature—empty neon-lit streets whispering too many secrets at once for me to understand.

The rain's hammering down like nature's own confession

when I pull up to Parker's place. The yellow crime scene tape is still twisting and turning, fluttering in despair like dying wings in the wind. The house squats in darkness, its windows are black holes in a rotting face, sucking me into their abyss. Lightning dances behind it like a grim brutal poem of death.

I pull the flashlight from underneath my seat before stepping out of the Diplomat. My shoes sink into puddles and mud as I approach the porch. Inside the industrial lights are gone, only my flashlight beam illuminates the scene from outside the window.

The door is sealed with yellow crime scene tape in an 'X' pattern, and an official Miami Police notice officiates the warning to not trespass. I lift the tape with one hand to avoid cutting it while I use my pocket lock pick to pry the door open. The rain and humidity has affected the wood of the door substantially, making me put in extra force to pull it open. The creaking sound it makes as it opens becomes an unexpected satisfaction, like one of those daily pleasures one usually takes for granted.

Inside the house is a tomb. The coppery reek of blood still lingers, mixed with the musty sweetness of decay and something else—something ancient, like feathers rotting in wet soil. My flashlight beam cuts through the gloom, catching dust motes that dance in descending swirls like tiny microscopic vultures. Then I see it again. There on the wall where it still gleams, written in drying blood is:

HOMO HOMINI VULTURIS

Lightning strikes and flickers through the windows, each flash making the letters dance, turning them into something alive, pulsing with what feels like primal fear. Beneath it the blood-scrawled symbols and glyphs look black under the cold beams of light, ancient runes speaking a language older than sin.

I sweep my flashlight beams to the floor where the twelve zodiac signs enclosing the body lay, the middle now empty, the signs seem to shimmer in the cold sporadic light, like living constellations trapped as dark stains on hardwood floors. The whole room is surrounded by numbered markers, greasy smears where the crime scene technicians dusted for prints, each one a testament to scientific futility against something supernatural.

My fingers trace the air above Aries—Sarah's sign. The warrior. The ram. My throat tightens. The place is familiar in an unforgiving way. But something's different now. The darkness seems alive, breathing with an ancient malice that makes my neck hairs stand, like death itself has taken up residence in these walls.

As I move deeper into the rooms my mouth fills with a metallic taste that grows stronger, mixing with the musty smell of the empty house. The blood feels different tonight—thicker, darker. The cancer's calling card, written in my own corrupted cells. Maybe that's why I can see him now, why death recognizes death. I feel like a ghost, my footsteps echoing in the hollow spaces.

A sudden gust of wind rattles the windows. The sound echoes through the empty house like distant laughter. Another lightning strike beams its light through the window, illuminating the

blood-scrawled phrase like a neon sign. My hand moves to my .
38, fingers wrapping around the hardwood grip. The copper taste
floods my mouth even stronger now. When I wipe my nose, my
left hand comes away wet and dark—the blood flowering on the
white gauze bandage like a crimson confession.

A sudden rush of vertigo hits me, and I brace myself against
the nearest wall, feeling the cold plaster against my palm like a
corpse's skin. Blood continues trickling down my nose, a warm
and sweet dance of copper pennies. I continue to catch the blood
with my left hand's bandage. The beam of my flashlight wobbles,
and for a moment—just for a moment—I swear I see a swift
movement in the shadows. Something massive. Something with
wings.

As I straighten myself against the wall, feeling my heart
slamming against my ribs, my gun half drawn. That's when I hear
it. A soft scraping sound, like talons on concrete, coming from
the doorway approximately fifteen feet across from me. I
unholster my gun, raising it to eye level; my left hand holds the
flashlight underneath it. I move my hands toward the sound. But
all I see is a dark swift motion.

"Show yourself," I growl, but my voice sounds wrong—
distorted, like it's being filtered through cemetery dirt.

Lightning strobes. The doorframe fills with nightmare—
feathers black as cemetery dirt, wingspan wider than a man is tall.
Not quite bird, not quite human. The vulture. Death's oldest
servant. Each transformation leaves behind a stench of
moldering feathers and grave soil. My lungs fill with it, coating
my throat like old pennies left too long in the rain.

Its wings unfurl like sheets of night, spanning the width of the doorway, each feather a slice of darkness that drinks in what little light remains. A dark heavy liquid drips from its elongated beak, leaving obsidian pools on the hardwood floor. The bald red head alternates between human and bird for a few seconds until it settles on vulture, snapping toward me, its beak too fast, too sharp. Deep black abysmal eyes—ancient and hungry lock onto mine, pools of primordial darkness that reflect centuries of death.

"Beautiful isn't it, Tom?" The voice is wrong—human words from an inhuman throat, scraping against the air like bone against stone. "You appreciate my work, don't you, Detective? That's why you've returned."

I know that voice. My gun and light follow it, but the creature moves with impossible speed. The beam catches a section of its massive shape, black feathers gleaming a bluish tint under the moonlight that seeps in through the windows, each feather edge sharp enough to slice shadows.

For a moment it stands there, unafraid and impossibly large, its hooked beak reflecting my light like a polished obsidian stone. In the blink of an eye it's in the hall, a silhouette against lightning-lit windows. The profile shifts—beak and feathers receding and melting into skin like wax under flame.

For just a moment, I see his face—Stein's face—twisted in that same rictus grin from my vision at Goldstein's bookshop, but now there's something more, something ancient behind those eyes.

"Stop right there!" My voice sounds hollow in the empty

house, echoing off walls that seem to drink the sound. "Don't move!" I struggle to steady my shaking hands.

The thing that is both Stein and vulture takes a step forward and laughs—a sound like grinding bones in an ancient tomb. "You still don't believe, do you, Detective?"

Its talons clock against the hardwood floor as it steps closer, each click a death knell. Each step brings with it a wave of dizziness, memories flooding my mind like sewage from a broken main: *crime scenes, victims, blood, the Sanskrit verse—*मृत्युः सर्वहरश्चाहम्*—'I am all-devouring death'.*

I struggle to maintain my balance, my body betraying me as the cancer dances with my decay. The closer he gets the weaker I feel, as if he's pulling my life force through those ancient eyes.

Its black mesmerizing eyes shift red—baring an ancient hunger that's swallowed civilizations. "You should be rejoicing, Detective. Redemption is at hand. My work is almost done. And you shall be my witness."

I squeeze the trigger. The gunshot is loud and deafening in this enclosed space, the flash briefly illuminating corrupted shadows that writhe on the walls.

Lightning flashes again revealing an empty space where the creature stood. The laughter echoes all around me, from room to room, moving deeper inside the house, a sound that carries centuries of decay.

My feet move before my brain can process, the academy's training carrying me through the dark doorways.

Each room is a moonlit nightmare of shifting shadows. The vulture always just ahead, just out of sight. Wings scrape walls like knives on bone. Feathers brush against my face, each touch cold as a corpse's caress. Stein's laugh bounces off walls—off every surface, a symphony of madness.

Inside the master bedroom, I stumble backward, slipping on something wet. My flashlight beam swings wild as I fall, catching glimpses of the walls now covered in Sanskrit characters, bleeding down like black tears. My hands and gun are dark and wet, slick with something that feels older than blood.

The copper smell intensifies, mixing with the stench of ancient feathers and rotting time. I stand up to see the vulture before me. A wave of nausea and memory fills my solar plexus. The hairs on my back stand up like soldiers at attention before death. My training takes over again and I fire one more shot.

The vulture moves fast—faster than my bullets, faster than thought. I have just four shots left before I need to reload. I back up against a wall, feeling the cold plaster against my spine like a tombstone. The vulture scurries out of the room, leaving behind a trail of darkness that seems to eat the light. I bolt after it, chasing it through the house. It leaves its scent wherever it goes— carrion and guilt, decay and memory.

It looms past me, its wingspan blocking out what little light remains where I stand, each feather a testament to deaths I've yet to witness. I follow it with my light beam.

It perches about twelve feet in front of me. In the depths of its eyes I can see reflections of every crime scene, every victim, every sin—a catalog of corruption that spans centuries.

"Stop! Or I'll shoot!" I command with an authoritative voice that withers with a terminal sickness, my words as hollow as my remaining days.

It opens its crimson-stained beak: "The signs I left—I left them all for you," the voice echoes around me, each word dripping with ancient malice. "Every victim. Every sign. It's all for you. My final gift—the septagram is almost complete." It moves again, swiftly disappearing before me like smoke in a hurricane.

I follow the voice back into the living room and into the hall, my footsteps echoing like funeral drums. There in front of me the vulture materializes from ethereal smoke, each particle arranging itself like a puzzle of nightmares. It cocks its head to one side, a gesture so familiar it makes my skin crawl—pure Stein, studying me like a specimen under glass.

Another step closer. Its beak parts again, and Stein's voice emerges from it: "The wages of sin is death, Detective."

I squeeze the trigger. Another shot splits the air. Another empty space where death should be. The terrible laughter continues—circling around me—mocking me, a carousel of horror spinning faster and faster. I turn checking every corner. All I see is black smoke—toward the back door, writhing like living shadows.

My heart pounds so hard I can barely hear, each beat a reminder of borrowed time. Blood runs freely from my nose now, splashing my white shirt, the floor—each drop a ruby marking time's passage. In one swift motion I swipe my already blood-stained left hand underneath my nose, picking up the long dangling clots with my bandage. My gun hand shakes as I lay it back on my flashlight hand as a base. Moving forward, I chase the black smoke, down the hall through the back door and into the backyard.

Outside, the rain hammers down on me, washing the blood from my face and hands like nature trying to cleanse a sin. Lightning turns the world into a series of frozen images: The black smoke now materializes into the vulture under the torrential raindrops, each transformation more visceral than the last. From all fours, rising up, Stein's face emerges from within the feathers like a nightmare being born. The large wings that spread against the jet-black clouds, now recede into his back, bone and feather melting into flesh.

"I've got you—you son of a bitch. On your knees, now!" The words exit my mouth with a dying authority, each syllable tasting of copper and regret.

"I am all-devouring death," he growls. The words boom like thunder, but the voice is pure vulture—a screech that devours my eardrums, centuries of carrion-feast distilled into sound. A loud ringing inside my brain torments me.

With impossible speed he begins to morph back into the vulture, each transformation more fluid than water, more terrible than nightmare. I empty my gun at the shifting shape. Each muzzle flash reveals something different, like a grotesque slideshow: The vulture's savage beak dripping black blood. Shoulder blades becoming wings, flesh peeling back to reveal midnight feathers. Stein's feet becoming talons that could rend souls. It leaps from shadow to shadow, moving with incredible speed, dodging every bullet like they're moving through molasses.

Then—nothing. Just rain and darkness and the taste of failure.

To my left, headlights sweep the street through my peripheral, cutting through the rain like searchlights in purgatory. Screeching tires on wet asphalt. A car door slams, the sound sharp as a gunshot in the rain-soaked night.

"Tom?" Cordero's voice sneaks through the downpour, uncertain as a prayer in hell.

I turn to find my partner approaching cautiously under the rain, crouching halfway, looking in all directions, gun drawn, but it faces the ground. Water streams off his service weapon, each drop catching the strobing lightning.

"You okay?" he asks, his voice tight with concern.

"QRU," I say—our police code for 'okay'. The lie tastes like old pennies in my mouth.

He holsters his gun, the leather creaking with wetness. "What the hell happened?"

"You're late, kid." I manage, trying to steady my breathing, each inhale scraping my lungs like feathers made of glass.

"My mother fell. Got the call from my wife right after I hung up with you. Had to wait for the paramedics, get her to Mercy." His eyes move from my bloody nose to the empty gun, reading the story written in violence and desperation. "You want to tell me what the fuck is going on?"

I look back at the house, at the shadow where the creature vanished, still seeing afterimages of wings against my retinas. "You wouldn't believe me if I told you, kid."

"Try me."

We're getting soaked, so I walk back over toward the back

entrance of the house. Cordero follows me closely, his footsteps in the mud echoing like muted drumbeats. I figure I can shift this around. Avoid the hassle of the story.

"Your mother," I say carefully, with sincere concern, deflecting like I've done since Sarah died. "She okay?"

"Yeah, wife's with her." He shifts his weight, glancing back inside the house through one of the back windows, his reflection ghostly in the rain-streaked glass. "What did you find in there?"

The events tumble inside my head like bones in a fortune teller's cup. Stein's words pulse venomously through my veins, each syllable burning like cancer.

"Nothing," I lie, holstering my empty gun, the metal cold against my hip.

His eyes narrow slightly, cutting through the rain and bullshit. He knows I'm holding back. I've only fired my gun once in the years we've been working together. "Come on, Tom. Don't fuck with me. What the hell did you walk into?"

Lightning flashes again and for just a moment, I swear I see something move behind him, inside the house—a dark shape with wings spread wide, patient as death itself. But when I blink, it's gone. He notices my facial expression and turns back to stare inside the window again.

"You're fucking scaring me, Tom. If you're not going to be straight with me, I have to tell Jacobs. He'll want a report." His voice softens. "Why don't we avoid the bullshit. You can trust me. You always have."

As much as I want to be angry at him, I know he's reacting the right way. Gotta put myself in his shoes. The kid's a good cop.

Just like his father. He goes by the book, even when the book's pages are splattered with blood.

"All right, kid. But you're gonna think I've lost my shit."

"Too late for that," he says with a chuckle that doesn't quite mask his concern.

We enter through the back door, locking it behind us, then exit through the front, each lock click echoing with finality. Moving toward my car, I give him the story, my words cutting through the rain like confessions. "Look, this scene had a lot more to work with than the previous ones. Figured I'd catch something I may have missed. So I arrive, get inside, and I see—feel—something moving. Then the shape becomes clear—its fucking face shifts from vulture to Stein and back—it speaks—repeats something from our sessions. I tell him to stop, but the asshole moves faster than my bullets. Then vanishes into thin air. And this isn't the first time. Stein's our guy—the vulture—I fucking know it, kid. But I have nothing to bring him in on. And Jacobs doesn't want us touching Stein unless we get solid evidence."

Cordero's gone pale. I can tell he wants to believe me. But this supernatural phenomena thing is fucking with him in ways he's never been fucked with. That's what all that religious upbringing does. Makes people superstitious. Afraid of what they can't explain.

He finally speaks. "That's fucking crazy, Tom." After a long pause, he continues, "Look let's keep this shit hush hush. We'll have to plan something out. Maybe we can trail him for a few days, set up some surveillance. When we catch something solid we take it to Jacobs. He'll get the DA to issue a warrant and we take him in."

He's right. "I see no other way around it, kid. According to Goldstein's theory he's running out of time, the eclipse happens this weekend."

"Yeah. We have three days until the eclipse."

"Good. We'll sort the details out tomorrow, kid. Go be with your old lady. She needs you. It's late."

"Thanks," Cordero says, with a handshake, collapsing his elbow and leaning in for a hug.

He walks to his car, plops in and I watch his taillights disappear into the rain, two red eyes swallowed by an abyss. The Sanskrit verse burns through the sutures in my skull and makes its way inside my brain, setting it ablaze. My nose trickles scarlet drops again, merging with the rain. I think about Rachmaninoff's second symphony. Sarah and I attended a live performance of it in the Miami Beach Convention Hall for our fifth anniversary. It was a rainy night just like this one. We kissed under the rain.

I stumble back into the Diplomat, soaked and tired. The reflection in the rearview mirror reveals my decay—my inescapable end. I wipe what's left of the blood stains on my nose, it comes off easily with the rainwater that's still on my hands. I look at my watch it's 1:54 a. m.

The engine turns over with a growl that I feel in my bones. It shakes my marrow, tickling the cancer that's eating my lymph nodes. It reminds me of the guilt that torments me, one I haven't quite figured out, but that weighs like lead in my gut.

I pull away from the curb, into the drenched night, leaving

behind the yellow crime scene tape that dances with the rain and wind.

In my mind, the vulture's red eyes still burn, and Stein's voice echoes with promises of judgment and death. One I'm actually looking forward to, because he's running out of time, and so am I. The truth is I'm already dead, I just haven't stopped breathing.

25

The weak afternoon light bleeds through the Homicide Bureau's venetian blinds like a gunshot victim, its bands of amber and shadow striping my desk with cagelike bars that remind me of the frustration circulating my bloodstream. The Bureau's air hangs heavy with stale coffee and resignation, thick enough to trap the ghosts of unsolved cases that haunt these halls.

Last night's rain still echoes in my skull—the drumming against windshield glass mixing with the thunder of my heart as I watched Stein's impossible metamorphosis. The memory feels both razor-sharp and oddly distant, like a dream that clings to the edges of consciousness. Could anyone else have seen it? The way his form twisted against the storm clouds, feathers black as midnight spreading like ink in water? But when I blink, the images scatter like startled birds.

My coffee's gone cold, bitter dregs swirling at the bottom of a Styrofoam cup while another dying camel dangles from my pale dry lips, its smoke reaching to the heavens, making intercession for my sins—some I can't quite remember. Across the bullpen,

VULTURE

Cordero hunches over case files, his shoulders taut with the weight of unseen burdens. His fingers press against his temples in slow circles, as if trying to contain thoughts that threaten to escape. There's something familiar about his posture that twists my stomach, though I can't say why.

I stub out the cigarette, my hands shaking with what I tell myself is merely fatigue, but know deep inside me to be perpetual fear. I watch the ember die like the little hope I have left inside me, devoured day in and day out by the cancerous cells that plague me. The cancer's a wildfire spreading through my swollen lymphs—competing with the fire that burns behind my eyes—an iron branding of the Sanskrit verse—मृत्युः सर्वहरश्चाहम् —'I am all-devouring death.'

The verse appears in my dreams now, carved into Spanish moss bark and whispered on the wind. Dr. Stein knows its power —must know its significance. The way he looked at me during our last session, his eyes reflecting something ancient and hungry . . . unless that too was just another hypnotic trick. Lately, time feels fluid, minutes stretching into hours or condensing into seconds without warning. Sometimes I catch my reflection in the station windows and don't recognize the man staring back.

Anxiety is a cyclical hell—one that mocks its victims with the fear of death and the lie of its own immortality. The case files before me tell a story I know by heart, yet somehow the details shift when I'm not looking, like words rearranging themselves on the page. They're tiny vultures circling closer around me, their shadows falling across my desk, across my mind. I can feel them watching, waiting. For what, I'm no longer sure. But I'm certain about Stein. I have to be.

Lieutenant Jacobs's voice slices through my thoughts like a razor blade. "Vogel! My office. Now." The words scatter the vultures nesting in my mind.

I rise from my desk, my joints creaking like old floorboards. Cordero's head snaps up at the sound, his eyes meeting mine for a fraction of a second before darting away. That familiar twist returns to my gut. The walk to Jacobs's office stretches endless, each step of my dirty shoes echoing against the linoleum like a countdown. The other detectives pretend to be absorbed in their work, but I can feel their eyes following me, their whispers trailing in my wake like cigarette smoke.

Jacobs perches in his doorway, his dark blue uniform black as pitch, backlit by the dying afternoon sun. His silhouette reminds me of something—a shape from my dreams, perhaps, or a shadow glimpsed through rain-streaked glass. But before I can grasp the memory, it slips away, leaving only an aftertaste of unease, like copper pennies that play hide and seek inside my mouth.

"Close the door," he says as I enter. His voice carries the weight of decisions already made. The creak of the rusty hinges sounds like a jail cell closing. As he sinks into the seat behind his desk, I can't help but notice he's aged a decade since the last time I saw him, worry lines engraved deep as knife wounds around his mouth.

The office constricts around me, the walls threatening like the sides of a coffin. Jacobs settles into his chair, leather creaking like old bones beneath him. A familiar folder lies closed on his desk—

thin, manila, unremarkable. Yet something about it makes my pulse quicken.

He exhales deeply. "Sit down, Tom." He gestures to the chair across from him, his wedding ring catching the light. The gleam reminds me of Stein's glass-eyed birds in darkness.

I sink into the black cracked leather chair, its rusty ancient springs beneath groaning with the aches of a dying man's last breath. The chair mocks me too. I fight the urge to reach for the cigarettes in my pocket. My hands want to shake but I don't let them—I just grip the armrests.

Jacobs stares at me for a long moment, his face a mask of exhaustion, frustration, and something else—pity, maybe. Or fear. The folder on his desk seems to pulse in sync with my heartbeat.

"Tom," he begins, then stops, rubbing his face with both hands like a praying mouse before the python strikes, wrapping him in a tight death hold until his heart stops, slowly swallowing him whole. The gesture reminds me of Cordero at his desk, and that twist in my gut tightens into a knot. "Want to explain why you discharged your weapon at Parker's place last night?" His voice is quiet, like that mouse about to die. "Or why you were even there?"

I think about Cordero. He must've told Jacobs, even though it was his idea to keep last night's events between us. Betrayal is a heavy burden, but sometimes it feels heavier on the betrayed. For a moment, I'm silent, the truth sitting heavy on my tongue, those copper pennies dancing around like the shameless whores of Miami's nightclubs. Then I finally speak: "I had a lead,

Lieutenant. Something about the Sanskrit markings—"

"Stop," Jacobs says, holding up one hand, his eyes locked on mine like a wolf on its prey. "You know what I got on my desk right now? Incident reports. Dozens of neighbor complaints about frantic screams and gunshots. The city's on edge with all this Satanic shit the media's pressing. Plus, we're short on patrol officers. You know this. The neighbors kept calling in about the same incident, asking why we were taking so long. We couldn't get an officer out there to Parker's place until three a. m."

"Lieu—"

"Three fucking a. m., Vogel." He cuts me off. "Do you know how bad this makes me look? I've tried throwing you a bone, but it's come back and fucked me in the ass. You catch my drift? Because it smells like shit. I can't stand the smell of shit, Vogel. And right now it's all I can smell."

"Stein," I say, "He's—"

"Yeah, Stein," he cuts me off again. "Stein gave me a call this morning, expressing concern about your mental state."

The name sends a jolt through my spine. Behind Jacobs, I can see shadows dance across the wall—or maybe they're feathers. I blink and they're gone.

"And frankly," he continues, "everyone else, myself included, Tom, has been quite concerned with your condition, not just the cancer, and the nosebleeds, but the way you've been since the accident, it just seems like you aren't yourself anymore. Your dizzy spells. You didn't think anyone would report it? Look, Tom, anyone can have an off day, hell, Alvarez was spilling his guts out the day the first vic was found. That shit was gruesome. I

understand. No big deal. It can happen to any of us. But you—
you're just not doing well. I can't have you working like this,
Vogel—not without making it official—getting Stein to sign off
on you after you've worked with him—in official terms—and he
signs off on you."

My jaw clenches tight enough to crack teeth. "Sign off on me?
Stein's the fucking vulture, Lieutenant. The evidence—"

"What evidence?" Jacobs growls, his fist comes down hard on
his desk, rattling his nameplate. "Your judgments are off . . .
you're going off . . . off the fucking rails . . . and off this fucking
case . . ."

"But Lieutenant—"

"Shut it, Vogel!" He interrupts. "You're lucky I'm not making
this come down harder on you! You've broken into a crime
scene, for God's sake! You think I don't know about your
hallucinations and supposed psychic visions? That's precisely
what got you into this mess!

"You've wrongfully accused one of the most important assets
to this department—who's very politically connected, I might
add—of being a serial killer—and you've been lucky enough he
hasn't pressed charges for your unprofessional behavior during
his questioning—in fact he's been nothing but cooperative and
concerned about you—to top it off—you're firing at shadows and
rambling about supernatural transformations to your partner.
What would you have me do? Keep you on the case so you end
up killing an innocent victim due to one of your hallucinations—
thinking it's some sort of psychic insight?"

I feel a deep scar of betrayal sink into my solar plexus.

"Cordero told you."

Jacobs holds a look of concern in his eyes. "Of course he told me. He had to, Tom. You're scaring him. Hell, you're scaring all of us."

The room suddenly feels too small, the walls constricting. Outside, dark clouds gather like thick smoke, announcing incoming rain. Miami's sky looks sick, as terminal as my illness. Something presses down on my shoulders. It feels like a lead blanket, just like the night of the accident, and I recognize its name—grief. I dig deep down, searching for the right words that'll convince Jacobs to give me a chance to close this case. I'm so close.

"Listen to me," I lean forward, desperation clawing at my throat, whispering to avoid screaming. "The Sanskrit verse inscribed on Parker's left forearm. It matches a plaque Stein has in his office. The septagram pattern he left at the last scene, the zodiacal signs he inscribed in blood—it all connects. He's planning something, Lieutenant, something for the eclipse, and we're running out of time."

"What Sanskrit verse, Vogel? There isn't anything inscribed on Parker's forearm. I've studied the file—seen the body. Horowitz is still working on the full report but there isn't anything like what you're saying. You sound crazy."

I stay silent, doubting myself for a moment, doubting everything I've seen and experienced until now. But then assurance sinks in. I know I'm not crazy.

Jacobs's eyes slowly scan me, taking in my whole disheveled state. "Look at yourself, Tom, you're a mess. The cancer, the meds, losing Sarah and Emily, this case—it's all taking its toll."

The mention of their names hits me like a freight train. Jacobs's face triples. The room starts to spin, and for a moment I swear I can see feathers drifting through the air. I close my eyes and pinch the space between them with my thumb and forefinger. "Don't do that, Lieutenant. Don't treat me like I'm crazy."

"I don't think you're crazy, Tom, but you need help. Stein—"

"Is a goddamn murderer!" I cut him off, the words exploding out of me, sending fresh blood trickling from my nose. I swipe at it with the fresh new bandage on my left hand, leaving a crimson streak that flowers into a horizontal evergreen of blood.

Jacobs watches me with eyes that scream with concern. He pulls a manila folder, slides it across the desk. "Everything's in there if you want to see it. Incident reports. Stein's professional opinion. But my decision is final."

His words are body blows, each one stealing the air from my lungs more than the previous ones. "You can't do this to me."

"I'm not asking, Vogel. Badge and gun. Now," he says, not meeting my eyes. "You're off the case. Effective immediately. Suspended—pending a full psych evaluation."

The words land like a death sentence.

"Jesus Christ, Tom, don't make this any more difficult than it already is."

My hands move without permission, unholstering my .38, unfastening my shield from my belt and sliding them both gently across his desk. Like dirt on a coffin.

"Look, it's only temporary," Jacobs says, but we both know it's a lie. "You get your pay, so don't worry about that. Get some rest. I'll give you a call when some of this blows over in a few days. We gotta do this right, Tom. It's policy. It's the right way. We'll have to schedule you in for a full evaluation with Dr. Stein. It's the only way you'll get back on."

My legs feel like concrete when I stand. "You're making a mistake. We're running out of time. Two more people are going to die. He's gonna finish the septagram by the time the eclipse occurs this weekend."

"Tom, please." Jacobs gestures me to exit his office. His eyes are two wrecking balls.

The walk back through the bullpen feels like the *Via Dolorosa*, every eye tracking my movement is a whip slashing my back. Cordero rises halfway from his desk, mouth opening to speak but I wave him off. I can't bear to see the pity in his eyes.

Outside the rain's pouring down as strong as my grief. The smell of sulfur is thick enough to drown in. I slump inside the Diplomat, dropping my head against the steering wheel. The leather's warm against my sick feverish skin. As I sob, I think about this godforsaken city, of its secrets, and the curse that runs through its loins.

I sit up, my hands shaking as I turn the key, the engine turning over with a growl that sounds too much like the vulture's laugh. My skin's gray like the sky in the rearview mirror, decay eating at the edges reaching my hollow eyes. The cancer's winning, spreading like Spanish moss on an ancient Miami oak. But the certainty of what's coming is deadlier than my fate. The weight of the lives I won't be able to save presses down on me—

drowning me in concrete quicksand. Miami's got a way of turning honest cops into ghosts—and I'm already halfway there. But without my badge and gun, I'm nothing—just a dying man in a dying city. The truth is that in Miami, we're all carrion, waiting our turn. And I'm waiting for the darkness to claim what's left of me. If Miami's taught me one thing—it's that even shadows can kill.

I pull out of the parking lot, tires throwing up sheets of water like angel wings. Sarah and Emily's headstones will be rain-slick when I visit—cold marble witnesses to what a man will do when he's got nothing left to lose. Their silence is all the permission I need. But the truth sits heavy in my gut, like a cancer made of certainty and fear. The weight's a decision I already know I'll be forced to make. The wages of sin is death—and tonight somebody's account comes due. Stein's got a tab to settle with me. My badge is gone, but the untraceable .38 in my glove compartment's got just enough bullets to balance the books.

26

The wet asphalt road spreads before me like the Red Sea, bleeding beneath the Diplomat's wheels, each street a dying heartbeat counting down my remaining time. Memorial Cemetery looms ahead, its iron gates like broken teeth against Miami's rotting skyline.

Rain hammers down with the intensity of a confessional, each drop another sin seeking absolution. The whitewashed headstones and stone angels are nebulous shapes that melt between the swipes of the windshield wipers.

The afternoon's grey seeps into my bones—poison merging with the grief that burns in my gut like battery acid. The truth about Stein festers like the cancer inside me, spreading through my lymphs like Spanish moss claiming an ancient oak.

The cemetery's lot drowns beneath sheets of rain, empty except for a rusted pickup whose owner must be laying flowers on some unfortunate soul. My mind replays Jacobs's words as I kill the engine near the familiar bend. The silence that follows feels like a coffin lid closing. My hands are trembling against the steering wheel's cracked leather, studying Pedro with his sun-bruised skin, huge gut, and thick black mustache, lurking in his guard shack through the rain-streaked windshield. He's still there, still looking like that old fortune-telling machine at the fair, his dark face and large eyes floating behind glass. Today, I can hear his predictions whispering through my tinnitus—describing a future written in cancer cells and swollen lymphs.

I march through rows of headstones, my mind continuously replaying Jacobs's words, each syllable settles over me like a burial shroud. Everyone thinks I'm crazy—the dying detective chasing shadows and monsters. But they didn't see what I saw at Parker's place. Didn't watch Stein's face melt into that ancient vulture skull, his laughter scraping against the air like bone against stone. The truth sits in my gut heavier than the cancer, but without my badge, I'm just another madman in Miami's endless rain.

Lightning splits the sky, vulture wings rippling through from horizon to horizon. Water streams down my face and raw grief claws at my throat with each step closer to their markers.

My shoes sink into mud as if the earth itself is trying to claim me early as I make my way down the familiar path that cuts through the heart of Memorial's oldest section, where Spanish moss drapes the oaks like funeral shrouds. I've walked this route so many times I could find their graves blindfolded—twenty-nine steps past the angel with the broken wing, turn right at the weeping willow, then straight ahead until my heart starts to splinter.

The thin mist that usually clings to the gravestones has turned to sheets of rain, and the familiar scent of damp earth and wilting flowers fills my lungs. West Flagler Street's traffic sounds distant, muted, like it belongs to another world entirely—one still concerned with the business of living.

The air is thick with decay, the kind of stench that seeps into your bones and never leaves. It reminds me of the Sanskrit verse that perpetually burns behind my eyes, haunting me: मृत्युः सर्वहरश्चाहम्—*I am all-devouring death*. Their headstones rise from the sodden earth like accusations, the rain runs down the darkened marble in rivulets that look like tears. Or blood.

The ground beneath them has turned to black mud, swallowing my shoes like quicksand as I approach. Sarah and Emily Vogel. Beloved wife and daughter. The words are harder to read now, more than ever before, today this truth cuts deeper than stone. The dates blur in the rain, but I know them by heart —like I know the taste of copper flooding my mouth, like I know the sound of Stein's laughter scraping against Parker's walls. Lightning flashes again, and shadows dance across their names like vulture wings, mocking me. Daring me to end it all right now.

I drop to my knees in the mud, not caring about the water soaking through my suit pants. That's when I notice it—their names are bleeding, dark liquid seeping from each carved letter like fresh wounds. The Sanskrit verse continues to pulse behind my eyes in time with my heartbeat: मृत्युः सर्वहरश्चाहम्—*I am all-devouring death*. The nosebleed starts without warning, copper pennies flood my mouth as time starts to slip—the graves blur and sharpen, blur and sharpen. Sarah's voice cuts through my

224

skull: "You know what you have to do, Tom." The Sanskrit verse fights its way back, pushing Sarah's voice aside, carving itself into my retinas. It burns stronger than the bile that exited my mouth two nights ago. Stein's laughter echoes in my skull, mixing with Sarah's voice until I can't tell which is which. Stein's voice momentarily overpowers Sarah's and scrapes against my bones: "Beautiful, isn't it, Detective?" The vulture's red eyes bore into my soul.

The dizziness hits me again, stronger this time. I stumble, my left hand sinking into the muddy ground, the only thing keeping me from dropping face first into Sarah's headstone. The ground fills with rain and blood—my blood. For a moment I'm floating in darkness, circling down deep in an abyss, I'm weightless—all I can feel is the rain, and the pain of everything I've lost. I will myself to blink and I'm back, both hands on the ground now, feeling my body wearing tissue-thin, like the membrane between life and death.

"Sarah, I'm so sorry," I whisper, the words drowning in rain. "I can't—" The rest dies in my throat as movement catches my right eye—a dark blurry shape at the edge of my vision. I whirl around, pushing myself up—unsteady on my feet—but there's nothing there. Just shadows and rain and the endless rows of the dead.

Silence.

Only the rain speaks.

Suddenly, a shadow twists between the farthest headstones to my right. At first, I think it's Pedro making his rounds, but the shape twists wrong—too large, too fast against the darkening sky.

I turn, checking all around me.

Nothing.

It's gone.

But I can feel fiery, burning eyes on me, watching, waiting. The same presence I felt at Parker's place—the ominous tension that filled every crime scene.

The vulture's presence—it's here.

"I know you're here," I call out into the darkness. My voice sounds wrong, distorted by rain and fear. "Show yourself, you son of a bitch."

Lightning flashes and there—sixty feet out to my right like some grotesque gargoyle—is a shape too large to be a normal bird, too wrong to be human—he stands there: Stein—his silhouette transforming against the rain. His face shifting like melting wax, human features elongating into that terrible and ancient vulture skull. His smile is an empty beak, no teeth but full triumph, mocking my grief, my failure, my dying body. From his mouth a laugh emerges, it sounds like bones grinding against stone. It pierces my soul—echoing between the headstones, impossible to pinpoint.

Against the dying light behind it, wings unfold like sheets of blackest night, spanning wider than ten feet each. The bald red head swivels toward me, eyes reflecting an ancient primal hunger. Unforgiveness coiling around him like a serpent around the caduceus. In the strobe of lightning, its form shifts and writhes—feathers becoming flesh, beak melting into familiar features. Stein's features.

"Beautiful night for redemption, isn't it, Detective?" The voice is heavy and terse—human words scraped raw by an inhuman throat. Each syllable is molten lead pouring inside my skull.

My legs move automatically, scrambling through the mud toward the Diplomat. I yank open the glove compartment, reaching for my burner—another .38 Detective Special—it sits atop a stack of white napkins from the diner. By the time I turn back, gun in hand, he's moving between the tombstones with impossible grace, each lightning flash revealing him closer, then farther, playing a game of supernatural hide-and-seek.

I give chase, slipping in the mud, bruising my ribs and standing back up with inexplicable strength—as I run, my lungs burn with each breath. My joints scream—the scream of cancer's victory—but I push through it.

Rain and sweat and blood mix on my face as I follow the dark shape deeper into the cemetery's older section. As I make my way through the dense woodland, Spanish moss whips my face like funeral veils, and somewhere ahead, that bone-scraping laugh echoes off whitewashed stone angels.

"Stop! You son of a bitch!" I roar, but the words cascade out weak, breathless.

I spin around, searching the shadows between headstones, but there's nothing. Just rain, the weight of darkness and the echo of its laughter.

Blood cascades freely from my nose now, hot against my cold skin. "Come out and face me, asshole," I growl, my heart pounding out of my chest.

The thing that is both vulture and man takes a step forward, talons clicking and scraping against a concrete section of the nearby mausoleum. Each click is a clock's second hand counting down what remains of my vitality. I turn toward the sound but my .38 shakes so badly I can barely aim. Then it vanishes into black smoke, leaving only its lingering, haunting voice to torment me.

It laughs again—a sound like maggots writhing in dead flesh. "You still don't believe, do you? Even now?" Its form ripples and shifts, feathers melting into skin, then back again. "Look closer, Detective. Look at what you've become. The signs were there all along, Tommy boy. Every victim pleaded for your belief. Nonetheless, you shall witness my work, it is almost complete."

A laugh lingers there for a moment and then it's gone—dissolving into mist between one heartbeat and the next. I spin around, gun raised, but find only rain and shadows. My legs finally betray me, and I stumble against a tombstone, chest heaving. The .38 feels too heavy, like an unforgivable sin as I slide it into my empty holster—it's a weight that replaces my badge and marks my fall from grace.

I drag myself back to the Diplomat, collapsing into the soaked driver's seat. I wipe the water that streams off my face, unable to tell anymore what's rain and what's blood. The Sanskrit verse pulses behind my eyes, burning through my corneas; its relentless fire reminding me of my own decay and the fear Stein carved into my heart: *I am all-devouring death*—grows boundless.

Anger and frustration surge through my bloodstream; my hands shaking as I grip the steering wheel. Surveillance. That's the solution. Follow him, document everything, catch him in the act. Even if Jacobs won't believe me, even if Cordero thinks I'm insane—I'll get proof. Or I'll put him down myself.

The rain hammers down harder as I start the engine, each drop silent against its growl mixing with thunder. As I pull out of the cemetery, my mind's already mapping out Stein's home in Coral Gables, planning entry points, sight lines. The cancer can have what's left of me after I finish this. After I make him pay. Behind the fiery verse that burns my eyes, Stein's laugh scrapes against my skull: "Beautiful, isn't it, Detective?"

27

Coral Gables spreads before me like an open watery grave, its manicured lawns and Spanish tile roofs bathe in the sulfuric rain and the amber of bleeding streetlights. Water drums on the diplomat like distant wings fluttering; the wipers are the two failing arms of a drowning man. They reach for the heavens, seeking salvation like I seek tangible evidence that proves Stein is the vulture. Anything that proves to Jacobs that I'm not crazy— evidence that'll grant me my badge and gun back. Without it I'm nothing—I can do nothing—at least within the official sanctions of Florida law. But if Jacobs thinks I'm just going to sit back, watching and waiting while more people die—while Stein continues his ritualistic cleansing of Miami's sinners—he truly doesn't know me like he thinks he does.

I park the Diplomat a block from Stein's house, sinking into shadow beneath a banyan tree whose roots crack the sidewalk like arthritic fingers. I kill the engine as I watch black evening clouds descend upon me through sheets of thunderous rain. The large two-story colonial—all perfect angles with a manicured lawn—squats behind two large ancient oaks dangling Spanish moss. It's a temple to old money and older secrets. God only knows what horrors must lay behind its impeccable façade. Just like its owner.

The house's windows are dark except for his study, where a warm yellow light bleeds through gauzy curtains. I can make out his hazy silhouette moving behind the rain-streaked glass like a vulture circling its next meal.

I can feel the cancer gnawing at my lymph nodes as I wait, each minute is a thousand burning raindrops piercing my bones reminding me of nothing but death. But tonight the pain feeds my focus.

At 9:45 p. m., the study light dies. Moments later, movement at the front door catches my eye.

Stein emerges, wearing a black sports hoodie instead of his usual suit. The respected psychiatrist is unrecognizable in this shroud of black that merges with the obsidian sky.

He strolls—with a measured grace that makes my skin crawl—to a gleaming black Mercedes; its like a moth waiting to take flight. My hands tremble as I grip the wheel—fighting to keep them steady. My knuckles go white.

When the Mercedes pulls out, I start the engine, but wait until it's three blocks ahead before following, my headlights off until I reach the first stop sign. It cuts through the black wet asphalt like a shark through dark waters, its taillights bleeding into the neon-drenched Miami night.

I follow him from the heart of Coral Gables' mansion-lined

streets, past coral rocks and sleeping castles into Miami's older arteries, where old concrete masonry buildings crowd together like mourners at a wake. I know I'm somewhere close to Coconut Grove, but I don't recognize the exact area under this torrential downpour. Each turn is executed with surgical precision taking us deeper into the city's maze, away from carefully curated wealth and into tunnels of darkness formed by banyan trees. To avoid suspicion, sometimes I trail him three cars back, the Diplomat growling in unison with the rage in my gut. When he suddenly cuts right, down a narrow alley, I nearly lose him—but the Mercedes's brake lights flash like demon eyes, guiding me into a hell-bound abyss.

I watch the Mercedes turn right and after four blocks it makes a left, its taillights bleeding red against dark coral rock walls. It pulls into a dirt driveway, in front of an old seemingly abandoned house tucked between two large ancient banyan trees with Spanish moss that hang just five feet from the ground. I kill my lights, easing the Diplomat forward until I can make out Stein's silhouette emerge from his car. Its shape is wrong—it seems to ripple in the darkness, twisting against the sodium vapor glow of a distant streetlamp.

My hand finds the .38 in my holster, its cold ivory grip is a comfort I can't describe. I turn to the passenger seat—my old Kodak is there, quietly resting until I reach for it. The camera's weight feels right in my hands, it's been waiting for this moment —I've been waiting for this moment.

Through my rain-streaked windshield, I watch as Stein makes his way toward the back of the house. I slide out of the Diplomat, letting the rain soak into my clothes. Every step I take feels like my feet are pushing through quicksand, my eyes fixed on the trailing shadows Stein leaves behind. The cancer is a hindrance to my stealth—I'm too tired, too weak, my breathing's too heavy, my movements too slow. I'm a fragile leaf the wind rejects, but I push through, willing myself to finish this.

Suddenly, Stein pauses, tilting his head toward the sky, then turning around, like a vulture scenting his prey. I quickly duck behind his car, heart hammering against my ribs, blood trickling down my nose, mixing with the unforgiving rain. By the time I dare to look, he's already moving on.

I follow him, keeping to the shadows. Ahead Stein disappears through an iron gate into what looks like some sort of abandoned courtyard. Ancient coral rock walls rise on all sides, dressed in strangler figs that coil around them with the anger of rattlesnakes. Large weathered stone statues of angels and birds adorn the place, the moonlight casts a bluish-green tint on their white surface. Upon the walls are ancient esoteric symbols and glyphs, just like the ones at the crime scenes; they seem to writhe under the lightning flashes. The place pretends to be some sort of church or place of worship, but it's something older. Darker.

Stein disappears inside the shadows. As I creep in closer, pressing myself against the wet stone, fresh blood begins trickling down from my nose. I catch it with my bandaged left hand, the gauze flowers black under the moonlight.

Lightning flashes and through the gate's bars, I watch Stein lighting candles in a pattern I recognize from the last crime scene —a septagram taking shape in trembling light. He hunches over a large rock lifting something sharp from the darkness—a ceremonial knife, its blade catches the candlelight like a sliver of ice formed in hell. It reminds me of death's scythe.

The chanting starts low, foreign words that sound like stones grinding against frail bones. It's Latin, but mixed with something else. Something older, something that makes my stomach churn and my vision blur.

Stein raises the knife skyward, like an offering to ancient gods. Suddenly, his form begins to twist—flesh melting into something black—like coal. His back hunches—its shape is too large—too angular—its edges shift between man and bird. His face begins elongating into that terrible beak. Black feathers sprout from his shoulders like giant organ pipes reaching toward the heavens. Wings unfold like black cathedral doors, spanning the width of the courtyard. For over five minutes he alternates between man and bird, like in an ecstasy of change.

This is my opportunity. I raise the camera, hands fighting to keep it steady. Another lightning flash and Stein's human again— just a man in a hoodie holding a knife. But the wings' shadow remains on the coral rock walls behind him, a frightening reminder of what lurks beneath his skin.

Before he can change into the vulture again, the flash explodes like lightning, freezing the transformation in cellulose nitrate truth. Stein whirls toward me, his mouth opens, a screech of metamorphosis splits the night like broken glass. I crash through the iron gates, the camera goes flying as his hands extend into wings, his feet into talons, and beat against me.

We collide, feather versus hands in a tangle of fury. I draw my

.38 but the vulture's faster—the gun slips from my hand landing a few feet behind me. Its sharp angular beak attacks my throat, my forearms are a weak shield of flesh. Blood drips from the sliced skin of my forearms onto my face, mixing with the rain. I turn and see the knife about six feet from me. I roll, grabbing it and thrusting it deep underneath its midnight feathers. A hellbound screech shatters through my skull.

The sharp talons find my injured arm, piercing through the healing wound. Pain erupts through me as the bandage blooms scarlet red. My scream echoes off the coral rock walls as the vulture lifts me, then slams me down—the knife ripping through its flesh, scattering across the soaked dirt and cracked stones along the path.

Through my pain-blurred vision, I see the shattered camera drowning in a puddle of rain and blood. My gun lays next to it, just three feet from my reach. The vulture looms over me, in a hell-like mirage, its form rippling between bird and man. Thick syrupy blood drips from the wound I inflicted, black as sin under this cursed moonlight.

"Beautiful, isn't it, Detective?" the words scrape against my eardrums, "you're so close now. Just two more unrepentant sinners. Witness me, Tommy boy, redemption is at hand." It tilts its head back in an ode to the moon. Opening its mouth like an ivory tomb, a sinister laugh emerges, the sound is like death itself.

I lunge for my .38, but by the time my fingers wrap around the cold wet grip, the courtyard is empty. The vulture's gone—dissolved into nothingness between one heartbeat and the next.

Only my pain and blood mark the night's violence as real. My camera's in pieces its evidence lost to darkness. For a moment the moon hides behind black clouds and the night seems to swallow me whole.

I stumble onto my feet, assaulted by the rain. Blood drips from my nose and forearms; my left hand's bandage is as black as the night. My feet are concrete cinder blocks, it takes me a little over five minutes to make it back to the Diplomat.

The drive home is a blur—the streets feel increasingly unfamiliar in this fever dream of pain and failure—my mind replaying what I've witnessed like a broken record. The wound in my left arm throbs in time with the wipers fighting the rain. The vulture's words won't leave my skull. Each strobe of Miami's neon that blurs past my windows is a judgment passed—a reminder of the evidence I almost had—the proof that shattered right before my eyes—just like the promises of safety I made my wife and daughter.

I park in my driveway, killing the engine but lingering in the darkness for a few minutes. The rearview mirror shows a man coming apart at the seams—but my eyes burn with purpose. Stein thinks he's won. But I'm not finished. Sometimes monsters wear human masks, and sometimes justice doesn't carry a badge.

The eclipse is a day away and two sacrifices are pending. One way or another, the vulture's reign of terror stops with me. Justice or vengeance, at this point I'm past caring which. This story ends with one of us in the ground—and I'm already halfway there. The wages of sin is death—and I'm ready to collect.

28

The whiskey bottle looms empty as a spent shell casing, its glass corpse catching Miami's moonlight through venetian blinds that stripe my kitchen in prison bars.

The Jack sits in my gut like motor oil, fueling this late-night cage of obsession. Sleep's a criminal I've stopped trying to catch. My hands won't stop trembling as I spread the case files before me, arranging and rearranging the crime scene photos in a cosmic pattern that mirrors the vulture's septagram. Scarlet drops from my injured hand stain the files like a reminder of my failures. Each image is a bloody constellation, one that dances just beyond my intuitive reach like smoke in a hall of mirrors. And the truth about his next victim lies somewhere in this galaxy of death—if I can decode it before he strikes again.

Outside, rain drums against the windows, a steady rhythm that matches the pounding of the Sanskrit verse inside my skull. मृत्युः सर्वहरश्चाहम्—"*I am all-devouring death*"—its molten letters scorch each one of my retinas with a fear that spreads as fast as the cancer that's consuming me.

This city's an ancient predator, one that gives birth to other predators. Changeling offspring that go bump in the night. Like the seemingly benevolent doctor, who tends to his patients by day and feasts upon their flesh by night. Stein's photograph bears back at me from the case file. His face bears a professional calm and psychiatric wisdom—but I know it's a mask—I've seen what lurks behind those eyes. Seen the vulture that screeches underneath that clump of human skin.

I snatch another Camel. The pack's crushed like my career. My hands struggle with the spark wheel. *Flick!* It finally flares in the darkness, momentarily burning away the shadows that enclose me—shadows that move when they think I'm not looking. I inhale, letting the nicotine navigate the weak rivers of my bloodstream. Its suicidal chemicals fuse with my cancerous cells, rejoicing in the wake of my terminal descent.

The puzzle on my kitchen table remains stubbornly incomplete, its pieces mocking me with their obstinate refusal to reveal their secrets—just fragments of red and black that dance at the edge of understanding, just like everything else in this goddamn case. I've been staring at it for hours, alternating between it and the files, watching as both blur together into a carnival of meaningless shapes, each one promising answers but delivering only questions that reflect back my own decay— cancer devours my body while obsession gnaws at what's left of my mind.

I know I'm close to the truth; I can feel it lurking just beyond my grasp. I should call Agent Chen. Maybe she could . . . No. The FBI won't play along. Not after Jacobs took my badge. Besides, what would be my play? Tell her I watched our esteemed department shrink shed his skin like a cheap suit, unfurling into something ancient and terrible—that he's targeting alcoholics with prior DUI arrests and conducting ancient and occult sacrificial rituals in the shadow of Miami's streets as some form of cultish redemption? With what motive? That his son was killed by a drunk driver eight years ago? That his grandfather was Adolph Steinburger, leader of an ancient cannibalistic cult?

Or should I mention his claim that he made amends with his son's killer, forgiven him, and volunteered his therapeutic services at the same AA center where that man attended as personal form of healing? Doesn't it make sense that he worked pro bono there with the intent of getting close to the victims? After all—all five victims attended that same AA center. No. It wouldn't jive. Technically speaking, these are all speculations because I don't have anything that ties Stein to the murders, other than his volunteer pro bono work and his possible motive. No prints, no evidence. His alibi at the Orlando Marriott checked out. Nothing makes sense, but I know he's responsible. My gut tells me so. Christ, maybe Jacobs was right. Maybe I'm losing it.

The phone rings, slicing through my thoughts, splitting the silence like a gunshot. I stub out the cigarette and seize it before the fourth ring, my throat tight with exhaustion.

"Vogel," I say, my voice thick like gravel.

"Hello Detective." The sinister voice is familiar. It hisses with static. Heavy. Cold. Distant. Like a record played backward. Yet the words are slow enough I can understand them.

"Do you know what's the virtue of the vultures?"

The question's words are sharp; they drill through my skull. I don't say a word.

"Patience, Tommy boy. Patience."

My fingers grip the receiver tight enough to crack the plastic. Fear and anger bubbles in my gut. "I know it's you—Stein—you son of a—"

A menacing laugh permeates through the receiver, its high static forces me to pull the phone from my ear. My fist's a steel trap, angry keratin teeth pierce my palm. "I'm going to finish you, motherfucker!"

"Tell me, Detective, do you still hear them? The vultures' wings at dawn?"

Something in those words ices my spine. Memories whirl in my gut. The tormenting whooshing sound preceded by tinnitus. It's haunted me for years, worsening after the accident. Are they vulture wings?

"Do you hear them now?" the voice growls. I hear them. But he doesn't doubt my experience like I do. "What about that haunting telephone ring? The desperate voice begging for help?" His laughs are talons scraping my eardrums. "Remember the vultures? How beautifully they descended? . . . how they helped you conceal the truth? . . . nature's janitors consuming the sins— evidence of loyalty to your partner. One insignificant life—a worthless one—because some sin more than others—isn't that right? Or is it that one sin is greater than another? Which one is it, Detective?"

The words are a sledgehammer to my chest. My sternum splays open. Blood no longer flows inside me. Only repressed guilt.

"Water, it cleanses all sins, doesn't it?" the voice continues, slow and heavy with static. "The rain and the river; they wash away all the evidence. But blood—it always leaves a stain in the soul."

The static on the line sounds too much like the beating of dark wings. Like drumming rain on asphalt. I can smell the sulfur hissing in my sinuses. My stomach lurches into heavy pain as the memory crashes through:

Three years ago. The phone yanking me from deep sleep. Cordero's voice cracking like a teenager's through what sounds like a war zone of hail pelting a phone booth's metal roof: "Tom . . . Jesus Christ, Tom. I fucked up. I fucked up bad." The storm's fury almost drowns his words.

Rain. Homestead. 4:30 a.m. A few miles from the Everglades. Acres of desolation. Cordero standing by his unmarked unit, hands shaking, breath heavy with stale whiskey. Steam rising from the crumpled fender like spirits escaping judgment. The trunk holding secrets neither of us want to name.

"I was getting a few things from Pop's place in Isla Morada," he says. Tears rolling down his face, mixing with the rain. "I stopped by Jefferey's pub on the way back. Just had a few drinks. He came out of nowhere . . . Oh God, Tom. What the fuck am I gonna do now? I'm fucked, man. My career's fucking over."

He opens the trunk.

My Diplomat's headlights reveal an old, deteriorated, and lifeless body. Male. White beard heavy with ocher stains. Sopping wet. Crimson streaks run down his head and mouth. Rigor mortis in its infancy. I turn the stiff's head to me. "Holy shit, kid. That's Drunkie-Pete. The pub's alley cat."

Cordero runs his hands through his hair, clasping them behind his head. He squats, head touching knees. Words of desperation exit his mouth. "I swear it was an accident, man. If we call this in, and they test me, I'm fucked, bro."

"Did you see any nearby cameras? Any potential witnesses?"

"No. No cameras," he says. "No eyes on me either. I checked carefully, that's why I loaded him in the trunk. I fucking panicked, man, didn't know what else to do. That's why I called you."

My voice is steady, despite the cold rain. "Don't feel too bad, kid. This poor bastard was as blind as lady justice. He probably walked straight into you. Of course, I'm sure the booze didn't help his judgment either."

"It's the fucking rain, man. My windshield was a blur."

"Listen to me, kid. We'll fix this. But right now you need to get yourself together. Now, help me get him in my trunk. Your car's not gonna make it to where we're going. We'll come back for it later. No one's gonna touch a city vehicle. Especially not out here in the middle of nowhere. Plus, I got some Homestead PD friends that'll throw me a bone if I need it. You're gonna be okay, kid. Let's roll."

Rain-slicked roads. Squealing tires. But the drive to the Everglades is quiet. Rivers zig and zag like tentacles into the veins of swamps. Darkness grows thick as tar before dawn. The wet body thuds as it hits the swamp grass. Large dark shapes began descending from the sky. Vultures.

"Nobody will find him here," my voice is clear and sharp in the rain, like broken glass. "The vultures will take care of it."

We watch through the rearview mirror as the vultures' black wings blot out the rising sun, ready to claim our offering—thinking we'd

VULTURE

buried our sins along with the body. But the wages of sin is death.

The memory fades and the line goes dead before I can respond. The room's still spinning and fresh blood drips from my nose onto my shirt. The truth settles over me like a burial shroud—my eyes turning over to the puzzle, just a few pieces missing, and now I can see it clearer.

Each black and red piece clicks into place: A vulture. Stein. That son of a bitch. He's been playing me since day one. Each victim's a hit-and-run driver. Each death a karmic settling of accounts. The Sanskrit verse's a laser behind my eyes:

मृत्युः सर्वहरश्चाहम्– *I am all-devouring death.*

Then the realization hits me like six ten-ring rounds of a .44 magnum: Cordero. He's next. Has to be. The pattern's so clear now I want to slap myself for not seeing it sooner. Stein's going to complete the sixth point of his septagram with my partner's blood. And I'd wager all my sins that I'm number seven.

I pull my revolver from the holster, checking its cylinder—six rounds, six chances to collect the wager of sin and claim redemption. The weight is heavy in my hand, heavier than my badge will ever be.

I check my watch; it's 4:30 a.m. Outside Miami's deluge waits for me, its empty streets ready to either drown me or wash me clean of my sins.

The Diplomat's engine turns over, its growl meaner than ever. As I pull out of my driveway, the streets blur together like watercolors in rain. We're all sinners in this city, consciously or unconsciously each one of us hides a secret. The night swallows

243

my headlights, but I know redemption waits ahead.

I floor the gas, the Diplomat's engine screaming like a tortured sinner. Each neon sign is a blur under this rain, a reminder that in this city seeing clearly is always a struggle. But tonight I see clearer than ever. Tonight, I bring balance to the scales. Tonight, I save my partner.

29

The deluge continues as dawn bleeds through Miami's gray-toned skyline. Everything blurs like a cheap camera lens smeared with Vaseline, decay and lost hope hiding behind the gaudy neon signs of Little Havana's cafeterias. The Diplomat's engine growls like a caged beast, cutting through streets empty as a broke gambler's wallet.

I'm stopped at the red light at West Flagler and 22nd when I see him. There to my right, across from me is Stein in his Mercedes. Through the rain-streaked windshield, his features contort—human to vulture in a heartbeat, beak jutting sharp as judgment, eyes burning red as hellfire.

Before the light changes, the Mercedes makes a right onto West Flagler Street, its red taillights are two demon's eyes bleeding into the darkness. The bastard's heading straight to Cordero's place in Flagami—the location of the sixth septagram point. My pale hands grip the wheel tight, trying to stop their trembling. A crimson river bursts through my nostrils, staining my collar. I feel the cancer gnawing at my swollen lymph nodes, but rage pushes me forward, bitter as Cuban coffee at midnight. I won't let him take my partner. Not tonight.

The Mercedes glides through black asphalt and dark waters like a shark tasting blood; always three blocks ahead, always just beyond my reach. Through his rearview mirror those terrible red eyes pierce the darkness, burning through the rain like acetylene torches. His face remains cloaked in writhing shadows until lightning tears open the sky, revealing that ancient vulture skull in all its horrific glory.

I chase him through rain-slicked streets, past shuttered storefronts where neon bleeds into a psychedelic smear. Around Southwest 57th Avenue, the Mercedes vanishes into the labyrinth of rain-swept side streets, leaving me alone with thunder's mocking laughter and the weight of my sins. But I know where he's going. And I'll be damned if I let him finish his fiendish work.

My heart's pounding as I approach Cordero's house. It emerges from an abyss through sheets of black rain, a mausoleum waiting for its next occupant. His white Diplomat sits in the driveway like a pale ghost. The front door hangs open, framing the darkness within. Water drums against the roof of my Diplomat like distant wings. I park at the curb, drawing my .38 from its holster. The ivory grip burns cold against my palm, its weight promising judgment as I step into the deluge, each drop another second ticking away on my partner's life.

The storm claims me for its own as rain pounds against my body like nature's own percussion section in this twisted symphony I'm conducting; my sodden trenchcoat heavy as a drowned man's burial shroud. The wind howls a devil's chorus as lightning splits the sky—cymbals in my requiem mass.

The house's darkness swallows me as I cross the threshold. "Cordero!" My voice echoes through the foyer and down the hall. Lightning pierces through the windows, painting shadows of dancing vulture wings on the walls.

I find him in the living room, alive but confused, backlit by the warm glow of a standing corner light. On the wall behind him is a mirror; my image blurs in it, contorting my face like a fun house mirror.

"Jesus Christ, Tom. What are you doing here?" His voice carries concern, but also fear.

"Are you okay?" I ask, still clearing the room with my .38.

"I'm fine," Cordero says, his posture is tense.

"The vulture," I say, lowering my gun. "He's coming for you, kid. Stein's on his way here. You're his sixth target. The Flagami point of the septagram." The words tumble out between ragged breaths.

"What the fuck are you talking about, Tom?"

Fresh blood streams from my nose, painting my shirt crimson. I wipe it clean with my gauzed hand. "He chose you. Just like he chose the others. He knows, kid. He knows what happened three years ago."

Cordero takes a step toward me, hands raised like he's approaching a wounded animal. "Tom. Bud. You're not well." He begins slowly walking towards me. "Now, why don't you just give me your gun and we go get you some help."

I retreat a few steps, my back almost against a wall. "Don't play stupid with me, kid. We don't have time for this shit." I signal him with the gun. "Now grab your shit and let's go before this maniac arrives."

He takes a few more steps towards me. "Tom, please, buddy. You're seriously scaring me right now. Let's go talk to Jacobs, he'll help you sort this all out."

"You don't get it do you, kid?" I ask, tapping the .38 on my right temple. "Remember that night three years ago, in Homestead—The old drunk—Drunkie Pete? You accidentally ran him over when you left Jeffery's Pub. You called me. I helped you clean up the mess. Stein knows, kid. He's the fucking vulture. And you and I are his next meal unless we stop him. Now let's roll."

Cordero's closer now, just a cold stiff's length way. "No, Tom —"

I wipe some more fresh blood from my nose. "Don't you get it? We left him for the vultures in the Everglades. That's why—"

"You're having a psychotic break, brother." Cordero's face is pale. His eyes swimming in tears.

"You were drunk, kid. And I helped clean up your mess. We're the two final pieces in his sick redemptive puzzle. He's taking revenge. He's all-devouring death. Don't you fucking get it?"

"Tom." His voice cuts through my skull like a blade. "That's not how it happened. *You* called me that night. It was *you*. Not me. *You* were the one who hit him. I helped you dump the body. We swore to never talk about it again."

The room starts spinning and everything blurs. The red filter descends and memories crash through my mind like broken glass:

VULTURE

Homestead. Jeffrey's Pub. Half a bottle of Jack clearing away the stress from Lawson's case.

The old drunk. The phone booth. Rain. Cordero's voice steady as stone: "It's okay, Tom. We'll fix this." The trunk opening to reveal the broken body. The drive to the Everglades. Vultures descending as we drove away.

"What?—No, no, no." The words taste heavy like copper and lead in my mouth. "That's not—

"It was an accident, Tom. It was fucked up, but we did what we had to do. You think that old drunk was worth your badge? Your career? You need to get yourself together."

Those last six words echo the past inside my skull. *"You need to get yourself together."* This time it's not me saying it. It's Cordero. *His hand on my shoulder. The rain enveloping us.*

"No!" I press the cold barrel of the .38 to my temple. My finger on the trigger. "It can't be—"

Movement behind Cordero catches my eye. The glitter of a knife I know all too well. The vulture emerges from the shadows, its ancient form rippling between bird and man, Stein's features melting into that terrible beak as wings unfurl like hell's gates.

"Get down!" I scream, raising the .38. The vulture—more beast than man—is on him in an instant. I squeeze the trigger. It roars six times, thunder and lightning in the living room. The vulture moves too fast, Cordero turns too slow. Where the vulture once stood, only black smoke remains, lingering heavy like our guilt. But Cordero—oh God, Cordero. He crumples to the floor, blood flowering across his chest like crimson roses.

"Fuck!" I curse, dropping the .38, falling to my knees beside him. I grab his hands in mine, tight. "Hold on, kid. Stay with me. Please stay with me."

"You," he gasps, blood bubbling like magma from his lips. "Why, Tom?" he gurgles, words drowning in a scarlet river.

His eyes go glass-flat like Stein's taxidermy birds as his last breath rattles out. He's silent like a tomb. My blood-stained hands tremble as I let his go, resting them upon his chest.

Something breaks inside me—reality splintering like a mirror —darkness swallowing me whole.

I stand to my feet, running bloody hands through my wet bald head. Clasping them at the base of my skull. Blood mixing with water. Confusion pumps through each one of my cells. I stroll to the window, seeing the storm growing stronger.

I hear a ripping and chewing noise behind me. I turn to see him there. That black oblong shape, its large clump of feathers hunching over Cordero's body. The vulture's back, feasting on my partner's corpse. Tearing into his flesh with gusto. He looks up at me, viscera hanging from his mouth. His blood-stained face holds that hideous rictus grin, rejoicing in death.

I throw myself at it, anger boiling inside me, erupting through my throat, spewing words of hate. We struggle in darkness, feathers and flesh and blood mixing on the floor. My hands find something sharp—the ritual knife—it plunges deep. I lift up with all my strength, cutting him from groin to sternum. Black blood sprays across my face as the vulture screeches—a sound like death itself. The body thumps to the ground, laying lifeless. Slowly, it shifts back into its human form—Stein.

I get back up, catching my breath. It feels like my life is

ebbing away. The world around me starts to warp and shift. I fight it, willing myself to stay present. I need to make this right. I need to call Jacobs. Show him the mess I've made. Show him I was right about Stein. Right about everything.

I move through the dark living room, looking for the phone. When I glance down, the vulture's body is gone—the creature I just gutted with savage intensity. No black feathers. No blood-soaked corpse of Stein. Just me, covered in Cordero's blood, white-knuckled fingers gripping a kitchen knife.

The room sways like a ship in a storm; I struggle to keep my balance. The vulture reappears, larger than ever, writing on the wall in Cordero's blood:

HOMO HOMINI VULTURIS

But as I watch his fingers scrawling the bloody words on the wall, his hand becomes my hand. The words flow from my fingers like a confession.

Memory floods back like acid: *Every victim. Every confrontation with Stein—it was me. Every phone call—just me, talking to myself.* The puzzle pieces align with terrible clarity. The Sanskrit verse burns behind my eyes, brighter than ever, melting my corneas: मृत्युः सर्वहरश्चाहम्— *I am all-devouring death.* I was never hunting the vulture. I was becoming it.

Stepping back a few feet my eyes witness the horror of my work:

HOMO HOMINI VULTURIS

I turn to the mirror, and my breath stops in my throat. Thick, syrupy blood crawls down my face, heavy like my sins. Lightning strobes through the windows, and my features writhe in the glass —skin melting like candle wax, jaw extending into that ancient beak, eyes burning vulture-red. Another flash, and I'm human again, but wrong—my face a grotesque hybrid of man and bird. In the mirror's dark truth, I finally see what I've become: Karma's carrion priest. The vulture. All-devouring death.

More memories come flashing back, assaulting me: *my hands tearing Reyes's body open like a savage communion. Parker's viscera hanging from my mouth. Williamson's eyes, glazed and accusing.* Each death a ritual, each victim a drunk driver who escaped justice.

The septagram is nearly complete—Cordero was the sixth point—I'm the seventh—the witness I—my subconscious— needed—the mirror to show me my sins. The cancer's not just in my lymph nodes—it's in my soul. The vulture was never Stein. It was *me*. Always me. Born in the Everglades that fateful dawn, fed by subconscious guilt, grief and rage.

I stumble out into the deluge, my mind fracturing like stained glass. The Diplomat waits like a faithful hearse. I know what I have to do now. Where this has to end. The same spot where it all began—where the vultures first claimed my soul. There's no one left to finish this but me.

30

Miami bleeds into swampland as the Diplomat growls down the Tamiami Trail, its headlights barely piercing the deluge. The rain falls like judgment—black, relentless, biblical—turning the world into running ink.

My windshield wipers wage a losing battle against heaven's tears as the cancer writhes inside me like a nest of vipers, each turn of the wheel sending fresh pain through my lymph nodes. But it won't get the satisfaction. I've got my own ending planned.

Twenty minutes to the spot. The same cursed blotch of earth where I dumped that old drunk's body—an offering to the vultures—three years ago. Cordero's blood cakes my face, my hands, my sleeves, my soul—black and thick like crude oil. The Sanskrit verse burns behind my eyes with renewed intensity: मृत्युः सर्वहरश्चाहम् *I am all-devouring death.*

Now I understand its truth with terrible clarity. Death was never my enemy; it was my reckoning. Every victim—just echoes of my fractured mind trying to balance cosmic scales.

The radio crackles with static that sounds like beating wings. I reach to turn it off, but pause—the white noise reminds me of those phone calls, of conversations with myself in my kitchen. When did I first spread these dark wings? How many nights did I circle above Miami, searching for prey, not realizing I had become the very thing I hunted? The very thing I punished throughout my entire career. The cancer gnaws at my insides, but this truth devours me whole.

Through the rain-beat windshield, the Everglades stretch endless and dark, a primordial soup of sin and redemption. Cypress trees loom like ancient judges, their Spanish moss swaying in silent condemnation.

Lightning splits the sky with divine judgment, documenting my final descent. Each flash a door into nature's own confession booth. Like cosmic alchemy, droplets morph into falling feathers that beckon me forward.

The turn-off appears like a memory of guilt barely visible in the storm's strange pre-dawn light. I ease the Diplomat onto the muddy track, its wheels seeking the invisible grooves I carved three years ago. The suspension groans under the weight of my sins as I navigate the narrow path. Ahead, storm and eclipse conspire to darken these final moments, sealing my fate like a tomb.

I park in the exact same spot, tires sinking into unforgetting mud. The engine dies with a shudder that echoes through my bones. This is it. The place where I abandoned both the drunk and my humanity. That first sin birthed all the others, a cascade of death flowing from this cursed spot. Every murder since, every ritual killing—just failed attempts to wash away that first sin. But blood doesn't wash away blood. My nose starts to bleed—

my body confessing what my soul already knows.

I exit the Diplomat, the rain washing the drying blood from my body. I tap the warm hood three times—a last goodbye to my faithful companion—catching my blurry reflection on the windshield.

I stroll through the muddy ground until I reach that same sinful spot. The pocket knife opens with a soft click that carries across the black water. Its blade catches the first hint of dawn, sharp as truth. Memories flood back with each heartbeat:

That old drunk sprawled beneath the banyan tree, vultures already circling above. Reyes spread-eagled on cold concrete, chest cavity splayed open like an offering to ancient gods. Villaverde's eyes widening with recognition in his final moment. Williamson's screams echoing through empty storefront halls. Sokolov's form transformed into sacred geometry. Parker's final breath escaping like a whispered prayer. My partner's bewildered eyes as understanding came too late. Each death a ritual, each victim a stepping stone on my path to becoming.

My hands are steady as I draw the blade vertically along my veins, guided by phantom gold lines that snake across my forearms—collecting the wage of my sins in full. Each drop marks my sins like a confession, each splash is redemptive absolution. The rain guides my offering into the swamp's dark altar.

I stumble to the nearest cypress, dipping my right index finger into the weeping cuts on my forearms, tracing the open veins, gathering their dark offering, before writing those ancient words onto waiting bark:

HOMO HOMINI VULTURIS

Man is a vulture to man. The crude letters gleam like molten crimson—they'll remain long after the vultures finish their feast. A warning etched in blood. A confession. Maybe both.

The world starts to blur at its edges as my life force drains away. Above, the storm parts like a curtain, revealing the moon's dark shape beginning to devour the sun. Through the growing darkness, I see them gathering. Dark silhouettes descending from the eclipse-stained sky, their wings making that sound I've heard in my dreams since that first rainy night. That whooshing that haunted me, that I blamed on anything but the truth. My brothers have come to claim me—black angels against the dying light—witnesses to both my end and the sun's temporary death.

Lightning flashes again, and I count them—seven vultures for seven souls taken—myself included. The septagram completes itself in the sky above me as they circle lower, their shadows painting the ground in shapes that mirror the ancient glyphs. My vision blurs, blood loss defeating the cancer, melting the world away, but the pattern crystallizes with perfect clarity. I've always seen it, always known it, when I thought I was hunting it.

"Tom. . . we've missed you."

Sarah's voice pierces the darkness like divine light through stained glass. She stands at the water's edge, beautiful as the day I met her, untouched by the rain that falls everywhere else. Emily beside her, both haloed in light that dims the approaching dawn. They're smiling—not with judgment or accusation, but with understanding. With love.

VULTURE

"It's time to come home, Daddy," Emily says, her small hand reaching out. The light around them pulses with each word, warm as summer sunshine.

I take one step toward them, then another, each movement lighter than the last. The cancer's agony, my guilt, my madness—all of it stays behind in the mud with my bleeding body. Blood trails from my wrists like crimson ribbons, but I feel no pain now. Behind me, I hear the vultures landing, their wings folding like ancient church doors closing at dusk. They'll cleanse what remains, just as they did with that old drunk three years ago. Justice has a poetry to it, if you look deep enough.

The cancer's gone now, dissolved like morning mist. Emily's hand radiates warmth like divine grace. Sarah's fingers find my other hand, washing away the last traces of sin. Their light grows brighter, pushing back the darkness, until the swamp and the vultures and my broken body seem like distant memories.

Emily's smile is the last thing I see as my body settles into the mud behind me. The light consumes everything—the pain, the guilt, darkness. Below us, the vultures begin their ancient work—consuming sins. Nature's janitors, doing what they've always done. The wages of sin is death, but the gift of God is eternal life.

Beautiful, isn't it?

Photo by NB Photogrpahy.

A. M. BLANCO is a novelist and screenwriter residing in South Florida. A dramatist and prose stylist with a poetically hypnotic and cinematic voice, he combines dramatic storytelling with noir, crime, suspense, and horror to create visceral narratives.

Connect with him:

www.instagram.com/a.m.blanco

Connect with us:

www.9thhousebooks.com

www.instagram.com/9th_House_Books

www.youtube.com/9th_House_Books

www.x.com/9th_House_Books